# LIFELINE

# LifeLine

*A story of lives shaped by connection and
acceptance, perseverance and love.*

## Bobbi Donovan

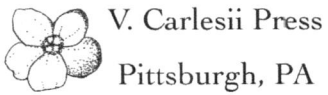

V. Carlesii Press
Pittsburgh, PA

The loom from which the tapestry of LifeLine materialized was strung with observation and woven with imagination. The characters and situations, therefore, may resemble people or circumstances you know, since our lives may vary more by timing and degree, and less by substance. This similarity is based solely on our shared humanity and does not reflect actual events, individuals or their lives. In other words, any resemblance to actual events or places or persons, living or dead, is purely coincidental.

Though written with sensitivity, LifeLine contains subject matter related to eating disorders and sexual assault that some may find triggering.

For a historical perspective, LifeLine was finalized during the global COVID-19 pandemic of 2020-2021.

To contact the author, email BobbiLeeDonovan@gmail.com

Cover photograph by Roberta Donovan
Cover design by Erin Burkett
Cover art technical assistance by Joel M. Donovan
V. Carlesii Press logo by Molly Donovan

Printed in the United States of America
Published by V. Carlesii Press
First Printing December 2021

ISBN 979-8-9852331-0-0

*For all the real lives at loose ends and
the people who cherish them*

# PART ONE

# 1. On Your Mark

Abby returns to standing and toggles the glistening chrome handle downward. A glow of satisfaction brightens her face as she watches her masticated dinner circle before flowing into oblivion. While the basin replenishes, she turns on the spigot, cups her hands and fills them with cool, cleansing water. Brought to her lips, she takes it in. A simple swish and spit. A gentle wipe. Her graduation day continues.

Abby revisits her mirror and recites her valedictorian speech making sure to enunciate each word to counter the effects of the college's less-than-ideal public address system. Her family might not listen. Her best friend, Ellen, will. The universe put the two girls in the same fourth grade class. They had social awkwardness in common and a compulsion to please. They didn't know "teacher's pet" was a derogatory label. They wore it with pride. They stayed close through junior high, their academic bent and Girl Scouts cementing their friendship. Eventually, the pull of new interests diluted what they shared. So by high school, Abby's participation in orchestra and Ellen's in choir kept them connected during the concert season, but didn't suffice as their last summer of youth faded with the daylight. Now, as top of her undergraduate class, Abby hopes the note she wrote to share her news reached Ellen in time.

Turbulent weather taunts the late spring evening. The setting sun slips behind the encumbered clouds just above the horizon as the flood lights of the stadium struggle to compensate. The dean of Abby's school swells with pride. His emotions rise not from a superficial affection for Abby but in the admiration many share of her rare combination of compassion, intelligence and unwavering determination.

"On behalf of myself and the entire faculty, I am thrilled to introduce a shining graduate of the Psychology Department, Miss Abigail Thompson, valedictorian of Trinity College's class of 1981."

The audience of gathered families and friends watches Abby stand and walk deliberately, haltingly to the center of the dais. As the crowd applauds, she approaches the podium with her head held high and her notes quaking. Anticipatory silence settles as she takes a deep breath. She places her notes before her, steadies her hands alongside and scans the expanse. She feels her energy surge as her listeners connect. "Good evening to all of you. Congratulations to the Trinity College Class of 1981! It is with great humility and deep honor that I address you all, on this momentous occasion."

Abby spent weeks writing and refining her sentiments, reading them to herself silently, then before her mirror, reciting them with frequent glances to her notes, then without. Tonight, with her heart pounding in her chest, all her hopes come to fruition. She overcomes her natural reserve and delivers her speech, line by line, with skill and conviction.

"We come to this day, with our hopes outstretched, our hands prepared for giving back. Our lives have been fashioned by loving parents, devoted professors, supportive friends. Until now we have been receivers, accepting from others their gifts of time and talents. Beginning today, we will enflesh the wisdom that it is indeed better to give than to receive. We enter the world's tapestry of life as teachers, physicians, scientists, artists, dreamers. We enter to encourage youth, to support the aged and to make the transition between the two as life-giving as possible. We enter the world's tapestry of life with tentative steps, gaining confidence with each success achieved, each failure overcome. Our paths are determined not so much by our past as by our willingness, our determination, to embrace the changes that embrace us—both those pursued and those uninvited. Beginning today, we become irreplaceable, undeniable strands in the world's great tapestry of life." Resounding applause rewards her. She smiles. *I did it.* "Thank you."

The bored-yet-proud in attendance carefully navigate the bleachers and wander into the parking lot, where those-who-chance-to-notice hope the angry sky will hold its liquor a few minutes more, giving the good-humored pandemonium, claps of congratulations and hugs of farewell their chance to swell through the throng of graduates and visitors. Ellen wanders among the buzzing crowd until she hears a faint but familiar voice. She follows the sound to a circle of Abby's adoring fans surrounding her and her family.

She sees Abby's father, Russell, never one for providing or enduring compliments, wearing his boredom in his posture. Her brother, Mark, stays close and compact. She watches Abby's mother, Chloe, brush the hair from her daughter's brow preparing Abby to lend her subtle smile to others' frames and albums. For a brief second, Ellen catches a glimpse of something close to satisfaction in Abby's stature. She has gained admirers, much to her parents' amazement.

As the crowd around Abby dissipates, Ellen surprises her from behind. "Hi Abby!"

Abby's eyes widen and smile. The reunited pair share a hopping squeal of joy, a moment of sweet awareness and a heartfelt embrace that only lifelong friends can exchange.

"Els, hi! You made it! I'm so happy you're here! Mom, Dad, you remember Ellen Kincaid. From my high school days?"

"Hi, Mister and Missus Thompson. Hi, Mark. You must be so proud. Abby, your speech was so authentic and touching. Sheer poetry. Can I have a copy, maybe? I'll keep it forever."

"Sure. I'll mail a fancy version to your mom's house, okay?"

"Perfect. Have you gotten their final answer? Are you still leaving Brookfield and moving to Boston to be a radio announcer?"

"Actually, I talked to the station manager again and they liked the tape I sent of the show I did here. The open-format, call-in show. They're willing to let me give it a try. I'm calling it 'LifeLine.' People can talk about anything that's on their minds. A place to unburden. It's just a small station, but it's a start. I can't believe my experience here and being valedictorian actually paid off."

Ellen bubbles with excitement that Abby's hard work has laid a promising path before her. "That's great! You'll be amazing. I've decided to head east, too. I probably won't be able to afford even the suburbs of Boston, but hopefully I won't be too far away and we can visit every once in a while."

"That would be fantastic. I don't expect to make it home very often. It'll be so nice to have you nearby. Once you get settled, call me at the station. WTOK. Okay?"

"Okay. WTOK. It was nice to see you again Mister and Missus Thompson. Bye, Mark. Goodbye, Abby. I'll see you soon. I love you."

Abby and Ellen hug again, each resisting letting go, each resisting stepping away into their waiting unknown.

# 2. Lava For Air

Two hundred miles northeast of Brookfield under the same waxing moon, Debbie dresses nervously, taming her boisterous locks and minimizing her long limbs. She checks her clock. She checks her make-up. She checks her clock, again. She seats herself on the edge of her bed and hugs a stuffed bear to ease her anxiety. First dates. Moments pass slowly giving her mind license to wander back to the day they met. She and her housemate, Megan, lounged on beach towels studying under a tree in the center of campus—their way to celebrate the first sunny day warm enough to sit still without freezing in place. He and his friend strolled over and playfully praised their fortitude. Countless chance encounters and inconsequential conversations followed and finally reached a critical mass. So, after three weeks of earnest dinner invitations, she finally accepted. First dates.

Debbie's focus returns to her anxiety at the sound of a car pulling up and idling. A beep. She takes a quick glance out the window and sees him running to her front door, his coat lifted over his head to protect his first-date preparations. She grabs her wrap and umbrella and heads into the dimming light of the late spring evening. He shields only her from the building storm with

6

her umbrella meant for one. At dinner, he insists she order without considering the cost. They laugh and gaze across the table with hope. As the conversation tapers into monosyllables, he asks for the check.

Once outside, the black clouds racing across the night sky burst under the weight of their load, sending the fleeing couple splashing through unavoidable puddles toward the refuge of his waiting car. Debbie's shoes dissolve. Her garments cling. He starts the engine. With wipers set to rapid, he drives steadily through the pelting rain that fuels rushing streams, carrying fallen branches, untethered toys and forgotten trash to lower ground. He parks the car. Debbie wipes the condensation from her window. Unable to recognize her surroundings, she shifts uncomfortably toward her door. He grabs her arm. Cracks of lightning and claps of thunder assault the air and drown out any possibility of relocating. He lies about love. In the cacophony, only two hear her screams as Debbie twists from the lips and wrestles from the grip of the creature in the seat with her. He grips her tighter. Debbie retaliates with kicks and bites. She hears a rip as her cold, wet dress falls from her shoulder. He fulfills his will. In agony, she staggers out of the car and collapses onto the flooded gravel below. He opens the rear door. Debbie looks up and, seeing the satisfaction on his face, spontaneously regurgitates her meal at his feet. Disgusted, he pulls her up and pushes her into the back seat where she lies trembling, her knees pulled to her chest, her quaking hands gripping opposite elbows and holding them tight. With the deed done, he nonchalantly checks his rearview mirror then turns the radio louder to mask her moaning. He drives her home.

# 3. Get Set

Any casual observer walking past Abby's bedroom would agree, no one excels at the strategic art of packing more than Abigail Thompson. Even as a child, she mesmerized fellow scouts as she, a demure Mary Poppins, removed countless items from her pretzel-can sit-upon. For her, arranging life in containers to travel two hundred miles and start again feels therapeutic. After twenty-two years of building frustration and three weeks of unbridled anticipation, she appreciates the promise she made to herself to break free from the ensnaring vines choking her family tree. Hours pass. Closets and drawers give up their contents, as suitcases, boxes and bags take them on. Finally, she loads a few treasured books, records and mementoes into a cardboard box, then stuffs her favorite plush animals alongside as filler. In the end, she stares deeply into her mirrored gaze before the backdrop of her soon-to-be-abandoned childhood surroundings. The time has finally come to leave them behind.

Long-distance apartment-shopping leaves so much to chance and the imagination. Against all odds, delight fills her face and music erupts from her heart as Abby drives her burgeoning car down a lush, tree-lined street and stops in front of a quaint, side-by-side duplex with vibrant, summer flowers neatly lining the front walk. She checks the address again. *70! This is it!* "Nice!" She looks both ways before opening her car door, careful to avoid the kickball game happening around her. Strewn maps, empty cups and food wrappers are left for later. Adventure awaits. The neighbor's yard and sidewalk teem with playing children of all ages. She finally feels like an adult.

Reading the landlord's letter again, Abby finds the front door key "inside the hollow rock below the pink azalea." *Clever.* She takes a deep breath and unlocks her door for the first time. "I'm home." She quickly realizes what it lacks in size it makes up for in style. She admires the hardwood floors, French doors, window seat and fireplace. She immediately imagines the placement of her furnishings in the empty rooms: "Table and chairs will fit nicely in the kitchen, sofa here, stereo there." *Stereo!* "Music!" Before anything, her music. Her source of solace and inspiration. How much she owes to the alchemist who turned vinyl into concertos! For now, she props her transistor radio on the window sill and tunes it till she finds the public station. She immediately loses herself in free dance and twirling in the resonating space. Her eyes sparkle as she hums along. No one interferes. She alone gets to choose.

Feeling energized by her freedom, she returns to her task. Ordinarily, unpacking lacks the flare and anticipation of packing. Not this time. Not for Abby. Her unparalleled skills shine. She learned something enduring from her mother so, last in/first out, cleaning supplies. As the sound of children and summer breezes pour through the open windows, she gives the cabinets and surfaces of the kitchen and bathroom a quick wipe-down. In no time, she fills them with her favorites and makes them her own.

After multiple trips between car and threshold, her remaining belongings encircle the apartment. *Enough for today.* No use moving forward until her furnishings arrive in the morning from the department store in town. Nudged by hunger's flirtation, she walks intentionally to the kitchen to find a package of cookies. She removes a carton of milk from the refrigerator. Methodically, she consumes the entirety of both. She disappears into the bathroom. A moment later, she grabs her purse and walks rejoicing out the door and into the celebratory sunshine. Time to explore.

Abby strolls past yards cluttered with inverted kiddie pools, leaning bicycles and waving sprinklers. She instantly contrasts them to the manicured and desolate showpiece that surrounds her home in Brookfield. Tidying parents and winding-down children greet her with a wave and a "welcome." Painfully shy, she nods and smiles, but continues on. As she turns east, her gaze falls upon the long, Giacometti-ish shadow cast at her feet by the setting sun. "Hah!" She smiles. *Getting there.*

Another turn delivers her to a shaded avenue lined on both sides with a menagerie of quaint storefronts. She meanders along the cobbled sidewalk, cupping her hands around her eyes to peek in the windows of each shop along the way. A hardware store, an antique dealer, a laundromat, a dry cleaner and, a wave of refreshingly chilled air takes her breath away as the door of the corner grocer closes behind her. She grabs a shopping basket at the threshold and leisurely, attentively strolls each enticing aisle. She grins. As she passes by the entrance, she trades her basket for a cart. Drenched in bliss, she surrenders to temptation and buys a variety of irresistible items to last the night and morning. Struggling to manage the two awkward bags, she crosses toward home and mindfully takes in all the beauty surrounding her. *My life is so blessed.*

Back in her neighborhood, she notices a centralized mailbox pavilion. *I'll bet that's what the other key is for!* Thankful for an excuse to give her quivering arms and cramped hands a rest, she sets her parcels down at one end and searches for her compartment. Preoccupied by the hunt, she accidentally stumbles over a festively painted stone placed along her path. "Ouch! Oh." *That's one way to keep them from blowing away.* She gathers one of each supermarket circular and manufacturers' coupon flier from beneath the stone and tucks them in her bags. *These will come in handy.*

Once home, Abby prepares her meal. While it simmers, steams and bakes, she sets up a campsite in her living room. She uses her sit-upon as a seat, stacked boxes as her table, piled towels and blankets for her bed. Simplicity suits her. Anything but the oppression of Brookfield suits her. Against the soundscape of Bach, she sits quietly and savors her first meal in her own home. A momentary visit to the bathroom once again affirms her independence. After a quick shower and weigh-in— *147*— she digs through her belongings for a T-shirt and soft shorts. "These will do fine."

Dressed for bed, Abby sits cross-legged on the floor and, by the beam of the streetlight, opens a pristine journal, presses back the binding and begins to write.

> *July 1, 1981, Dear Diary, I live in Boston! Mattapan, officially, but Boston. My life is so blessed. I cannot believe I get to decide. I'm camping out in my own living room while I wait for my own furniture to come tomorrow!! What would dad say about that?! I'm so excited to get started with my new life.*

She rearranges her padding and envisions all her tomorrows as her mind drifts toward gratitude. "Holy Father God, Mother God, my life seems like mine right now, but I know it is still in your hands. Please watch over me as I move forward. And if I start to climb too high, please, catch me if I fall. Amen."

An abrupt knock at the door awakens Abby from an uncomfortable position. She opens her eyes to radiant light pouring in the undressed window, flooding the room with warmth. "Coming!" Abby grudgingly realigns her body and clambers to the window to see a delivery van parked out front. "There's a sofa and two men on my porch. Yippee! Yikes, men?!" Abby quickly clears the room of her makeshift accommodations, wraps her scantily clad body in a bedsheet, and opens the door. "Good morning!"

"Abigail Thompson?"

"Yes, that's me. I'll get out of your way." Abby steps aside as the sofa becomes hers.

"Where do you want this?"

Abby watches in awe as all her imaginings materialize before her eyes. "Yes, that goes right there. Yes, thank you. Yes, please, there is great!"

As the street lights glow on, marking the end of another day, the hum of activity, from squealing, hose-soaked toddlers to blaring, boom-boxed teens, ebbs from yards, toward sidewalks and through doorways. Peace settles in. Even by her own measure, Abby's first two days prove remarkable. The surroundings she considered foreign yesterday now feel familiar. The vacant apartment, her inviting home. *I'm doing this.*

With all her pieces in place and personalized, she finishes stacking meticulously folded corrugated cardboard on her front stoop. A hefty first load for refuse pick-up. *I hope they don't mind. I wonder if there's a nearby dumpster.* While the day's shadows succumb to the vanishing sun, Abby half-heartedly wanders down her street in the opposite direction, this time taking note of flower combinations she finds appealing, and committing them to memory for her first visit to the garden center. As she rounds the corner home she spots a large refuse bin in the lot on a dead end street. *Noted.*

Led by a rising moon, Abby returns home to indulge her freedom once again. Music. Bach. Candles. Lots of them. Dancing. Abby relishes every choice she makes, every decision which no one un-decides. She voraciously delights in this day's celebratory grocery choices. Ice cream. Fudge sauce. Whipped cream. Pretzels. Cake. Abby enlivens her senses with food, relishing the textures and flavors, aromas and beauty. Her nourishment's expulsion creates its own satisfaction; last-in-first-out restores her mind to calm.

As the gentle night breeze chills to comfortable, Abby undresses and examines her body in her full-length mirror. Robotically, she steps on the scale, waits for it to settle and smiles. *146.* Crisp sheets and satisfaction embrace her as she snuggles among the well-worn plush of her youth. She opens her journal to the next blank page. As she begins to write, her chest swells with a combination of pride, joy and contentment. Spontaneously, her expression transforms to gratitude.

> *July 2, 1981. My little place feels like home. My furniture came and fits great. I'll take the rest of the weekend to really get organized, but I get to do it ALL!! Then on Monday, I'll drive down to the station to get acquainted. This is really happening! Just being away from the stress of home would be good enough.*

Recording the day's modest yet monumental achievements calms her spirit and seamlessly leads her to implore her higher power. "Abba Father, Loving Mother, thank you so much for the joy I feel in my heart. Help me to be a source of comfort to those around me. Please, catch me if I fall. Amen."

She hugs her pillow as her thoughts lose form and context and a nighthawk chorus accompanies Brahms to serenade her to sleep.

# 4. Shooting Gallery

Across town, Cathy Morgan sits alone on a park bench in Boston Common under a struggling street lamp. Cliques of cocky teenagers rip along the footpath on boards and skates, dodging joggers and older couples walking hand-in-hand, all extracting the last hours of pleasure from the fleeing day. July 2. Her father's 58th birthday.

Cathy distractedly pens today's entry in her log book as moments of deep and distant thought punctuated her writing. She recalls walking these same paths safe and serene, her hand tucked securely in that of her dad. They bonded here. As a toddler, she challenged his patience, constantly seeking the tiny creatures hidden under rocks and decaying branches. As a teen, she tested his resolve, discussing the boundaries that kept their ancestors at a safe distance from success. As a woman, she expanded his imagination, fulfilling her dreams before his tired eyes. She dreaded his lingering transition toward death. She dared not envision its aftermath. The loneliness.

Soft tears drift over the banks of her eyes. She brushes them away with resignation. So much change to process. Alone. Minus her dad's presence, reasons to visit their home seldom meet the threshold to motivate her effort. Her mother, Beatrice, parented more with dominance, less with forbearance. She found fulfillment in her role as wife, mother and homemaker, and assumed Cathy would follow her lead. Cathy confounded those expectations and in so doing, estranged her unintentionally, but significantly just the same.

After months of effort, the distance between them lingers. Still. She closes her book and places it in her briefcase. She pulls a compact mirror from her purse and checks her makeup for evidence of fallen tears. She stands and turns her attention and herself toward home. She has a dinner to prepare.

The moon's brilliant beams cast long shadows through the picture window framing Cathy's view of the nearby park. She proudly incorporates worn, though meaningful, pieces among the ultramodern furnishings of her not-so-humble abode—pieces that she has treasured since childhood: her grandfather's wood carving and grandmother's handwoven rugs, her mother's terracotta water pitcher, her father's favorite pillow.

Not everything reflects her decorator's prescribed color scheme of rusty earth tones and dusty blues, but blindly obeying the rules has never been Cathy's *forté*. She pays close attention to her inner voice and trusts it to guide her on a path that resonates in her soul. Such independence tests her relationships, especially with her mother. For Cathy, "To thine own self be true," tends to give unconditional love a run for its money. Still, spending quality time with Beatrice remains a priority, however difficult the scheduling or the conversation.

A knock starts Cathy's heart pounding. She wipes her hands on her apron, inhales deeply, opens the door and welcomes her guest. "Hello, Mother. It's good to see you."

Beatrice enters, wearing the ever-present chip on her shoulder with pride. "Hello Catherine. It's been a while since I've seen your place."

"Yes, it has been. Not much has changed. Dinner will be ready soon."

Cathy returns to her refuge over a bubbling saucepan, her back to the disquiet, stirring in more ways than one. *Oh, God, conversation. I could feign complete focus on making dinner. Or, or I could be really brave and broach a few simple opening questions.* The guilt of staying silent eclipses her trepidation. "How have you been, Mother?"

"I still have so much to keep me busy. Thank you's, insurance policies, meetings with my attorney. It's all so draining." Beatrice walks around the elegantly set table. Suddenly, an exasperated exhale breaks the silence, reinforcing what Cathy has dreaded since extending the invitation.

Straining her peripheral vision so as not to turn her head an inch, Cathy glimpses Beatrice stop momentarily and straighten the table linen. Determined to restore her composure, Cathy recalls her yoga instructor's favorite command. *Breathe.* She inhales silently but deeply and ventures back into the fray. "What about your friends? Have you gone out with them?"

"Well, yes. We see each other once a week." With the table cloth meeting her reproachable standards, Beatrice lifts the water goblets and examines each for spots. She scornfully strides to the kitchen and deliberately unhooks a dish towel from the rack. She returns to the goblets and polishes both.

*Breathe.* "Well, I'm glad you were finally able to come over. Sorry I was so late. My last clients were determined to see that home on Eastcrest. I couldn't say 'no.' Then I had an errand I had to run."

"Do you honestly expect to continue this real estate thing? You're rarely home and when you are, your phone never stops ringing. How is that conducive to a family? I mean, what man wants that?"

"We've been through this, Mother. You're living your choices, I'd like to live mine."

"The life I live isn't good enough for you?"

"Could we please put this aside for tonight?" Cathy turns back to her meal preparation. *That escalated quickly.*

Beatrice picks wilted blossoms from the table's centerpiece. "Have you ever considered wall-to-wall carpeting? There's a new fiber Shirley says wears like iron."

"I prefer grandma's old rugs."

Without so much as a transitional breath, Beatrice plows ahead. "But the centers are practically worn through, and hardwood is so difficult to keep dusted. Not to mention…"

"Mother. Dinner's ready."

"Your attitude is unbecoming, Catherine. Rather offensive in my humble opinion."

The meal, though selected and prepared with her best intentions, falls short of Cathy's expectations. Beatrice stays conspicuously silent. Her most cunning critiques arrive that way. With her dutiful daughter role executed, Cathy casually ushers her mother to the door promising to keep the time between visits shorter. They exchange an obligatory hug and say "Goodbye." Cathy feels a surprising burst of energy as soon as she turns the latch. "Clean-up."

Morning shows no mercy. Cathy overindulges the leniency of her best friend—always there to give her exactly what she wants most in life—more time—until the fourth whack, when her snooze button goes from "best friend" to "worst enemy." Bob

Edwards' voice crooning out the headlines on "Morning Edition" offers no help at all.

Getting mere snippets of tortured sleep last night only exacerbates today's pre-work race against the clock. Sure, clean-up took longer than usual. But it never fails. Her mother's visits, though customarily short, always generate a pinball game of unresolved issues that clang and ricochet in her brain no matter how dark the room or quiet the surroundings.

Unlike her manicured company spaces, mounds of classic and classy a-lines, button-downs, hand-wovens and relaxed-fits occupy every horizontal surface of Cathy's disheveled boudoir. The disarray attests to too many red-eyed endings of too many sixteen-hour workdays. She considers taking her Barnum & Bailey act, of chugging lukewarm coffee while mascaraing her eyes and steaming her resurrected blouses, on the road. "I'm so late. A blazer. That's what I need. A man? Can you imagine? Please! A family? Oh, no. Taking care of myself suits me just fine. Where's my seersucker?"

Cathy hurriedly yanks each hanger along the walk-in's rack searching for her prize among the garments. "Pooh! I know I hung it up." Ruing using her snooze button at all, she returns to the tallest mound and tosses through the layers again, finding her wrinkled jacket at the bottom of the heap. "Seriously? This looks worse than the blouse. Tonight. Tonight this mess is gone. And not because of you, Beatrice." She glances at her clock. "Good God, I'll never get to work on time!"

# 5. False Start

Abby learned more than packing, fire-building and camp songs in scouting. She learned her motto: Be prepared. So today, one week before she starts at WTOK, Abby executes her dry run. She energetically rises from horizontal, gleefully matching her alarm's enthusiasm.

A twinge of hunger guides her to the kitchen. Breakfast foods lie in wait. Cereal with milk. Donuts with custard. Eggs with ham. Toast with butter. Juice with pulp. Eating and drinking as much as she wants of whatever she wants epitomizes Abby's independence. She glories in it. Her consumption this morning leaves empty boxes and cartons piled on her counter. Her skin stretches over her abdomen. Her breaths are shallow and between her breasts. But not for long.

Abby's solution flows like clockwork. She need only think about regurgitating and it happens. Practice makes reflex. No gross fingers down the throat. No gagging. Not anymore. A simple tilt over the commode and relief. Cleansing her insides of the accumulation of her binging illustrates her power to control something in her life. She depends on it.

Raised with God and the saints as her constant jurors, and her father's mantra ringing in her ears—*Remember 1 Timothy, modestly and discreetly.* —there's no surprise that Abby's wardrobe lacks knits and darts. Still, her self-esteem inches up when she views herself, front and back, in her relaxed choice for her first visit as a staff person to WTOK. "Adulthood away from dad's watchful eyes certainly has its advantages." Abby grabs the satchels of snacks she packed for the occasion and heads downtown.

Navigating the streets of Boston proves a challenge all its own. "No wonder the expression 'you can't get theh from heeah' is a Boston classic. It's true!" One way streets confound her sense of direction but Abby maintains her composure and holds her tongue despite the haranguing she takes from fellow drivers. *Note to self, allot at least an extra half hour for commute.* Nearly an hour after exiting her front door, she finally arrives. Her nerves settle once she puts her car in park. "Did it. Just enough time for a little nibble."

Abby turns to her three-bag supply of cheese curls and a half-gallon of juice in the front seat with her. Her ritual begins. She opens a bag of snacks and counts out fifteen, placing each one in her mouth and melting it individually. Time for a drink. Then fifteen more pieces. Another drink. Fifteen more. Drink. The importance of repeating her practice illustrates to her that, although food dictates the whens of her life, she decides the what. Her ritual ends. When she opens her car door to enter the building, nothing edible remains.

Abby pushes the stairwell door open and emerges, face glowing, with a hint of perspiration around her edges. *Not bad for a free workout.* An interloper no more, she smiles to see members of her future community hard at work through the station's wall of glass. Her gaze loses focus remembering the day of her interview, how her pulse raced and her palms sweat just being in this lobby. Her nerves nearly got the better of her. Now, she feels an ember of satisfaction ignite her confidence. She lingers in its benevolent glow.

The churning and gurgling of her digesting food waken her from her daydream. Determined to dispel the resultant wisp of worry, she checks her watch, "Nine twenty-four. Still early," and quickly scans the scene for the ladies' room. *This will just take a minute.* She slips inside for a quick cleanse. Returning to the hallway, she straightens her seams, brushes back her hair and takes a deep breath. She catches the glance of the receptionist who runs to the door to greet her. "Abigail, welcome back! I'm so glad you got the job!"

Abby struggles to overcome her shyness. "Thank you. I am, too. When Linda called, she said it would be okay for me to come in before my official start date so I could get acquainted with the staff and equipment."

Taming her enthusiasm to reflect Abby's reserve, Renee slows her pace. "That makes sense. The control room's a mystery to me. But if you've got any questions about the rest of the station, just ask. Are you from around here? I'm sorry. Renee, Renee Lang."

"Of course. Nice to formally meet you, Renee. Please call me Abby. Not really. I grew up near Brookfield, in southwest Connecticut, about two hundred miles from here. I've visited Boston several times, though, and always enjoyed it."

Unable to maintain her composure for long, Renee swells with the pride of a local. "Yah, it's a wicked great city. Lived here my whole life. Food, night spots, concerts, just check with me. I'll introduce you to the crew." She turns and leads Abby through the labyrinth of vacant desks toward the site of her coworkers' daily catch-up.

Just as she arrives, her phone rings. So, before launching into introductions, she pivots and retraces her steps to answer it.

Abby follows but stops at a respectful distance. Renee adopts her official voice, "WTOK, may I help you? Yes. No. You'll have to call back when he's on the air."

Abby waits, timidly, unsure how to stand professionally and whether to acknowledge she's eavesdropping.

Renee's voice develops an edge. "It's station policy not to give out personal numbers. Tomorrow evening, between six and eight. You're welcome. Goodbye." Shaking her head, Renee hangs up the phone and winds her way back to her charge. "People call me when they can't get through during the shows, expecting to get the host's home number." Renee misreads Abby's knit brow and curled upper lip as affirmation. "I know. I know. We'd lose all that crazy squabbling. They don't realize that's what keeps ratings up, up, up." Remembering where she left off, Renee resumes her tour. "You met Ms. Warner when you interviewed."

"Linda? Yes."

"Right. Then we'll start with the folks at the coffee station."

Once Abby wades within the audible radius, their lively conversation fades to welcome the stranger among them.

"Hey, folks. This is our new talk show host, Abigail, sorry, Abby Thompson. Abby, this is Donna Miles and Gordon Hampton. Donna is one of our journalists and Gordy is our daytime control room guru. Abby starts next Monday with the new call-in show." She glances at Abby for confirmation, "It's called LifeLine, right?"

"LifeLine, yes." Determined to appear at ease, Abby reaches for Donna's hand. *Pretty cool. Make eye contact.* "I'm pleased to meet you, Donna."

Donna automatically engages her journalistic prowess, "Have you worked in radio before?"

"I volunteered a few years at my university's station. I expect some things are similar."

Gordon checks his watch then shakes Abby's extended hand with a congenial grip. "You'll fit right in. We're all rather young at heart. We've been running a syndicated show in your slot. We can use that block to show you the ropes."

"After you review the hardware with Gordy, you and I can grab lunch and I'll fill you in on the software."

Despite her efforts to fit in, Abby's expression this time clearly betrays her confusion.

Donna chuckles, "The people."

Surprised by the invitation, Abby struggles to formulate a believable response. "I appreciate the offer, Donna, but I still have some last minute errands to run. I would like to come back and watch the room in operation, though. Do you think the next host would mind?"

"The Plant Lady? She won't mind at all. But watch out. She'll send you home with more seedlings than you'll know what to do with."

Abby's reflex to please engages. She smiles with no idea why.

# 6. Theater-in-the-Round

From the relative calm of her momentary sanctuary, Betty hears her husband, Harry, tell their three children to "keep it down." He taps at the door then tiptoes in. "Hey, honey, I'm leaving. Ben and Sandy are fed and dressed, and just watching TV. Joey's building as always. I'll be home on time. Have a good day. Love you." He kisses her gently on the cheek. Her cue to respond.

She winces against the blazing radiance blasting into the bedroom around the edges of the drawn blinds. "Bye, Harry. Have a good day. Love you, too." *Another Monday.*

Betty pulls back the covers and drags herself to standing. Her loose-fitting shirt and baggy pants drape over a body left for dead. She arrives at the bathroom mirror and examines her puffy eyelids. Running the water till it turns cold, she fills her cupped hands and splashes her weary face. Again. Again. Again. She dries it lightly. Unsure how to accept the woman looking back at her, she closes her eyes and inhales to fill every crevice of her lungs. She imagines rising like an escaping balloon, floating above herself, her home, the clouds. Her senses blur. She exhales, reversing her buoyancy and slowly reconnects her mind to her body. She opens her eyes, manages a smile, mindfully locks in the proper persona and exits onto the arena stage of her life.

After ten years of marriage, she knows how to smooth rough edges. She knows how to make the best of it. She knows something about expectations and the value of exceeding them, even if it hurts. She also knows about armor. For more years than she admits to herself, neither sunlight nor moonlight, nor lightning, nor fireflies—no wavelength of nature—has penetrated the armor guarding her true self from view. Even under the performer's spotlight, she reveals only her protective shell. Trapped inside, she wrestles with silent thoughts, unspoken words and unrevealed expressions, constantly aware of the upheaval they hold at bay.

Open windows and screen doors offer some relief from her claustrophobia. Thank goodness for summer. At least Betty has her children around her. She can take them to the park or do an art project. Creativity. Exploration. Skills and talents no longer dormant—for a few months, anyway. *Papier-mâché* puppets were today's adventure. So wheat paste and newspaper, paints and brushes clutter the kitchen table. But now, dinner preparation takes center stage and things need to get moving, starting with the dishes in the sink.

Betty knew after her first child that full-time motherhood would hold her heart. She didn't understand it would also hold her back. She readily admits she has no exceptional talents, but notices even her mediocre ones drifting away. She mindlessly fidgets with a cast iron skillet of home-fried potatoes as they sizzle on the stove. *Focus.* A pot lid spurts steam on the back burner. *Turn down the heat. Focus.* The air hums with the mash-up of Joey singing "Somebody Come and Play" along with the television over her rendition of "It's Too Late" in full Carole King mode. *Flee. Focus.* Without warning, Joey has the only accompaniment. "Who turned off the stereo? Joey?"

Betty takes a deep breath, relaxes her chin and shoulders, rests her grandmother's spatula on the skillet's blackened rim and leaves the kitchen to investigate. She arrives just in time to see Joey rush from the scene of his crime and plop down cross legged in front of the television. With the conviction of one falsely accused, he looks up at her and starts to plead his case. Betty stops him with a frown and a shake of her head. *Darling boy. You're so new at this. I went through two rounds of the terrible twos before you were so much as a glint in your daddy's eye.* Her expression says she sees right through him. His expression says he knows it.

His toddler indignation fades to regret. "Sorry, Mommy."

"Please, don't touch the buttons, Joey. Remember I told you, I like to hear my music, too." Betty powers on the stereo and loosens her body, heels to hair, to the rhythm. "It's too late. It's too late. It's too late." While transported to another universe, another reality—*Breathe deep. Relax.* —her three children exchange glances ranging from concern to amazement, wondering where she's gone and when she'll be back. The spell vaporizes when the faint smell of something burning drifts past her. *Shit. Shit. Shit.* Silently, she rushes to the kitchen to find smoke trickling from the broiler. She turns the knob, yanks the drawer open and drops to the floor in despair.

Sandy hears the broiler door slam and comes running to help. "Mom, are you okay? Do you want me to call Dad and ask him to bring fast food again?"

Surreptitiously wiping a single tear from her cheek, Betty rises and does her best to hide her thoughts as well. "Oh, sweetie, thank you, but no. He's already left. He'll have to go back out. You go play, honey, I'm fine." *How can all this be too much and yet not enough?*

Within minutes, Betty hears Harry's footsteps on the stairs. Right on time. She waits for his kiss upon her cheek. Right on target. She yearns for any change at all. "Hi, Harry. How was your day? I burned dinner. Sorry."

"Hi, Betty. Yes, I could smell it when I came in. Do you want me… "

With the dexterity and cunning of a cephalopod on a mission, a nervy thought escapes through a chink in Betty's breastplate. "I'm going out to get fried chicken at the deli. Are you okay with the kids?"

Harry works quickly to make sense of this disorder in their routine. "Ahh, sure. Are you feeling okay? Another long day?"

Betty's public persona regains control and replies with a smile. "I'm fine. I just got distracted by the kids, is all."

"I can understand that. Well, sure. We'll get the table set and be ready to eat when you get back."

Halfway to her destination, Betty pulls into the lot of an abandoned building. With the twist of the key, her composure breaks. No words form, no thoughts surface, no demands of self or others dilute her simple sadness expressed by nearly silent weeping. Just weeping. Freely. Finally. She weeps knowing she loves and is loved by her husband. She weeps knowing she loves and is loved by her children. She weeps knowing she loves the roles she plays as wife and mother, sister and daughter, cousin and aunt, granddaughter and friend. Then finally, she weeps admitting her fault, "What's wrong with me that this is not enough?" She listens for an answer that does not come.

Disappointed by the silence, Betty repositions and restrains her inner voice deep, safe below the surface. She feels it settle into the niche reserved for it specifically. Tinged with regret, she applies an airtight seal above her heart to keep it from getting any more ideas. She restarts the engine and resumes her role.

Betty checks her reflection in the mirror before opening her car door. The reddened tint around her eyes testifies to her truth, overriding her silence. "Shit!" *Lucky the line's long.* She steels her nerves and averts her gaze to avoid connecting with the deli's exiting customers. "I can do this." From her position at the back of the line, Betty stares at the illuminated board above the netted, shaggy heads of the bag-fillers, scouring it for textures and flavors that will satisfy her family's hunger for nourishment and hers for relief. She advances, oblivious.

"Can I help you, ma'am?"

Her trance breaks. "Yes, what's new on your menu?"

# 7. Bang

After ten days of arranging, rearranging, decompressing and ritualizing alone in her apartment, Abby resigns herself to make an unannounced visit to see her family in Brookfield. With passing tail lights as her only distraction, memories of life before her "awakening" sharpen into focus. How tidy to believe, all those years, that every child in her class lived in a "perfect" family of four—to envision all dads as dogmatic and pious perfectionists, all moms as obedient and subservient to dads, all parents sleeping in twin beds and all brothers as inevitable favorites—rendering her experiences as a girl in the Thompson family "perfectly" normal and acceptable.

She shakes her head, reliving the embarrassment of her sheer gullibility. She sighs, reaffirming her eventual explanation—how her family's isolation and insistence that friends visit there, kept her illusion pure, her view of reality warped.

Her mental meanderings next drift to her brother's steady rise to success despite his serious vision impairment, and then to the hundreds of days and nights she led him, like a guide dog, to ensure his safety. She ponders the moment she realized her brother's congenital birthright, reinforced in this most concrete way, would cement her lower status forever. When she understood, at her vulnerable age, that because she had her sight, in her father's opinion, accomplishments in her column would always pale. Always.

Frustration wells up as she remembers all the efforts she made to please, always to please, but never pleasing. Nearing her destination, Abby wipes her emotional slate clear and consolidates the strength of her newfound attitude, determined to rise above the past and introduce positive energy to her household.

Abby pulls into a parking spot in front of their home. Despite the late hour, she sees the familiar silhouette of her father, head bowed to bill-paying, at his desk. Being a Friday night, she knows she will find her mother on her knees in front of the refrigerator, moving leftovers to the front and wiping surfaces of sticky. Abby grabs her overstuffed overnight bag and briefcase and breathes deeply and slowly as she hesitantly approaches the house and puts her key in the front door lock. "Home."

As she crosses the threshold, her arrival earns a glance and a grunt from Russell. Determined to practice her resolve, she returns his coldness with a warm, "Hello, Dad." Not enough to thaw him. Abby looks around the familiar room with fresh sensibilities. The quality and quantity of everything she surveys so exceed the surroundings she chose for herself in Boston. *Home?* Chloe hears the front door close and emerges from the kitchen be-gloved in yellow latex, takes one look at Abby and momentarily drops her composure.

"Hi, sweetheart! I wasn't expecting you."

They linger longer than usual in a sincere embrace that more than compensates for Russell's scowl.

"Hi Mom! I wanted to surprise you. My place seemed kinda lonely. So, here I am."

"Wonderful! How have you been? How's your apartment? Are you enjoying Boston?"

"It's all going well. I'm starting to feel more comfortable, actually. My apartment is just the right size, and it's in a cute community. I haven't met anyone my age yet, but my neighbors are friendly."

"You must be starved. Can I fix you something?"

"No, that's okay, but thanks."

"Your face looks thinner. Have you been eating? Let me fix you something."

"No thanks, Mom, really. I ate before I left Boston. I'll wait for breakfast."

"Are you sure, honey?"

Russell's short fuse smolders to its base. "For God's sake, Chloe, the girl said she's not hungry. How many times do I have to hear it?"

*What was I thinking?* "Thanks anyway, Mom. It's been a really long day. I'm gonna go to bed. But we can catch up in the morning, okay? Goodnight."

Chloe longs to move past pleasantries, but relents. "Okay. Goodnight, honey."

Abby picks up her belongings and heads toward the stairs.

"I made up your bed for you, in case you came to visit. There are towels in the closet." Humbled by stating the obvious, Chloe concedes, "Of course you know that. Sleep well."

Sensing Chloe's yearning, Abby lovingly returns to her mother for another embrace and a welcomed kiss. Within earshot of a stifling chill, their eyes say all their voices may not.

*Thanks, Mom. I appreciate you.*

*I'm glad you're here.*

Abby opens the door she has opened thousands of times. She flips the light switch that still sports the "Abby" count-cross-stitch plate-cover her grandmother, Elizabeth, made for her. Moved by her mother's love, she realizes Chloe has done her best to re-create a welcoming space where her space used to be. But absent her posters and plush, Abby feels like company. Her home, yet not her home. Nothing she chose to bring with her bridges the gap. Most of it will be consumed before sleeping.

Nearly exhausted but driven, she undresses and views herself front to back in the mirror. Despite her unsettled emotions, she manages a smile. *Getting there.* Once dressed in a loose-fitting nightgown, she takes a seat on her floor and carefully muffles the zipper as she silently opens her overnight bag. Soft, quiet donuts are first.

While she indulges, the insights that surfaced between homes stir revelations of wider breadth. She recalls the gratification she felt upon learning from Ellen that her peers believed "the Thompsons live in 'utopia.'" It came as no surprise, really. She knew her home's putting-green front lawn rivaled any country club course. Its spring and autumn floral shades mimicked the pallets of Impressionists. Its vegetable garden produced only produce, not weeds. Its window shutters always flaunted the year's new color. The ding-free cars in its garage never aged more than two years nor went two weeks without a wax. Table linens and upholstery fabrics on its furnishings were richer than royalty. Its water was always hot, its lights bright, its locks secure. Anyone seeking weaknesses in the external features of the Thompson home left frustrated. There were none. Russell saw to that.

She relives the day her hubris deflated to dismay when, having abraded its idyllic surface with new awareness, she saw her family's centerfold-of-a-home-interiors-magazine life with new clarity—as a pristine facade for the dysfunction that lay beneath—a family forced into rigid, constrictive molds: the

33

breadwinner, the homemaker, the favored and the second-born. She realized Russell saw to that, too. As she finishes the last of her confections, she realizes he still does.

Saturday mornings highlight the Thompson role-divisions more clearly than most. As patriarch, Russell enthrones himself confidently at the head of the formally set table overseeing the efforts to please him from behind the early edition of the *New York Times*. Chloe, active for hours, tends to the cutting boards, skillets, juicer and percolator as the sizzle of smokey bacon, the tang of fresh oranges and the aroma of brewing coffee create a symphony for the senses. Mark, in training for his role as man-of-the-house, practices this week's hymns at the piano, indifferent to the happenings around him.

The absence of the second-born has yet to become routine. Russell still resents it. Mark still fumbles due to it. But the effects of Abby's move fall heaviest on Chloe. Only her heart and hands experience the loss of her supportive daughter. Yet, for better or worse, having her home again stirs the layers of latent disquiet that had nearly settled since her departure.

Mark breaks the silence from his place in front of his keys. "Mom, was I dreaming or did I hear Abby's voice last night? Is she home?"

"Yes. She got in after you went to bed, must have been around ten. Didn't you hear her in the bathroom this morning?"

"I heard someone. I didn't know it was Abby."

Asserting his authority, Russell barks out, "Call her. Breakfast is ready."

"Abby! Breakf…"

"Not from here, Mark. Go tell her."

"Abby, get up! Breakfast!"

Once Mark is safely away, Chloe's concern gets the better of her. "Take a good look at Abby when she comes down. I think she's losing weight."

"You worry too much. She misses your cooking. She won't starve."

Chloe diverts her eyes to hide her frustration as Mark reenters and reports in. "She didn't answer and her door is locked."

"Locked? Then she goes without. Let her get good and hungry. Then she'll show some respect for her mother. Let's eat."

Mustering her intent to be heard, Chloe passes the serving dishes and fills the juice glasses and coffee cups. "She hasn't eaten since Boston. She's probably just fallen back to sleep."

"Sleeping or not, this family will not stop in its tracks because she decides to drive back here at all hours. Bow your heads. Bless these gifts, Lord, received through Your bounty."

"Amen."

Contrasting the atmosphere one floor down, Abby's room is dark and serene—home, yet not home. While tensions below volley between concern and disdain for her well-being, here she feels nothing of the sort. She knows her goal and how to reach it. She is in control. Finally.

Aware of how observant and persistent her brother can be, Abby painstakingly avoids the hallway's creaking floor boards as she leaves the haven of her bedroom. She needs a few more minutes to herself. She enters the bathroom, gently closes and latches the door behind her and turns on the light. She has perfected her technique so as to barely make a sound as the food she so consciously consumed flows into the commode. She finishes. Her secret remains. A simple flush, a rinse and dab of her mouth and face, and her public day begins.

Hiding so basic a secret challenges Abby's full range of diversions. No one notices her first trip upstairs following her serving of reheated pancakes. She blames her next absence on feeling "a little gassy" after a grilled cheese sandwich and homemade tomato soup. Thankfully, no one dares to question her abrupt departure after dinner when she mentions "my time of the month." She exhausts her supply of plausible excuses after Sunday breakfast, just in time to say "goodbye."

Relieved to be back home in her apartment, Abby sways with the music as she joyfully stirs a pot of steaming vegetable soup. She serves herself a generous helping, then another, and another until only tomatoey residue remains. Satisfied with this evening's binging phase, Abby walks past three empty soup cans and two empty cracker boxes—laying crushed on the counter—and makes her day's last visit to the bathroom. The routine of purging does not diminish her gratitude for this way to consume all she wants and suffer no consequences. She makes quick work of her dishes and divides the empty containers between trash and recyclables.

Her nightly practice continues with a shower followed by a naked visit to her mirror—*Abdomen, buttocks, thighs, arms.* —and scale, "One forty-three." *Getting there.* Sleep calls her name as she puts on her nightgown and climbs longingly into bed. By the flickering light of her bedside candle, she begins her next journal entry.

> July 12, 1981, Dear Diary, How to summarize today? If visiting home taught me anything it's that binging and purging are so much simpler when I'm alone. Privacy is good.

She takes note of the happenings in and around her, and analyzes them to release her mind from racing.

> Here my body gratefully absorbs the sounds, sights and flavors of my little personal refuge. Muted

*Bach, vased azalea cuttings, vegetable soup. There I felt like the strained knot in mom and dad's clandestine tug-of-war. My weight, my faith, my intentions. But, all of it adds up to a life. All of it, if I can live it honestly, helps me understand and relate to my world and to others. First day tomorrow!!!*

She closes the book as her recorded thoughts flow into prayer. "Holy Father, Holy Mother, bless my family, and my friends. Be with me as I start down a new path toward a destination I've never even imagined. Please, catch me if I fall. Amen."

# 8. State of Unrest

Thirty-eight days. Exhaustion, from five weeks without sleep, magnifies Debbie's agony. Shame, for being so naive, restrains her connecting. Her eyes perceive light without acknowledging it. Her ears garble the vibrations they encounter. Her skin recoils at the slightest touch. Her tongue regrets its role. She would gladly halt her breathing to quash the haunting memories of his rancid odors burned into her brain. Debbie's senses became weapons that night, in the pouring rain, in the front seat of a rapist's car. Their lethal ends face both directions.

Driven by fear, Debbie avoids human contact whenever possible. She flees instead to the only truly safe place she knows, at least in daylight. Isolated, among the headstones, with a clear view of her surroundings in every direction, here her exhales sometimes tend back toward automatic. A welcomed breeze stirs the leaves on the surrounding sycamores. But, gentle air currents lift both the fragrant aroma of bright, vased flowers marking loved ones lost, and the putrid acridity of wilted, moldy remnants left too long.

Such dichotomies occur to Debbie every time she visits the cemetery where her beloved Nana rests. Rebirth and decay.

Confrontation and resignation. Love-making and date-raping. Alone on her knees, as she tends to the weeds and leaves of grass that escaped the blade on mowing day, she pleads for relief. "I can't go on like this, Nana."

Weariness collapses her to her haunches. Her body releases forward, rocking rhythmically, front to back to front. Her forehead rests on her knees. Her eyelids lower. Her breathing slows and deepens. Relaxation saturates her muscles... a sudden flinch as her reflexes resist gravity's pull and she awakens again. A chill. A fright. And with the threat of the impending sunset, Debbie hurriedly gathers her belongings and drives away.

The chill follows Debbie home. A hot shower could serve two purposes. By the diffused light entering through her bathroom door slightly ajar, evidence of Debbie's lasting trauma abounds. No longer do pretty somethings provide joy. Only dust covers the shelf. No longer does viewing her face bring the slightest satisfaction. Newsprint covers the mirror. Not only does she wait to drop her heavy terry robe till the last possible moment before entering the steaming shower, she does so only with the door and her eyes tightly shut. But in the end, these futile efforts do little to mask the memories that haunt her waking and nightmares. *Will I ever feel clean again?*

# 9. Off the Block

Alarm. Covers off. Feet on floor. Play Johann Sebastian Bach. As her fantasy materializes, Abby feels well-prepared for her first day as a professional radio personality. Her best outfit hangs freshly laundered and pressed, ready for wearing. The script of her opening remarks, tucked safely in her briefcase. Her emergency food and drink, stashed on her car's passenger seat. As for the show itself, preparation relies on living consciously and listening intentionally. Those, for Abby, come naturally.

Abby sashays into her kitchen with a lilt and a spin. Johann, summer breezes and sunshine have that effect. Her refrigerator gives up its contents to the toaster and skillet. Pop, crack, sizzle, drizzle. Breakfast! Planning makes perfect. "Thank you, God, for this beautiful day and whatever it brings!! Amen."

Her methodical consumption once again reinforces her sovereignty over the morsels on her plate. Bite by bite, extracting every waft of aroma, every pocket of flavor. Control. Pausing, to let the feeling of satiation register, she inhales high, shallow breaths. C-o-n-t-r-o-l. Her fingers and lips twitch as her nourishment longs for its ultimate repository. "Enough." Feeling her power surge, she purges.

Neat and complete, she enters the next phase of her morning routine cleansed and energized. Abby's spirit dances on the strings' melody line as she dons what she promises will be the final tan and gray pieces in her wardrobe. "I'll get there, one step at a time." Fed, cleansed and dressed, Abby takes one more look in her mirror. "Humility be damned. Starting today, LifeLine will forge its place in history!"

Abby emerges from the stairwell, carefully avoiding any eye contact with Renee who, though on the phone, surely has her radar tuned to Abby's arrival. *Dry runs have value.* Elusively, she slips into the restroom to rid herself of the half-digested snacks from her car's front seat. "Success. Here I go!"

As she opens the station door, she overhears Renee's parting words, "…to come in as soon as she arrives. Yes ma'am." Renee's excitement pours out at first glance. "Well, good morning, Abby! Big day!"

"Good morning, Renee. Yes, it is!"

"Are you ready for your radio debut? I just spoke to Ms. Warner. She'd like to see you as soon as you drop your things."

Abby's complexion blanches.

"It's nothing to worry about. She likes to give pep talks, 'confidence builders,' she calls them."

"I wasn't planning on meeting with Linda. Do I look all right?"

"Sure, you look great! Besides, anything goes around here. It's radio."

"Okay. I'll put these in the studio."

Abby deposits her parcels and returns to Renee's desk. "Should I go in by myself?"

"Of course. It's nice to have you on the team."

Despite her clear qualifications, Abby lugs her apprehension toward the door ajar. The effects of her father's browbeating linger. *Breathe.* She gently knocks and nudges the door open several inches. From the threshold, she views the familiar inner sanctum. Fresh flowers. Family photos. Fabric curtains. She feels the color returning to her face. Linda drinks coffee from an oversized mug while waving Abby forward.

"You asked to see me?"

Abby sheepishly enters the room, and stays near the door, waiting for a formal invitation to move forward. Linda joyfully provides it. "Good morning. Please, Abby, come in. Sit down. Welcome to the WTOK team! Are you excited for your first day as a radio professional? You've got so much potential. It will be a delightful challenge to keep one step ahead of you."

Abby responds with gratitude and, willing it so, muted confidence. "Thank you so much for this opportunity, really. I'm just so honored to be here, to have my own show. Giving people an outlet for their private thoughts, I mean, I'm grateful you liked the idea. I just hope I can live up to your expectations."

"Be yourself and you'll do fine. Listen, Abby, Boston is a bit of a hike from Brookfield. If you ever need anything, I hope you'll feel free to ask anyone here at the station. We really look out for each other."

"I appreciate that. Thank you."

"Good luck today, Abby."

"Thank you." Reassured, Abby leaves the office smiling. Renee glances her way and flashes a cheery two-thumbs-up. Abby responds in kind. She enters the studio and closes the sound-proofing door behind her.

The room's floor-to-ceiling plate glass window overlooks a lushly wooded area. The fresh green leaves of early summer hang motionless in the placid air. Abby absorbs the innate energy of her surroundings as she seats herself and edges closer to the microphone. She puts on her earphones and quietly opens a folder containing her prepared script. The "ON AIR" sign lights. Gordon, in the adjacent glass-enclosed control room, flashes a smile and a "You're on."

"Good morning, Boston. I'm Abby Thompson. Welcome to the inaugural edition of LifeLine, a radio program directed by you. We all have thoughts we're reluctant to share, even with those closest to us. Sometimes, especially with those closest to us. Without an outlet, these thoughts lie fallow. This is your outlet. This is where we nurture your thoughts and give you an opportunity to grow. I invite you to share what makes you human. The situations in your life that generate exuberance or agony, pride or fear. The number is 555-WTOK. To get things started, I'll tell you that I'm new to the Boston area. Are there any places I need to visit in the next few days that will provide my rites of passage? We have a call. Hello, welcome to LifeLine, the airwaves are yours."

"Welcome to The Hub, Abby. You're gonna want to go to Filene's Basement. The place is always crowded with bargain hunters but…"

Driving home, Abby basks in the thrill of Gordon applauding each time he switched off the mic, of Renee squealing as she greeted "Our new star!" and of Linda and even the Plant Lady taking time to congratulate her on a job well done. Upon arriving at her apartment, the impulse to make a call to Brookfield and share her joy ebbs and flows as her soaring enthusiasm and wounded pride arm-wrestle to a draw. On one hand, she knows moments like these should warrant a family celebration or at least a heartfelt "Good for you!" But, recalling her recent visit — her father's judgmental temper, her mother's capitulation, her brother's disinterest — dulls her excitement.

After quarreling with herself for more than an hour she makes a decision. "They knew it was today. They can call me." Uneasy with her choice, but resolved to maintain it, Abby turns her attention to her to-do list hoping for a distraction. She cooks and enjoys a delicious lunch topped off by a decadent dessert. "Eat, check." She replaces digestive tract gurgling with silence. "Purge, check." She presses tomorrow's garments and hangs them on the shower rod. "Prepare clothes, check." She yields her body and soul to Handel's restorative care. "Unwind. Damn. This isn't working. It's not even four o'clock! Laundry. I'll do laundry."

Abby tosses bath linens and undergarments, worn-once blouses and bed linens in her immaculate laundry baskets. She counts out an oversupply of quarters and dimes and drops them into her shoulder bag. "Walk or drive?" She lifts the baskets. "Better drive."

Abby sits quietly, fixated on the "wash, rinse, spin" lights as they announce the progress of her belongings' adventures. Giant rolling dryers toss and tangle the sheets and leave delicates hidden inside blouses, willfully clinging by ionic charge. She checks her watch. *Five-thirty. I guess I'll fold them here.* On her way out the door, she remembers the corner grocer. "Maybe just a few things."

Her prolonged outing complete, Abby trudges in the door with baskets full of fresh linens and groceries galore. She freezes the ice cream, refrigerates the meats and shelves the non-perishables. She remakes her bed, closets her towels and hangs her blouses. Within no time, her thumbs twiddle. "Okay, now what?" She wanders to the kitchen and peruses her purchases. "I guess it's time for dinner." Eighty-nine clicks of her clock's minute hand later, while drying her lips after her day's final cleanse, Abby convinces herself to take the risk and make the call. "They knew it was today. Maybe they're wondering how it went."

She cozies up on her sofa and dials by candlelight. "Hi, Dad. My first show was today. The callers were all really friendly. I kept the phones lit up for two hours and I know the best places to visit. It's exactly what I inten... Oh, sorry. I forgot about the game. Are the Red Sox winn... Is Mom there? Can you tell her and Mark I said 'hello?' Goodnight, Da..." Breath withdrawn and heart empty, she replaces the receiver as her shoulders and spirits deflate. She extinguishes the candles and resigns to fill her gaping void with a trusted servant. "Rocky Road."

She sits at the table in the dark and opens the family-sized carton. She draws her spoon over the soft surface and watches the luscious, lumpy curl form. She extends her lips over the sweet, chocolaty creaminess, compressing it with her enraptured tongue against the roof of her mouth and isolating the salted nuts hidden within. "This is working." Peace restored, Abby's head bobs and catches as she scrapes the last remnants of melted pleasure from the carton's seams. She distractedly licks the spoon till it reflects the glow of the streetlight. Time to cleanse, again. The mere thought reinforces her sense of tranquility.

Having removed the contaminants within, she undresses and steps into the shower to remove the contaminants without. She delights in the ecstasy of steaming water pouring down her back and through her hair while lathering limbs and torso with a fragrant bar. "Ahhhhh." Stepping out, soaked impressions form on the thirsty tufts beneath her feet as she towels her hair and body. *Weigh-ins must be dry.* Her mirror, her scale, and therefore, she, herself, do not disappoint. "One forty."

Her nightgown and bed yearn for company. Once seated, her journal receives the first thoughts of its new entry.

> *July 13, 1981, Dear Diary, First day at WTOK! I'm so glad I did a dry run last week. I knew what to expect driving down and parking. My coworkers seem to think I did a good job, for a rookie.*

*Hooray!! Renee and Gordon, even Linda and the woman who comes on after me, were smiling. Dad, of course, wasn't interested enough to turn off his game. Oh well, families need more than blood to bind them. But who knows? LifeLine could be a hit!*

Writing the details until her vision softens, she happily slides under the sheets. "Holy Father, thank you for this day. Thank you for the people I met and for the relationships I've begun. Please bless my friends and, yes, my family. Please, catch me if I fall. Amen."

# 10. Serpentine

With summer in full swing and her savings and pay in her pocket, Abby sets out to do a little seasonal spending. First task: Wardrobe. She scours the racks at Filene's for garments that finally reflect her personality —turquoise and coral, red and orange—to replace the drab tans and grays bestowed upon her by her parents' decree. As she loads up her arms and heads to the dressing rooms, she remembers having fear of an omnipotent God injected into every aspect of her childhood. "God is watching." "God can hear you." "God knows your thoughts." How she accepted these statements as fact and as threats. To tighten the straight jacket one notch more, as a female, she carried the responsibility to avoid arousing sexual tension in the men and boys around her. Based on her experiences as an adolescent, she accepted, "If you fail, boys will force you to have sex with them," as fact and as threat as well. As a result, below-the-knee hems and oversized blouses comprised the entirety of the outfits chosen for her and by her. So powerful an indoctrination leaves deep scars, for despite her expanded and personalized understanding of God, she hears those voices, exhumed from her childhood memories, haunt her style choices still. "Modestly. Discreetly. Cover your sexual zones." She smiles —*That's a lot of fig leaves.* —tamps them down and pulls the room's curtain closed.

Abby undresses and views her slimming body in the three-way mirror. *Wow, I need a set-up like this at home.* She turns front to back and front again and nods in approval. *Getting there.* She slides proudly into a size 12 knit skirt. *Nice. Fits perfectly. So I need that in a size 10.* She tries on pants in size 12 and knit tops in size 10. She returns to the rack and finds each piece in the next smaller size. *How much fun is this?!*

With bulging shopping bags on either arm, Abby hops in her car and heads to Symphony Hall to purchase tickets to three Boston Pops concerts at Tanglewood. She hands over cash and slides the tickets into her wallet, imagining packing a picnic lunch and enjoying the sunshine and live music on her own terms. Her heart swells with joy. Every step she takes feels lighter.

Back at her car, she checks her watch. *Where next?* As if on cue, she senses a tender reminder stir in her abdomen. "Ahh! Where shall I lunch?" She thinks back to a Boston family vacation a decade ago. *Where were we? Our waitress was hysterically rude. Dad got so angry. He does not handle disrespect well.* Unable to recall, she lets her budding confidence shine and asks a passerby. Upon hearing "Durgin-Park in Faneuil Hall," the full memory floods back of the casually dressed waitress, cracking her gum and sitting down next to Russell to take their order. *She insulted his button-down shirt!* Abby chuckles at the thought. "We were on vacation, after all. Durgin-Park it is!"

Abby's appetite builds during her meandering trip back toward the Waterfront. "There it is! Durgin-Park!" She eagerly takes her place in the lengthy queue of lunchtime locals and tourists intent on enjoying delicacies found only in New England while surrounded by sights and sounds that go back hundreds of years. Her mouth waters in anticipation. Finally, the travel-weary hostess escorts her to a seat by the kitchen. From her vantage point, Abby witnesses every plate of steaming food heading toward its destination. She fidgets in her seat and checks her remaining cash. Her obvious impatience attracts the attention of a brawny woman, sporting a well-soiled apron, who arrives pen and pad in hand. "Yah, whaddaya want?"

Abby giggles, "I'd like a shepherd's pie, the clam bake, a side of fries and broccoli. Could you stagger the entrees, please?"

# 11. Asides

Mother Nature has her in a headlock, but Betty's determination, to fight to her last breath, endures. Someone told her weeds have more leaves than flowers. By that definition, her entire quarter-acre is a weed bed. Between the overgrowth, the sun-bleached toys and the moss patches, her dream of a showpiece yard gets more unlikely by the day. Tending her tiny herb garden, however, presents a reasonable challenge with a more promising outcome. And being outdoors, singing along to songs on her favorite station while the kids play a game indoors, feels like a blessing from above. Suddenly, her revelry snaps to the crescendo of a spirited, yet unfamiliar, symphony. She deflates. "Hey! Who changed the station? Ben? Sandy? Who? Joe—y?"

In frustration, she removes her muddy gloves, bangs the accumulated soil from the tread of her shoes and enters the house. "Joey, I've told you so many times not to touch the buttons. I like to hear my music. Don't touch the buttons. Do you hear me? Ben, please keep Joey busy playing a game. I need to make some progress outside. Thank you." The two formidable creators, Betty and Mother Nature, resume their *pas de deux*. Both know which one is the lead.

Though summer is still in full bloom, Betty already dreads the change of seasons. *I need something creative to get me through the darkness.* Aware of the consequences of acknowledging its influence, she suppresses the voice within. *Focus on now.* She pinches back the white blooms from her bolting basil plant. The sharp fragrance, one of her favorites, cuts through her longing. "Maybe we'll have pesto on pasta tonight?" Her calm returns.

By mid-afternoon, Betty begins her daily struggle against the effects of her sleep-deprived nights. Her pace slows. Her mind fogs. Her patience ebbs. The voice resurfaces. Her willpower frays. *Dinner. Focus on dinner.* She moves through the prescribed steps to prepare, serve and clean up after the meal. Harry expresses his customary gratitude. She expresses her customary "my pleasure."

Tucked between homework and baths, pestering and conceding, Betty hears but abruptly stifles the voice in her head. *Now is not the time.* Longing for the dissonance to end, Betty counts the hours, then minutes, until the household sighs to silent. *One voice, my voice.* She sighs along.

Middle-of-the-night moments of quiet solitude offer some compensation for Betty's insomnia. For during such precious times, her mind turns reflective to summon her inner voice. She listens as it sorts through shopping lists, conjures up craft ideas and dictates poetry. Yes, poetry. Her sole opportunity to bare her soul, if only to herself. Tonight's composition provides no comfort, save that her wayward thoughts, thus freed, now reside on the page. Harry shifts his supine position the moment a tear tumbles to her journal's cover. She wonders if he senses her despair. She wipes the cover dry. He settles. She wonders if he ever will.

# 12. Duck and Weave

Nature's promenade from summer to autumn follows a well-trod path toward cooler days and warmer hues. Clothing Abby purchased for temperate days takes up residence in drawers and racks, below and behind cozy corduroy and stylish wool. Finally, fashion works in her favor. This season, layers make the woman. Her style and wardrobe illuminate the glow of self-assurance Abby brings to every show.

After less than three months, she no longer hesitates to trust her instincts, but rather, engages her audience as a confidant. Accustomed to her now-normal, she keeps her ritual disguised but not hidden. She lives free and captive simultaneously. And at the microphone, she thrives. "Glen, thank you for that great story of your latest camping adventure. Next up is Jo. Good morning. Welcome to LifeLine, the airwaves are yours…"

Nearly three hours since her last meal, the pang of hunger scraping at her empty stomach distracts her from her caller. Road construction this morning interfered with her pre-show feeding, so urgency dictates an especially hurried departure from the studio as the Plant Lady takes over as host. Abby releases an inaudible exhale as her theme music overlaps her farewell. "… Thank you for calling, Jo."

"Thank you for your show, Abby."

"My pleasure. Another hour of LifeLine comes to a close. LifeLine offers you the opportunity to share your humanity—the extraordinary, the mundane and everything in between. Every weekday, between ten and twelve, the WTOK airwaves are your LifeLine. Thank you, Boston. *Time for sustenance. Avoid eye contact.*

Renee and Donna watch astutely as Abby gathers her belongings. After weeks of observing Abby's weight loss and strategizing how to intercept her before she bolts out the door, they finally have their golden opportunity. Coordinated by nods, they move in tandem like wranglers toward a wayward calf. Renee times her stall tactic impeccably. "Abby, don't run out. You had a call from Ellen Kincaid. She said you'd recognize her name. She left her number."

Abby reluctantly slows her pace, despite her lightheadedness, at the mention of her dearest friend. "Did you say Ellen Kincaid?"

"Yes. Ellen Kincaid." Renee, dawdling, slowly relinquishes the pink message as she uses her date-night "tell-me-more" expression to root Abby in place. It succeeds. As always.

"We've been friends since grade school."

"Really? That's amazing! She said she meant to call sooner but, well. She said she's moving to, hmmm, where did she say? She said…" Frail and clumsy though they appear, Renee's intentional fumbling and vapid lines nonetheless tether Abby motionless, giving Donna the opportunity to appear nonchalant, calm and non-threatening in her coincidental arrival.

Donna's peer-standing conferred the next phase of their intervention to her. "Hey, loved the show. That guy, Glen? was hysterical. I know more about lean-tos than I really need to. And your last caller, Jo, was so sincere."

Abby feels a personal conversation unfolding, a luxury she seldom affords herself. *I can't do this. Not today. You know how to wrap it up. Keep walking.* "That's what gets to me, too. It's as if we put windows in their hearts. I'm so pleased to be a part of it."

Donna winds up and lets loose her language lasso. "Join me for lunch? My treat. I'm going down to the wharf for clams."

Abby dodges its landing. "Sorry. I'm going to a watercolor class at the museum. I usu…"

Foiled, Donna tries another tack. "I didn't know you were an artist."

Determined to maintain her privacy and reach the exit, Abby deflects again. "It's more a hobby than anything. Anyway, I usually just grab something on the way. But thanks for asking. Maybe next time?"

Seeing her opportunity dissolving before her eyes, Donna resorts to unvarnished interrogation. "Sure. Don't mind me asking, but are you doing okay?"

"I'm great. I love my job. Boston's a wonderful city."

"I hope you don't mind me saying, I mean, I can't help but notice your weight. I have a friend…"

Abby's defenses simmer. She recycles her standard reply. "It's not a problem. I put on a few extra pounds at school. I'm just getting back to where I was."

Donna persists. "If you ever want to talk."

"Thanks, but, I'm in control."

"Control? Keep my offer in mind. If ever."

Within arm's length of the exit, Abby makes her move. "Thanks, Donna, I will. Gotta go."

Abby mindfully slides the message paper into her pocket, then puts her full weight into opening the station door. Regret distorts Donna's face as she gazes back toward Renee, shrugs and shakes her lowered head.

# 13. Dress Rehearsal

As October kicks in, without the chatter and laughter of interacting children, Betty does her best to entertain Joey singlehandedly. But monotony's rhythm has settled in, again. Her focus narrows to a weekly routine that numbs longing. She shops on Mondays. Does laundry on Tuesdays. She irons on Wednesdays. Cleans surfaces Thursdays. She vacuums on Fridays. Tidies on Saturdays. She plans menus on Sundays for the week ahead.

Today, as always, her connection to the living world flows over the FM airwaves. Pressing starch into poly-cotton collars and cuffs seems somehow bearable when she harmonizes to lyrics of her youth. Betty pushes and pulls her iron in a distracted daze as Joey constructs myriad structures from interlocking blocks tucked in the hanging gardens of Harry's freshly ironed dress shirts. Demanding the attention he misses, Joey tiptoes to the stereo, presses AM and presto, he's got it. Betty identifies the culprit by process of elimination. "Joey! How many times?" As she gingerly makes her way to undo the damage, the soothing sound of Abby's voice stops her short.

"Glen, thank you for that great story of your latest camping adventure. Next up is Jo. Good morning. Welcome to LifeLine, the airwaves are yours."

Betty leaves the radio dial set and robotically returns to her task.

"I've been listening since July and I've finally gathered the courage to call. With so many lonely people in the world I thought my story might help someone. I lived for five years wondering if I would ever find happiness again. My husband lost his desire for me. It took me a long time to come to grips with that."

Betty's stroke over the flattened sleeve stalls as her distraction meanders further off course.

"It wasn't until after he left that I realized my own potential to live. Now I'm in a fabulous relationship that thrives on me being me. Believe me, if I can come this far, anyone can."

"How did his leaving change you?"

"Hmmm. Well. It changed me in many ways because it freed me from constantly being judged. I have to admit, he had the better looks and personality, always smiling and joking. For eight years, I lived in his shadow in social situations for sure, but even at home. I was convinced my value relied on his opinion of me. So, the day he left, and for months afterwards, I felt empty and worthless. I carried more than my share of the blame, I can see that now, but at the time, I believed his leaving was all my fault.

"It should not have surprised me, but, without him around to criticize and overrule me, my personality was able to develop. It needed to. I needed to survive in the world. I treated myself better than he had. I forgave my shortcomings and worked to improve them. But, doing it without his badgering, meant I could learn from my mistakes without the intermediary step of feeling useless."

"Why did you stay as long as you did, if you were so unhappy?"

"I dreaded the thought of divorce. I knew neither of us was happy, but I thought being alone would be worse. His leaving was totally out of my control. My choice, at that point, was to stay broken or heal myself. I didn't do it on my own, but I did it. I called up a friend and neighbor who had gone through a break-up, too. We had a long conversation and she suggested a self-help book that she read, just to build up my self-esteem a bit."

"Exactly! Great idea! Being in contact with people who have gone through disruptive experiences not only proves that getting through is possible, you can also get ideas about how to move forward."

"Right. The book suggested figuring out affirming ways to spend my free time. So, then I started going out to hear music and for walks in the woods. All to find who I was without anyone's judgment. I found I had new interests and untapped talents. While I found me, love found me, too."

Betty catches the scent of scorched fabric. Bored with the consequences of excessive heat on flammable objects, a single eyebrow barely shifts. She uprights the iron, still transfixed.

"The struggle you worked through sounds heart-wrenching, Jo. Change always is. But, as you've shown us, if you can hang in there, the outcome is almost always an improvement. I know there are people listening who are a few steps behind you. Others, a few steps ahead. Your courage to embrace change is an inspiration. Thank you for calling."

"Thank you for your show, Abby."

"My pleasure. Another hour of LifeLine comes to a close. LifeLine offers you the opportunity to share your humanity—the extraordinary, the mundane and everything in between. Every weekday, between ten and twelve, the WTOK airwaves are your LifeLine. Thank you, Boston."

"WTOK? LifeLine? Well, Joey, finally your button-pushing paid off. Let's get some lunch." Betty rolls up today's singe victim. *This will make a couple nice rags.* "I just have to put these away." She lifts the fruits of her efforts from the bowing clothes rack. The wire hangers cut into her hand and strain her wrist under their weight. As she gratefully transfers the shirts to the closet, her gaze falls on a sequined memory hanging pristine in a floor-length dry cleaner's cover. She removes it from the rod, holds it up to herself and hums softly as she dances slowly around the bedroom. Her flight of fancy transports her to a younger heart and mind. Joey, hungry and curious, enters the room but remains unnoticed as long as his appetite allows.

"I'm hungry, Mommy. What are you doing?"

"I'm pretending I'm in love."

"I love you, Mommy."

"I know, honey. I love you, too."

# 14. Log Roll

Despite her protestations to the contrary, evidence of ordered chaos layers Abby's life. It's been nearly three months since her realization that weekly coupon circulars meant for her entire street are not deposited in individual boxes by the mail carrier. Having seen them left to accumulate, she thought it only frugal to make use of them herself. All of them. Twenty of each coupon. Thirty or more coupons. Weekly. Now, neat stacks of identical, name-brand crackers, cookies, condiments and cereal cover nearly every horizontal surface of her kitchen. Bags of snacks overflow cardboard boxes under the table. Two-liter bottles of soda encircle the room, two deep. This exaggeration of plenty combats Abby's near-constant, nagging anxiety. Though grateful that purging and flushing her meals satisfies her personal goals, watching a normal-sized grocery order float, rotate and disappear, several times a day, plucks at her thinly veiled fear of exhausting her provisions. With more than enough for today and tomorrow, food insecurity vanishes. Control.

Her evening ritual begins. Embraced in the vibration of Vivaldi, she loosens the stress of her day from her body. Arms sway above her head; hips catch the wave; feet, spread, take on her alternating weight; her delicate shadow dances on the floor, ceiling and walls, lit from behind by flickering candles. Once one with the symphony, she makes her way to the spigot to wash her hands, lathering to the elbow and rinsing till her skin glows. Her meal, consumed in installments, depletes her food supply by a negligible amount. Still, the crushed and discarded packaging fills her waste receptacle and recycling box. Time for this installment's cleanse.

Not only has Abby's coupon strategy provided her a means to support her goal of eating all that she wants, of whatever she wants, whenever she wants, but recently the necessity to rid her body of all food remnants gave rise to the invention of the "purge bottle." Not a true invention. Merely an adaptation of a common object. Abby leans over the toilet. Her reflex expels the nourishment consumed moments ago. She fills a two-liter bottle with water from the tub spigot. She drinks while the water continues to run. She leans over the toilet again. Again she vomits. She refills the bottle, drinks and vomits. The expelled fluid is clear. Control.

With the regularity of a metronome's arm, Abby lifts her clothing from her diminishing body and steps into the steaming shower. Her sinews and sighs give up the last residuals of today's challenges — the show and near showdown. *Take time to heal.* Her hands slide, soap-covered, over her defined shoulders and pelvic bones, breasts and calves. *Release.* She watches as the lather flows down the drain taking with it the grime of the day. *Cleanse.*

After drying hair and body, she walks, naked to her mirror and examines every contour, every hollow. Unfazed by today's incremental change, she steps on the scale. "One hundred and thirty pounds." *Getting there.* A sigh of relief. She calmly dresses in her nightgown and pulls back the covers on her bed. Seated, she retrieves her journal and a pen.

> October 1, 1981, Dear Diary, Perception is in the eye of the beholder. My coworkers are concerned by my weight loss. I gave my normal excuse. They seemed skeptical. I'll have to wear more layers.

As sleep once again imposes its weight, she slides to horizontal and reaches out to her Almighty. "Goddess of Heaven and Earth, preserve the good in the world against evil. Please, catch me if I fall. Amen."

# 15. Molten Emotions

One hundred and seventeen days. The wall clock's minute hand snaps to vertical as Debbie enters the Animal Physiology classroom. Camouflaged in oversized clothing, no make-up and closely cropped hair, her physical presence declares neither male nor female. Her wounded demeanor wards off anyone seeking to figure it out. She barely casts a glance toward even her friend and housemate, Megan, as she winds her way to her lab table in the center of the room. Jeremy, her lab partner, has already tacked the specimen to the dissection tray and reviewed the manual of the systems on today's assignment, cat anatomy.

Jeremy greets her with bright positivity. "Hi, Debbie. How are you?"

Determined to accomplish something, Debbie pushes out a reply. *I can do this.* "Hi. Thanks for setting up."

"No worries. I've got everything ready. Do you want to dissect or do the drawings?"

Horrified by the alternative, Debbie blurts, "I'll draw."

Jeremy uses his scalpel and curved probe to open the carcass and explore its contents "Okay, great! Respiratory system is first. So these are the lungs. Here are the three lobes of the right lung. One, two, three. Left lung, one, two, three. Easy enough. This tube must be the trachea. So this part here must be the larynx. And the mouth."

Debbie draws as Jeremy describes the components. "Is that it?"

"It must be. Am I going too fast?"

She tallies a win. "No, I'm getting it."

"One down. The next system is reproductive. I think we're responsible for the male and female systems." Jeremy calls over to the adjacent table. "Megan, do you have a male or a female?"

"A female, and pregnant at that."

"We have a male. Can we swap copies of our diagrams?"

"Anything to save doing this twice."

"Great, thanks. Okay, Debbie, are you ready?"

The wafting formaldehyde and dry heat tip Debbie's agitation into the red zone. She walks away to open a window and takes repeated deep breaths. *Relax.* She returns to the table nearly drained of willpower. Jeremy notices her vacant stare.

"What's wrong, Debbie? Don't you feel well?"

"Let's just get this done."

"Okay. If you're sure. It would probably be easier to start at the end. That'll lead us to the testicles. So, here's the penis. Look, here are those barbs Dr. Bob mentioned. No wonder the female screams during mating."

Debbie's eyes and nostrils widen; sweat drenches her sternum, face and palms; her breathing turns rapid and shallow. *NO!*

Focused on his task, Jeremy misses her silent transformation and continues his work. "This must be the right ductus deferens." He glances up. "You don't look so good. Am I doing something wrong?"

Debbie fights unsuccessfully to control her panic. "I, I, I just can't. I thought I…"

"If you'd rather, I'll draw and you can do the dissection?"

"I can't. Megan, I have to go."

Megan looks up from her notepad to see a blur rush out the door. Jeremy drops his tools, rips off his gloves and starts after her.

Megan calls him back. "Jeremy, wait!"

He reluctantly retraces his steps and implores Megan, "What was that all about? Is she sick?"

"Not physically. That I know of. It's been at least since we got back to school. It must be bad. But, she hasn't shared anything with me. She won't even let me in her room."

"So you have no idea? It seemed the dissection really got to her."

"Really?"

"Yah. It seemed to push her into a panic."

"Maybe, but lately she's always on the razor's edge. I can try again to help her. I will. She's just so fragile."

Desperate to be helpful, Jeremy racks his memory. "Do you know about LifeLine? It's a call-in on WTOK. Just before lunch, I think. I've caught it a few times. Maybe you could mention that to her."

"I'm willing to try anything."

# 16. Bumper Cars

Little in Cathy's life undermines her plans more effectively than car trouble. No wheels, no paycheck. Simple cause and effect. Only threats to her livelihood can persuade her to subject herself voluntarily to the ratcheting wrenches, dizzying fumes and contagious grease of the local auto repair shop, not to mention the cigarette exhaust saturating the waiting room. Only the abrasive metal-on-metal grinding of worn brake shoes on rotors could drive her here now, in the middle of a workday, with so many clients clamoring to see properties. Exasperated, she does her best to reason with the head mechanic. "Two days? Really?"

"That's the best I can do, lady. My brakeman called off. I can have someone look at it in the morning, but it'll be two days at least before it's done."

She eases into yoga mode. "Do you offer loaner cars?"

"Nope. Figure that's up to your insurance company. There's a phone on the wall if you need it. Phone book's in there."

Willing herself to be civil, she bites her tongue, "Thanks. Do you have change for a dollar?" Cathy lacks clairvoyance, but she does have an excellent memory. *Still, never assume a 'no.'* She deposits a coin and dials.

"Hi, Mother? How are you? Again? Uh huh. What did they say? That's good. So, do you need me to make a copy? I could do that, sure. For tomorrow? Fine. Mother, can I ask you a favor? I'm at the garage with my car. It was supposed to be done tonight. Now they're saying it will be two days. If I rent a car from here, it'll take hours for them to deliver it. Is there a chance you could pick me up? Right, I forgot about your class. I'll manage. I have some paperwork. Bye." *Breathe.*

Cathy feels her thermostat inching up. She follows the line of the eavesdropping service manager's thumb pointing into his office. There, among the billing statements, obscene calendars and family photos, she finds the Yellow Pages.

Red brake lights as far ahead as she can see. White headlights as far behind as she can see. Trapped in the middle with no exit ramp for miles. Gridlock. Such squandering of time brings out Cathy's worst even when surrounded by comfort. Now, in a stripped down, economy compact with a storm brewing, her patience frays. "Of course this was the only car they had left. No tape deck? What do they listen to?" Without an option, she resorts to the radio; anything to break the tedium. A click and knob-twist and a screaming guitar solo sends the dashboard, door panels and windows pulsating. She winces, turns down the volume and hopes for better on a pre-set button. AM button number-one broadcasts WTOK.

"Well, Clyde, do you have paper-hanging experience?"

"I've watched it being done. I was the gopher on that job."

Cathy's cynicism surfaces. "That should come in handy."

"There are lots of books at the library that can give you some hints. Maybe even talk to a professional."

"That sounds like good advice. There's a pro at the paint store I go to. I'll do that."

"Good luck, Clyde. Hello. Welcome to WTOK Home Update. Who's this?"

"Hi, this is Ron. I have a question about insulating this old farmhouse."

Cathy's cynicism re-surfaces. "This should be good."

# 17. Weight Lifting

Plan-full as always, Abby now grocery shops as soon as the stores open to avoid nosey crowds and judgmental stares. She has learned that onlookers, even ones who are able to ignore the juxtaposition of her diminished form and brimming cart, seldom see past her interminable check-out process with a coupon for nearly every item. At 7:00 a.m., she has the store to herself. The catatonic cashier totals the purchases and discounts for the coupons. Silently, they both pack the bags and place them in the cart. Abby pays with cash. Anonymity. She carefully maneuvers the overtaxed cart to the rear of her car and unlocks the trunk. Parcels from her previous stops crowd the space. She squeezes in as many additional bags as possible and places the remainder in the back seat.

Abby pulls up to her front yard, now overgrown with grass and weeds waving their empty seed cases in the breeze. She purposely avoids eye contact with the usual gawkers as they stop in their tracks to watch her trudge between car and kitchen, kitchen and car. Determined to maintain her privacy, she uses two five-pound packages of flour to prop her apartment door open and preempt any offers of help. Control.

When the last parcel finds a place on her floor, she returns to her car one final time with two empty grocery bags. One she fills with empty beverage bottles and cans — good for cash at the local grocery chain — the other with discarded wrappers. She locks her car, puts the trash bag on her stoop and brings the recyclables in with her. Dangerously exhausted, she collapses on the sofa. "Just a little nap."

# 18. Merry-Go-Round

All the way home, one after another, callers piqued Cathy's pique or tickled her fancy, softening the agony of the tedious bumper-to-bumper, gas-to-brake traffic. But, since jammed time usurped free time, neither Cathy's bedroom nor her morning routine show any sign of better organization.

Tightrope walking through the maze on her floor while nimbly monitoring the sloshing of her coffee, she topples back into the seat before her mirror. "Where was I? Why do I do this every morning? Who am I doing this for?" With one eye smokied, she whisks the wand across the other's lashes. The second coat goes high and wide as the sudden ringing of her phone jars her into stabbing a glob of black goo mid-lid. "Ugh!" She quickly lunges onto her clothes-draped bed to grab the receiver. "Hello? Yes. The Eastcrest home? Ummm. How's 11:30 at my office? Good. I'll see you there."

She hangs up and digs for the notepad on her nightstand. "The bank, dry cleaners. Oh, God, that paper for Mother, the seminar starts at nine. Forget the bank. No. Forget the dry cleaners. Okay, the paper, the seminar, the office." She looks down at her half-dressed self. Then, remembering the blotch. "First, cold cream and a tissue."

With the seminar underway and the room darkened, Cathy slowly edges the auditorium door open as she minimizes her presence and tiptoes toward the only remaining seat in the back row. She gently taps the shoulder of the man on the aisle who, without redirecting his attention, stands in response and clears the way for her. She quietly apologizes as she nudges past. "Excuse me. I'm sorry to disturb you."

"No problem."

Concerned some secret-to-success was revealed without her hearing, Cathy leans over and whispers as quietly as possible. "Did I miss much?"

"Nope." Feeling obliged beyond so abrupt a reply, the man leans sideways to elaborate. A hint of Cathy's perfume wafts his way and wobbles his composure. "Ah, um, those two are rambling on about real estate economics. How the industry is leaning toward agents becoming more than traditional agents."

Confused, Cathy shakes her head to rattle the marbles into place. She leans in to reply. A wisp of his hair tickles her ear, releasing a tiny giggle from deep within. She suppresses it before it surfaces. "Do you understand what they mean?"

Still distracted by her fragrance, he struggles to summarize the basics of the conversation Cathy missed. "The regional rep thinks with some targeted trainings, agents could improve the industry from the inside. The other guy thinks specialized education in economics is the best way to go." Unable to regain his focus—*Do I know this woman?* —he turns to face Cathy's perplexed visage. "I know, these meetings test the psyche, don't they? I'm Drew, by the way."

Cathy gleams—*He's cute!* —amazed to see this handsome man regarding her approvingly. "Hi. I'm Cathy." Caught off-guard, she attempts to conceal her attraction, but breaks into a stammer that instantly confirms it. "To think, I chose this over the bank and the dry cleaners, probably lunch, too. Come to think of it, cold coffee doesn't constitute much of a breakfast, does it?"

Drew does a quick assessment of the situation. He hesitates. And decides. *Carpe Diem!* "What say we give them fifteen minutes? If they haven't moved to a different subject, we go and get us both some breakfast."

Cathy wrestles with her curiosity to reestablish her normal priorities. "What about the rest of the seminar?"

"Have you ever left one of these better off?"

Lured by Drew's entreaties and the temptation of spontaneity, she surrenders with a smile. "I see your point. Fourteen minutes and counting."

Cathy and Drew admire the vibrant yellow, sun-drenched leaves of the *Ginkgo biloba* trees of Boston Common. The weeping willows and ornamental cherries join in the fashion show, boasting their feathery robes of autumnal gold. The familiarity of the couple's interactions belies the newness of their relationship. Oblivious to the world around them, they stroll leisurely to the lake, laughing and munching on breakfast sandwiches.

"In the middle of the photo session, she pushed me into this very lake." Drew chortles as he pantomimes being shoved and staggering. "The tuxedo, a rental, thankfully, was covered with black muck. I never did find the other shoe. I should have taken it as an omen. Six years later, we were emptying our nest egg into our lawyers' pockets in exchange for our freedom."

They find a bench in the sunshine.

Cathy, tickled by his antics, proves her attentive nature as well. "It seems like you've worked through the difficult parts."

"'Work' being the operative word. I buried myself in the job. I've got a stellar reputation, a little fixer-upper out of town and a four-door hatchback," he winks, "with a sunroof. The passenger seat's where I put my briefcase. It could be worse. We could still be making each other miserable."

"I never took 'the plunge,' so to speak."

"Never? How'd a beautiful woman like you manage to escape the clutches?"

"I've never been tempted to give up my hard-won freedoms. My life is the envy of my peers and my family, well, except my mother. Why would I want to clutter it with a man? No offense."

Drew smiles. "None taken. You don't miss love?"

Cathy's face grows sullen and introspective. "Hard to miss what you never had."

With his features drawn to center, Drew draws his neck back in disbelief. "Never? Really?"

"Pretty sad, isn't it? I'm not sure I'd know love if it showed up wearing a name tag. You can't avoid learning about pride, greed, sex. But somehow I missed the lesson on love." Cathy stops abruptly. "Wait a minute. What time is it?"

Drew checks his watch. "About quarter after eleven."

Cathy stands up, bringing Drew to his feet. "I'm sorry. I have to cut this short. I need to get to the office. Newlyweds."

They turn toward the parking lot.

"First-timers?"

"Definitely. They can't be more than twenty-five. They've got those blinding stars in their eyes. It's actually kinda cute to watch."

They walk for a while in silence mildly aware of the activity around them. Cathy reluctantly inserts the key to unlock her door. *I wonder what Beatrice would say if I brought home a white boyfriend.*

There is an ease in Drew's expression. *She's really interesting, and beautiful. I wonder if she'd go out with me.* "I enjoyed this. Maybe we could do it again sometime."

Cathy gets in but leaves the door ajar. "What, play hooky from another company seminar?"

"Not necessarily. Get together and talk. Just talk. I'll leave it up to you." Drew closes the door for her.

Through the glass, she sees him produce something from his pocket. Distracted by the possibility of an unplanned future, she fumbles then rolls the window down.

Drew hands it to her. "Here's my card. Think about it."

"I will. Aldrich?"

He nods.

She puts the card in her jacket pocket. "I'm Cathy Morgan."

"It's been my pleasure, Cathy Morgan. I hope to hear from you."

"Goodbye, Drew Aldrich."

She turns on the ignition.

Abby's voice fills the space. "Being abducted is an extraordinary story, Scott. Where were you when it happened?"

Drew watches as Cathy pulls away. She glances into her rearview mirror to see him glued facing her direction. She smiles. "That was certainly unexpected."

As she drives, she absentmindedly replays his words in her head—*A beautiful woman like you.* —filtering out the world around her. She stops at a light and, for the first time since starting her car, takes stock of her surroundings. "Pooh! I'm going the wrong way! I'll never get to the office in time." She tamps down her intrigue and ramps up her attention. Against her will, it falls on a deflated voice coming through the speakers.

"I guess I could at least do that. Thanks, Abby."

"You're welcome, Scott."

"Our next caller is Frieda. Welcome to LifeLine, the airwaves are yours."

"Hi, Abby. You can tell from my voice that I'm older than most of your callers. I'm ninety-one."

"It sounds like you have wisdom enough to share."

"The wisdom came too late. That's exactly why I want to talk to your listeners. I gave up the best years of my life to bitterness and resentment. My husband died a young man and left me with five children to raise. I carried that cross like a badge of martyrdom. I got so strong I forgot how to depend on others. I never loved again. I never let my heart soften again."

Transfixed, Cathy's reflexes steer her car into her reserved agent-of-the-month parking space. She hypnotically turns the key to accessory.

"I heard one of your callers yesterday say there are lonely people in the world. Lonely is a choice, not a destiny. At ninety-one, I wish someone had told me to choose love."

"Frieda, thank you for that. With so little time to just talk, many lessons that take a lifetime to learn aren't passed on anymore. Thank you for passing that one on."

"God bless you, Abby."

"Our last caller for today is Raymond."

"Last caller?!" The spell shatters. Cathy checks her watch. "Eleven fifty-two? Oh my God." She feels her string of awards snap as she rushes to her agency's door, flings it open and dashes inside. Moments later, her professional air restored, Cathy calmly escorts her young clients to the car. "Forgive the squeeze. Off we go."

The engine turns over, returning Abby's voice to the conversation. "That's all the time we have for today. I want to thank all our listeners…"

Cathy deftly splits her attention between the radio broadcast and her passengers. "So, you've settled on the Eastcrest home?"

"...especially those of you who called in. Join us every weekday between ten and twelve, when the WTOK airwaves are your LifeLine. Have a great day, Boston."

*Ten to noon? Got it.* Having made a mental note, Cathy switches off the radio to salvage the conversation and the sale.

Driving home. The tapering of another day. Cathy's brain juggles thoughts of this morning and afternoon as the last remnants of sunset give way to darkness. "Choose love? I could defend the Fair Housing Act doing a handstand. But love." She feels in her pocket for the three-dimensional proof of her memory. "Drew Aldrich." Finding it there, safe and secure, she surprises herself with a subtle smile and a sigh of relief. "Huh. Friendship? Maybe. But! But, I'll play it cool."

# 19. Soliloquy

In a nearby suburban kitchen, Joey hums along with the LifeLine theme song as he sits at the table making colorful modeling clay snakes and pancakes. Betty scrubs the oven's interior as today's surface. She works her way around the open door on her knees wiping caustic cleaner, now black with dissolved grease and carbon, from the inside walls. She pushes a fallen lock back into place behind her ear with the back of her gloved hand. *Choose love? What if you have love in every direction and it's still not enough? What then? How do you fix that?*

# 20. Balance Beam

Abby's weekly routine now operates on autopilot. Publicly enlightening strangers for two hours a day, secretly binging and purging for the remainder. But tonight, instead of providing solace, her trusty companions — clipped coupons and stacked groceries — prick at her heart. Tonight, it is more than she can stand. *Choose love?* She puts down her scissors and picks up the phone. "Hello? Mark? How are you? That's good. What have you been up to? Probably not till Thanksgiving. You never missed me before. We'll see. Is Mom there? Already? How's Dad? Oh, that's why you miss me. You need to find a way to move out of there. At least find a friend — Reverend Jim is not a friend — and get out as much as possible. You're surrounded by toxic men, Mark. You'll see that if you get out more." The words "Reverend Jim" churn up the dregs of a memory Abby hoped she'd buried beyond retrieval. "I should go. Tell Mom I called and that my work's going well. Bye. I love you."

Feeling even more disconnected from her family and with her thoughts venturing into treacherous territory, Abby reflexively replaces the receiver on the phone. She returns to the kitchen and carefully files the fresh coupons in their organizer to clear the table. "An apple pie and a pound cake will remedy this."

# 21. Carousel

Days have passed since a pebble named "Drew" dropped in the center of Cathy's placid, secluded pond. The expanding ripples have yet to settle. With him on her mind, patterns and assumptions float away as she putters around tidying her bedroom, sorting the clothes and closeting the shoes. She intentionally checks the pockets of the garments before she hangs them on the rod or deposits them in the hamper. Her delving turns up three quarters and a twenty-dollar bill. "I'm rich!" A fuzzy toothbrush and paste. "That's where they are!" And, eventually, Drew's business card.

"Friendship? I don't have time for a cactus!" She gently passes her finger over the embossed surface. Her brow un-furrows. *Choose love.* A hint of impishness turns her lips almost imperceptibly upward. "Still, I have to eat. Couldn't hurt to have company."

Cathy walks to the phone, picks up the receiver then quickly hangs it up again. Embarrassed, as if someone spied her apprehension, she picks it up again, dials six numbers... hesitates... "God, how old am I? Twelve?" She puts her finger in the dial across from the last number and pulls it around clockwise. Deep breath. "For pity's sake." She lets the dial unwind and bites her lip. *Ringing!!! Breathe.* "Hello, this is Cathy Morgan. Hi. We met—I'm fine and you? Actually, I feel, uh, rather like a twelve-year-old. Well, I figured we both have to eat, right? Breakfast? Tomorrow? I have a ninth-thirty appointment. I'll meet you there. Yes. Great. Goodnight, Drew."

Cathy hangs up the phone and smirks with self-congratulations. "That wasn't so difficult. Oh, my God! Eight o'clock? I'm not a morning person. So much for playing it cool."

# 22. Vault

Abby's breath crystallizes with each exhale. Boston Common takes on a melancholy mood once the yellows and auburns of autumn fall to await reincarnation. And, although the temperature dipped last night, and the sun just broached the horizon, Abby wants to capture it, needs to capture it, now. Balanced on a wobbly stool before her easel, she brings the colors to life, pallet in hand, the solids and mottleds of trunks and leafless branches, the grays and grayers of sculpted clouds. Her drawn face and fragile hands escape her oversized parka. She raises her hood against the wind.

Back in the heated studio, the chill of the Common still permeates Abby's bones. Wearing her parka helps, but not enough to compensate for her diminished form. She pulls her turtleneck up tight to her chin. The LifeLine theme music fades as Abby puts on her earphones and moves toward the microphone. "Good morning, Boston. Welcome back to LifeLine. It's one of those gray days we generally dread here in New England, mostly since they usher in the interminable winters. But, determined not to be broken, I defied the weather and planted my easel on Boston Common this morning. I used colors

I haven't touched since last November. Today, I look forward to hearing what remedies you've come up with for these dreary, late-autumn days. Our first caller is Monica. Welcome to LifeLine, the airwaves are yours."

"Good morning, Abby. On days like this I brew a pot of herbal tea, light every candle in the place, and curl up with my ferret."

"Your ferret? I've never heard of a ferret."

"It's the newest pet craze. They have different colored fur than a weasel but otherwise they're pretty close."

"It looks like a weasel?"

"Yes, but maybe it's a bit longer."

"Wow. Does your ferret have a name?"

"Yes, it's Fawcett."

"Fawcett? Ferret Fawcett? Clever. Well, good for you, Monica. Keep warm. Next up is Graham. Welcome to LifeLine, the airwaves are yours."

"Hi, Abby. Starting right about now, the second weekend of November, I start planning my next summer vacation. I've got books in front of me for Paris. Once I read up on all the sites, and make my reservations, I spend the rest of the winter imagining I'm there."

"I like it. Are you a world traveler? Or do you mostly stay in the United States?"

"As a kid, my family drove all over the country and visited the national parks. I've seen a bunch of them up close and personal, the best way to see them, in my opinion, from one of the official campgrounds. Now, as the planner, I'm intentionally picking places where I can see the postcard views, but also get to know how the people live. Their food, celebrations, entertainment. It's more expensive, but it's worth it."

"That sounds so worthwhile, Graham. And Paris is your next destination?"

"Yep, I'm going to spend two weeks next July in Paris. I'll spend another one touring the countryside."

"Wonderful. Thanks for sharing, Graham. Janice is our next caller. Welcome to LifeLine, the airwaves are yours."

"Abby, I don't know where I am. My fourteen-year-old daughter thinks she's pregnant. She refuses to tell me who the hell she's been with. I'm losing it."

"All right, Janice, you thought clearly enough to make this phone call. That's good. Where is your daughter? Can she hear the radio?"

"She locked herself in her room."

Abby moves in closer to the microphone and grasps it firmly to steady her hands. "Is that a safe place for her? She's feeling very isolated right now. Imagine, Janice, how frightened she is. She's a child with an adult problem. She needs you now more than ever. Janice, more than ever."

"She's only fourteen."

Abby focuses her vision on the air before her, convinced that imagining this conflict in three dimensions will inspire meaningful insight. "She's your daughter. It's important that you find some calm. You are her connection to the world. She needs to feel connected."

"Who would do this to a child?"

"Believe it or not, that's not the most important thing right now. You need to go to your daughter and actually embrace her. Connect with her. Everything else can come later. Can you do that? Will she let you see her?"

"I blew up when she told me."

"Go to her door and make verbal contact. Tell her you're going to step outside for a minute to clear your head and that when you get back, you'll need a hug. I bet her door will be unlocked when you knock again."

"I can do that."

"Find a friend or a family member to help you through this. If the situation is too sensitive for that, there are lots of professionals who can help the two of you. Or, call LifeLine again. The receptionist will get a message to me, even after hours. Pick up the phone, okay?"

"Okay. Thank you."

"We're going to take a short break. When we come back, we'll —"

Abby cues up the theme music as Donna runs toward the studio.

"— tackle the blue grays of Boston Novembers."

Between the lingering chill and the adrenaline rush, Abby shivers uncontrollably. She motions a concerned Donna into the room.

"Are you okay?"

Abby forces her hands down on the desk to steady them. "Yes. Yes, I'm fine. That was intense."

"Where did you learn all that?"

"I don't know. It just sort of came out. Did it make sense?"

Gordon knocks on the glass and points to the flashing phone bank.

"Yes, it was great advice. She sounded convinced. I wonder if she'll call back."

Abby stands and turns toward the door. "I need to talk with Renee. She usually puts people off. I want to make sure I get this one."

Gordon knocks again.

Donna intercedes, "I'll tell her. It looks like your switchboard is all lit up."

"I guess the subject has changed. I hope I'm up to this. Thanks."

Donna heads to Renee's desk as Abby resumes her place behind the microphone. "Welcome back to WTOK, I've got Nancy up next. Welcome to LifeLine."

"Abby, you may have just saved a life. When I was sixteen, I got pregnant. Instead of having a backroom abortion, I told my mother. She went crazy. That night I tried to kill myself. I would have bled to death if not for my brother. You're right. It's the isolation that can kill."

"How scary, Nancy. I'm so thankful your brother got to you in time. How awful for you both. People weren't meant to be alone in the best of times. We worry about pets left alone, and yet there are thousands of people in this city who seldom see an approving smile. But in times of crisis, it's vitally important that we stay connected. Stress interferes with clear thinking. Our minds can rush toward a cliff and if no one is there to grab us, we can end up plummeting beyond reach. Reaching out is something we all need to do, to receive and to give help. Thank you for your courage to share your story."

# 23. Pressure Builds

One hundred and fifty-six days. Debbie listens in rapt attention to the dramas unfolding on LifeLine huddled safely under the covers in her darkened room. With blinds drawn and shelves and floor devoid of dust and clutter, the cocoon she built suits her need for solitude and order. She hasn't seen her reflection, by design, for months. She knows her life is at risk. She knows Megan cares about her. She desperately wants to feel better. Accepting Megan's advice to devote time to LifeLine marks her first venture into the light. The glare nearly blinds her. Her determination to recover keeps her listening.

"Next up is Paul. Welcome to WTOK, the airwaves are yours."

"Hi Abby. I haven't really shared all this with anyone, but if I can maybe give someone out there some hope, then. I was just a little kid. Someone who I trusted to protect me, twisted my innocence against me and poisoned my childhood, and honestly, a big chunk of my life, with toxic sludge. He told me it was my fault, that I deserved it, and, because I didn't know any better, and was too afraid to tell anyone, I believed him. I was just a little kid. I believed him, that I was damaged before what he did to me, and worthless after. I feel my heart racing, even now, just talking about what a monster he was, to use twisted lies and shame to keep me quiet. To keep me vulnerable, available.

"I withdrew into a dark place and buried myself in shame and guilt and loneliness. He took away my ability to feel, to feel anything positive. Things that other kids did without thinking—laughing, playing, exploring, making friends—being hopeful—might as well have been happening in a fiery pit. I couldn't even imagine doing any of it, let alone, risk joining in.

"Eventually, I started acting out. At home and in school. Raging outbursts. Deep isolation. One of my teachers could tell something was wrong. And that's what started my long way back. It took years, years of hour-long visits in uncomfortable chairs, telling strangers the tangle of lies that had turned me against myself, had taught me to hate myself. Ever so painfully, those knots started to loosen. And each visit, I'd tug at another lie and unravel another toxic story. Until finally the light, that other people take completely for granted, took a stand against the darkness. And in those moments, I'd catch a glimpse of the other side. Where hope and joy and love were present.

"Honestly, it took years for me to step into that light, to risk trusting again. Yah, just to risk trusting again was a huge accomplishment. Once trust inched its way back, I was like a giant vacuum, sucking up anything that resembled acceptance or love. In the frenzy, I made some awful, self-destructive decisions—decisions that I know now, hurt other people, too. Trying to prove to the world and to myself, that I was strong enough and recovered enough.

"Having ripped open the rot, I kept digging into it, to get to the 'why?' of it. But there is no answer to 'why?' that will ever reverse the loss. I got into the habit of using it. I figured my story made me different—deserving of second and third chances, a justification for my cynicism, my toughness. It took many failed relationships to realize that by anchoring my story in the abuse, I was immobilizing myself. Again.

"So in the end, or the new beginning, I made the decision to let it go. Not to pretend that it didn't happen, but to choose to let it go and walk away. To know that my experience would always be a part of my past, but to know that it would absolutely not determine my future.

"I ultimately leaned into a chance for real love and that very love restored all the fallen pieces of myself that I'd lost. Thirty-three years later, I learned I could love and be loved. I honestly felt like I was given a chance to make up for lost opportunities. I keep facing forward now. Every single gesture of love, and I mean giving or receiving, heals me. Over and over, all over again."

"My heart is breaking, Paul. Thinking of you carrying all that torment in your childhood you. Crushing. But what an inspiration you are! What strength it took to keep going even when the struggle kept reinventing itself. It sounds like one breakthrough just led to another huge challenge. But you kept going! That is so strong. If you are open to sharing, what guidance can you give to others who feel paralyzed by their history of violence or abuse?"

"I guess my advice would be to do the work. It is all-consuming, to face what happened, but I don't think I could have felt worthy of love without seeing the abuse as a violation of me, not a part of me. I was no part of the 'why?' But I had to understand that to my core, and that's what the work helped me see. After I believed that, instead of the gnawing lies, that's when I could work toward asking 'What now?' instead of 'Why me?'."

"Right, 'What now?' That challenge alone can get you out of bed."

Debbie reaches out from under her covers to switch off this deeply visceral invasion. She retreats again, battens down the hatches and sobs.

# 24. Deus ex Machina

Betty stares at the plaster swirls encircling the central light of their bedroom ceiling. After ten years of nights on her naked back, she recognizes every shadow cast by each flourish, each dip. Harry buries his face in the crook of her neck. The force of his exhales assaults her ears and moistens her hair. "Ah, ah, ah." The bed springs accompany his rhythmic refrain. "Ah, ah, ah." His persistence pays off. "Oh! My!! God!!!" Satisfied, he withdraws and collapses in the afterglow onto his wife below. "That was great, Betty."

"I'm glad."

"Goodnight. I love you." He kisses her cheek and rolls off into his side-facing imprint on their mattress.

"Goodnight, Harry." Betty lies motionless waiting for the sleep rhythm of Harry's breaths to replace that of ecstasy. Despondence tightens its grip. She cautiously extends her left leg off the bed and slides free, careful not to lift her weight abruptly. Her ritual, of draining his ejaculate while she waits for him to settle, numbs her like no other. *Fifty more years.* Returning to the darkened room, she feels for her fleece, redresses and silently returns to her place beside her sleeping husband. She pulls her notebook, pen and miniature flashlight from between the

91

mattress and box spring and places them on her breast as her breathing deepens. Her mind clears of the cares of the day. Her inner voice rises to fill the void. *Maybe my poems are actually lyrics?* Intrigued by the thought, her creativity sets to work assigning melody where there once was none.

Betty stirs at the sound of Harry entering their room. She rolls over and feels her secret items still lying beside her under the covers. She hurriedly slides them to the floor and out of sight. *I must have slept.*

Harry leans over to plant his morning peck. "Good morning, Betty. I'll be home on time. Have a good day. I love you."

Betty feigns waking, incorporating squinting and yawning with finesse. "Oh! Good morning. It's time for you to leave already? I forgot to tell you, I have an appointment this morning. My mother is watching Joey. It won't interfere with dinner. I'll see you then. Love you."

Betty dresses in real clothes and ushers Sandy and Ben out the front door and onto their bus, lunches and backpacks in tow. Today promises variety. She hums a brand new melody as she readies Joey for his adventure with Grandma. Everybody wins.

Her plans today take her out on the town. Not on the town, precisely, but out, in the presence of adults, who are no relation. Close enough. She looks forward to her six-month dental exam. An hour of conversation, albeit mostly one-sided, with a pick or drill in her mouth. Still. The cleaning goes well enough, but a cavity needs a filling. The whirl of the tiny drill bit against her enamel sends chills from earlobes to fingertips. She grips the chair arms. White knuckles.

"Just one more minute."

"Ugh kah."

"There we go." The drill stops.

WTOK plays over the office speakers. When the whirling fades from her ears, Betty recognizes Harry's voice. Then Abby's. She listens with rapt attention as her dentist deftly completes the work he started, providing her a convenient justification for lingering.

"...don't know why. I can't seem to reach her."

"Step back. Think about the last time you heard her laugh."

"It's been so long."

"Okay, then, what brought out the best in her?"

"She liked to sing, all the time, and dance."

"Have you seen that part of her lately?"

"We have three children."

"Still, how can you help her get that spark back? Think about that and you'll find your answer."

"I'm afraid I've lost her."

"She needs to be happy, Henry. I believe we all need to be happy. When we're happy, and engaging our talents, we strengthen our strand in life's tapestry. You must let her grow."

"Let her go?"

"Let her grow. She needs to find her joy, to be free to explore her self. She needs to know that she, herself, has value. Give her time and gentle encouragement. Be prepared for change, both in her and in yourself. You can do this. You have love as your motivator."

"You've given me a lot to think about. Thank you, Abby."

"Thank you for your call, Henry. You can do this. Next up is Jacob."

With the children tucked in for the night, Harry takes his customary lie-down on the sofa. Meant as a chance to unwind before bed, tonight his mind churns. He replays Abby's words, "Think about the last time you heard her laugh." After hours of trying, he still comes up empty. He hears Betty noisily shuffling books and toys around him. But, terrified to confide his vulnerability, he feigns sleep, snoring and mumbling for effect.

With the children tucked in for the night, Betty starts her customary tidy-up in the living room. Meant as a chance to get ahead of the clutter, tonight she just shuffles it. She replays Abby's words, "She needs to find her joy." After hours of practicing, she still fears a failure. She sees through Harry's weak attempts to imitate sleep. Terrified to let the opportunity pass, she imagines the dreaded conversation one more time, then takes a deep breath.

"Harry?"

He cracks an eyelid.

She steadies her vocal cords. "I heard you on the radio today."

Bewildered, he pushes himself to a seated position and faces her, petrified. "Did you? I thought you had an appointment."

"I did. I am unhappy, Harry."

His worst fears confirmed, his eyes and expression suddenly drain of hope. "What can I do?"

"I need time away. I need time to create. Poetry, stories, songs."

Given a glimmer of a way back, pleading replaces his dismay. "I'd love to hear what you write."

"That's just it. I need it to be my own. Something separate from you, from us, from the family. I need to be just me, to find my own singular value."

Confusion roils his thoughts. "How can I help you if you need to be separate from me?"

"You can give me time to be alone. Time away from the children." Her voice catches and quivers. "I need to sleep alone."

Harry stares in disbelief and agony. "Sleep alone?"

Betty's voice breaks as the last remnant of her composure dissolves into exhaustion and desperation. "I'm disconnecting... I'm suffocating, Harry."

With Abby's words still circulating in his memory, "You need to let her grow, to find her joy." Harry sadly, haltingly relinquishes his pride and concedes. "I'm so sorry. But, but, absolutely. I don't understand, but if it's what you need, I'll make my bed up here. Have I lost you, Betty?"

"I don't know."

# 25. Fun House

A thin layer of frost partially obscures the view from Drew's picture window overlooking the barren trees along the coastline. The setting moon highlights the cresting waves as they massage the shore. The aromas of toasting batter and brewing coffee mingle and rise to greet Cathy as she descends the open staircase into the bustle of breakfast preparation.

Drew smiles looking up at her from the kitchen below. Wearing a man's silk pajama top, she flashes a smile while catching a glimpse of herself in the mirror hanging over a darkened, rustic fireplace. Unbeknownst to the other, a memory from childhood, of watching 1965-Hollywood's version of an unlikely couple dance in each other's arms, simultaneously surfaces. "Something good." Cathy grins and subconsciously hums the song's melody as she kisses Drew, "Good morning."

Drew immediately recognizes the tune and knowingly nods to himself. *I agree.* "Good morning, my dearest Cathy. You know, it's been more than a month and you still haven't let me make you a Bloody Mary for breakfast."

"I have difficulty enough controlling my outbursts. A shot of vodka and I'd be laughing all day long."

"Are you saying I intoxicate you?"

"You're so poetical."

Peeking around his bare shoulder, Cathy noses her way in. "It smells so good. What are you creating now?"

Drew gently kisses her on the ear. "I have this great Belgian waffle recipe. I thought they'd be tasty with the leftover strawberries." Drew opens his refrigerator and removes a plastic-wrapped bowl. "Hmmmm. A bit fuzzy. How does Vermont maple syrup sound?"

Cathy fills two cups with coffee. "Just so it's quick. Don't you have to meet a client at nine?"

"I've got plenty of time."

Cathy takes a seat. He serves her. "Eat up." Then himself.

Cathy's mood mellows. "You realize I have to tell my mother about us soon if we're going to spend any part of Thanksgiving together."

Drew kiddingly shares his thoughts: "Maybe we should hire someone to take our places at the family ordeals and we can escape to the mountains for a long, romantic weekend."

"My mother might not notice, but I'm sure your folks would."

"What if you come down with something 'really contagious' and call off. My parents would love to have us for the whole day."

Cathy wants to see the humor, but she knows better. "Mother has to be told. She might not react too harshly. She has been adamant about me broadening my life to include people. You're a people."

"I like to think so."

"She's never explicitly stated her feelings about interracial couples."

"How about implicitly?"

"Mother doesn't do 'implicit.'"

Drew's naivety bolsters his optimism. "She'll probably be happy that you're happy."

"Let's visualize that for a few days. Can you transmit good vibes?"

He tenderly kisses the palm of her hand sending a tingle racing to Cathy's core. "You should know the answer to that by now."

"Why do I stay with you?"

"Because I'm the best thing that's ever happened to you."

"Fuzzy strawberries and all?"

"Fuzzy strawberries and all."

# 26. Tunnel of Love

Preoccupied by today's daydream of being in Drew's embrace on some exotic tropical beach, Cathy struggles to stay rooted in reality. From experience she knows, with autumn's daylight hours on the wane and the holiday multifecta on the horizon, she needs to take every opportunity she gets to introduce clients to the properties in her region. She makes a valiant effort with the couple in the back seat. "That home has a beautiful layout and back yard. It needs some work in one of the bathrooms. But, structurally it's sound."

"What's the price on it?"

"I believe they just reduced it to fifty-four, nine."

"That seems high."

"Remember, you're also paying for this neighborhood."

"Where's the —"

Cathy's pager rings.

" —closest elementary school?"

"It's just down —"

It rings again. She checks the number. " —the block. Excuse me. May I?" Cathy quickly interprets an exchange of glances in her rearview mirror as the lead-up to a nod. Her pager rings again. She pulls over within steps of a public phone. "I apologize." She hurries to the booth and dials. "Hello. This is Cathy Morgan. Drew? Ahhhh. Well, it is a very fancy pager. You're funny! I've got clients in my car. What's so important? Fighting what urge?" She blushes. "Meet me at our spot in about, an hour? Goodbye, Drew." Cathy, flustered and distracted all over again, gets back into her car and does her best to restore her professional air.

Fifty-nine minutes later, as if on cue, the sun sends wedges of light through tiny breaks in the dense blanket of clouds, spotlighting Drew from above. He waits, as promised, on the park bench where he and Cathy shared their first meal. The warmth from the beams kindles his exuberance. Cathy approaches with a spring in her step. "Hello!"

They wrap arms and energy into their embrace.

Drew barely contains his joy. "Hi. Sorry about the interruption, but I had to see you."

Cathy grins from ear to ear. "It's so un-me to take a break in the middle of the day. My life is turned upside down."

"Is that good or bad?"

"Good or bad? It's great! I realize now I was living to work. Now, now I have urgent rendezvous in the Common. So, what's so important?"

Drew takes Cathy's hands in his and captures her gaze with his own. "Do you love me?"

"Do I love you?" Cathy pauses as her mind rummages for the words to describe this foreign territory. "Well, when I'm away from you, I want to be near you. When I'm near you, I want to be nearer."

Drew narrows the distance between them. "But do you love me?"

She looks hopeful. "Isn't that love?"

Drew tugs her arms gently as they slowly descend to the park bench. "I love you, Cathy. I adore our similarities and I cherish our differences. I long to see the person you become tomorrow and every tomorrow after that. And, I trust that there is no change that can separate us."

"That's love?"

"To me it is. With a healthy dose of passion, of course."

Cathy flings Drew's hands away as she dives in to wrap her arms around him with an embrace bursting with relief and joy. "I love someone! Yes! I love you! I can love. Kiss friendship goodbye. I can love!"

Drew takes Cathy's glowing face in his hands and, with confidence and yearning, kisses the woman of his dreams. "I want everyone we care about to know, starting with our families. I've told my folks all about you, so they have a pretty good idea. Your mother, no clue, right?"

Cathy reluctantly pulls away but reconnects with her gaze. "Right. I keep thinking about telling her. I figure she could react to news of you in either of two ways. She could admit that she's been virtually out of my life for the past decade and shrug it off. Or, more likely, she'll insist that her opinion is the only one that matters. In that case, she won't even want to know why I love you. She'll see your skin color and freak out."

"What if we don't tell her that right away?"

"Just rave about you for a week or so, then have you show up at her door on Thanksgiving with your flowing hair and hazel eyes? We'd go hungry. 'Go,' being the operative word."

Drew frowns at the thought. "My being white would be more important than your happiness?"

"Not only that, but the sheer audacity of my making a choice without her input. Still, there's no getting around it. I guess tonight is as good a time as any. Let's see if we can get reservations at that fancy, new, French restaurant, L'Espalier. Maybe we can win her over with luxury."

"It's worth a try."

"Is eight o'clock okay?"

"Eight works for me. I'll clear my schedule."

Caught up in the thrill of their thriving romance, Cathy conjures a thought. "I wish we could take the rest of the day off, go back to your place and celebrate."

"Why can't we? Don't you feel queasy?"

"Now that you mention it, I do have butterflies. I thought it was the love thing."

"I'll see you there."

Passersby remember their youth or imagine their future, just catching a glimpse of the passionate kiss unfolding in their corner of the park. Drew and Cathy part reluctantly and walk away in different directions. Cathy twirls with her smiling face to the heavens and arms outstretched. Drew, laughing, takes a sideways leap and kicks up his heels. Love wins, again.

Cathy cajoles the checkout clerk to sing along with her as they bag her groceries. She swells with delight and relief as she carries her parcels to her car. "Finally! Love in every cell and synapse of my being." Today, even luck goes her way. No hatchback in the drive. So, despite the stop, she still arrives first. She turns the key in the entryway lock and crosses the threshold cautiously, carrying her tote bags.

"Drew? Babe, are you home? Good." She quickly unloads her packages. "Oysters. Put them on ice. Candles." She places the candles on the end tables, the center table, the mantel and the floor. The mood turns romantic the instant she sets them alight. "Music." She unwraps an audio cassette and puts it in the player. "Ahhhh."

As she lets the music lift her away from her old self, she catches a glimpse of that self in the mirror. "A quick freshen up." She checks her watch. "Really quick." She runs upstairs and turns on the shower just as Drew pulls into his space. He opens the door and enters empty-handed. He looks around, grinning.

"Candles! Sweet! Cathy? Sweetheart?" He listens intently and hears the shower accompanied by his love singing her version of the tune in the air. "Perfect.' Drew slips out the door with his mind in a whirl. As he gathers his packages, he thinks of the hopes he felt denied his entire adult life. How he longed for a lover who believed in candor and honesty, compassion and generosity! How he equated beauty inside with beauty outside. How he needed someone willing to balance, really balance professional and personal aspects of living. Now, finally, he found her. And, finally, his fantasy of filling a celebratory space with roses comes to life.

Arms full, he returns with three long-stemmed boxes and a bottle of champagne. He opens the boxes and arranges the pink and white roses in every container he can find. Then he places the eleven red roses and a single blue in a tall, cut-crystal vase among the candles. He nestles the champagne in an ice bucket, the flutes in the freezer. "One more thing." He kneels before the hearth and builds a roaring fire. Standing, he glimpses his now soot-smudged reflection in the mirror. "Ugh." He bounds upstairs and knocks at the bathroom door.

A voice from within, "Friend or foe?"

"Lover."

"Come in."

Candles flow and flare warming the air and passions in the darkening room. Embers fade and blaze creating an undulating cityscape just beyond the hearth. Ice softens and melts having chilled the effervescent wine to its ideal. Oyster shells, absent their residents, overflow the crystal bowl. Drew and Cathy, welcoming of new possibilities, offer their entire bodies to each other with tenderness and intention. Love-drenched afternoon delight.

# 27. Uneven Parallel Bars

The shorter days of November invite the simple romance of candlelight into Abby's afternoon routine. A single flame flickers in the misty air precipitated by the shower's steaming hot spray. "Ahhhh." Silence. Abby pulls back the curtain and steps out of the tub. With water dripping and pooling over and in her new contours, she grabs a towel and dries her fading form. She returns the towel to its hook, dons her robe, pinches out the candle and navigates her way from the bathroom, through the corridor and into her bedroom.

Where once she had space to dance, she now has packages-a-plenty. Boxes, bags, bottles and cans, eerily well-organized by product and brand, thickly pad the perimeter of the entire space. Abby walks to the mirror, drops her robe and examines her body as she slowly rotates. She sees but doesn't see her shrunken breasts, her concave abdomen, her distinct jawline. She re-robes. "Getting there." *Feeding time.*

Long the repository for her grocery-shopping binges, the kitchen floor, counter and shelves mimic a grocer's warehouse. Abby wades through the narrowing pathway to the counter where she chooses four boxes of cereal then eases the refrigerator open to remove a gallon of milk. She maneuvers to pull out a chair and pauses before her first bite. "Thank you, God, for this meal. May it give me the strength to be of help in the world. Amen." She pours the cereal and milk into a bowl and eats ravenously. She pours another bowl, devours it, pours another and consumes it.

Eight boxes of cereal and two gallons of milk later, this afternoon's evidence of Abby's compulsions lies crushed and meticulously stacked on the table in her darkening kitchen, lit only by the beam from the bathroom light where Abby's cleansing flows like clockwork.

Seated on a step stool facing, knees embracing, the bowl of the toilet, she leans over and feels the soggy and masticated flakes and raisins mixed with gastric acid leave her stomach, flow through her esophagus, over her tongue and into the pool of water below. With the contamination largely reversed, she fills her purge bottle with tepid water from the tub spigot and guzzles half. She vomits. "Ugh." She repeats the process. Drink, vomit. "Eh." Drink, vomit. "Better." Drink, vomit. "Clear." She sighs, stands and steps on the scale. *127 pounds?* Expressionless, she disrobes and steps on the scale again. *126.* "Getting there." Exhausted and shaking, with the last phase of her day's last feeding complete, she bundles up again to wind her way back to her sofa, careful not to collide with the packaging lining the path.

Abby picks up her phone. She dials. "Hello? Hi, Mom. I'm fine. How are you? It's going well. They seem to be pleased. I'm thinking ahead to next week. Yes. I'll come home Wednesday evening, if that's okay. Don't hold it for me. I'll eat before I leave town. How's Dad? Tell Mark I said hi. Thanks, Mom. Bye. I love you."

Thankful for the season's early sunset and chilled beyond comfort, she gratefully readies for sleep. She dons soft, well-worn pajamas that now hang unnaturally from her shoulders and hips. She carefully pulls back the familiar blue, ruffled coverlet before collapsing on her bed. She reaches for her journal. By candlelight, she opens it, revealing perfect, minuscule printing.

*November 17, 1981, Dear Diary, Today I felt a heart break. A husband is terrified he's lost the love of his wife. People turn to me in such dire situations. I hope my words gave him hope and ideas.*

Her pen slows and slips from her hand. She closes the book and lays the pen alongside. She slides snugly under the covers, inhales a deep breath, exhales and connects with her faith. "Heavenly Mother God, thank you for this day. Please bless me, my family and all I interacted with today. Give us the strength we need to be images of your love and care in the world. Please, catch me if I fall. Amen."

The streetlight filters through the curtains separating Abby's hidden life from the world outside. She turns over, restless. She checks the time. 7:54. Hours since her last meal, she reluctantly responds to the persistent nudge of hunger. She slowly drags herself out of bed and cautiously walks toward the living room in virtual darkness. She approaches the television and turns it on hoping for some human companionship in one form or another. She clicks through the offerings to find every channel broadcasting mindless news, insulting sitcoms or violent crime shows. Disappointed, she turns it off. "Music." She goes to the stereo and turns on her salvation station. "Mozart. Ahhhh." Her spirit lifts with the vibration of the strings and reeds.

Abby navigates to the kitchen and removes a head of broccoli and a package of ground meat from her overcrowded refrigerator. While the meat browns, she cuts the florets into bite-sized pieces and drops them in the hot skillet. She flips the sizzling green and brown morsels in time with the symphony. Once cooked through, she wastes no time moving the hot pan to rest on the stack of collapsed cereal boxes. She lights a candle. She eats.

# 28. Demolition Derby

The knot in Cathy's fifth chakra tightens as she and Drew marvel, aghast, at the intimate ambiance of their surroundings. The melodious strings and reeds of Mozart do little to ease her angst. Seated back-to-back to their proximate neighbors, Cathy reluctantly whispers their shared disquiet across the candlelit café table. 'Maybe L'Espalier wasn't the best idea. Maybe I shouldn't have worked so hard to get a reservation. If my mother reacts badly, there'll be no way to hide it."

As the ornate clock on the wall strikes eight, a sophisticated woman crosses the threshold and hastily scans the restaurant's interior. As she hands off her coat to the attendant, she notices Cathy and points the maitre d' in her direction.

Her arrival captures Drew's attention. "Too late to change plans now. I think your mother's here."

Cathy looks over her shoulder. "Yes, that's Beatrice. Maybe, let's do our best to direct the conversation away from us until we enjoy our meal?"

"Sounds like a challenge, but I'm willing to try."

The maitre d' escorts a bedazzled Beatrice from the coat check to join her daughter and Drew. Cathy edges out of her seat and greets Beatrice midway with a warm embrace. "Mother! You look beautiful."

"Thank you. My, it's very crowded here."

Determined to make a reassuring first impression, Drew straightens his tie and his backbone. As the Morgan women approach, only one knows why.

"Mother, I'd like to introduce Drew Aldrich. Drew, this is my mother, Beatrice Morgan."

Drew and Beatrice nod, keeping their eyes fixed on one another.

"It's my pleasure, Mrs. Morgan."

Unable to fathom their possible connection, Beatrice replies with a socially civil, "Hello, Drew."

Cathy draws out a chair for Beatrice and nudges her in. Safely out of her mother's view, Cathy defuses her dread with a comical expression in Drew's direction. He stifles a smile as they gracefully seat themselves. Cathy's heart races in her chest. She does her best to hide it. "Have you been here before, Mother?"

"No, but I have read about the chef and owner in several magazines. I guess that's why it's so crowded. He's very highly regarded."

"This is, our-ah, my first time here, too. The chef has an interesting menu that…"

"Yes, I know. It's a four-course meal and dessert as well."

"Yes, exactly."

"So, Drew. What do you do? Are you visiting Boston?"

"No. I live…"

"He lives up north. We met at a seminar. So, what have you been up to lately?"

"Actually, several women and I have started a Bible study group. We met for the first time this week. I've known most of them for more than a decade. From back when your father was council president."

"Did you start with the Old or New Testament?"

Napkins dab, *fromage* forks engage and, with the plan to soften Beatrice underway, the wine and artistic delicacies that graced the table clearly worked their magic. Nevertheless, Cathy and Drew know Beatrice's virtual monologue—about the church groups and luncheons that keep her spinning in social circles— now needs to pivot toward a dialogue and their relationship before the check arrives. They order the Grand Marnier soufflé.

With plenty of time before the server returns, and hoping crediting Beatrice will ease the impact of her reveal, Cathy nervously dives in, head first. "I've been taking your advice, Mother. For the past six weeks, I've made some free time for myself."

"That's nice."

"That's because I met Drew. He also works in realty. We met last month."

"In October? You never mentioned him to me."

"Our conversations don't generally lend themselves to..."

Sensing the emergence of a negative vibe, Drew edges in between the waves. "Cathy and I have been spending much of our free time, together."

Beatrice pauses, as her assumptions regroup, and the unlikely pieces, slowly start to interlock, in an even less—likely—way. "Your free time?"

"Yes, our free time. A truly wonderful thing has happened, Mother. I found out I can love."

Despite Beatrice's strenuous resistance, the puzzle stubbornly merges into view as her decorum fragments. "Is this why you invited me here? To spring this on me?"

"I love your daughter, Mrs. Morgan."

"No. This can't be."

"And I love him, Mother."

"In love? With him? I can't, um, I can't stay here." Beatrice slams her napkin down and grabs her purse. An unfortunate busboy struggles to keep himself and his overloaded tray upright as Beatrice pushes passed on her way to the coat check. Impatiently waiting for the attendant, she glances back to see Drew rise to follow her. "I'll be back for my coat." She abruptly leaves the restaurant as Cathy pulls Drew back to the table.

"There's no point in going after her. She needs some time to think this through. I'll talk with her tomorrow."

# 29. Zoltar

As if to personify the tree limbs now barren of leaves, Abby's transformation between June and November screams for attention. Nobody answers. Certainly not Abby. In defiance of the momentum of her downhill drift and her daily struggle against her weakened state, Abby pours what remains of her vitality into her on-air confidants. "Good morning, Boston, welcome back to LifeLine, the show directed by you. Our number is 555-WTOK. Looks like we have some lines open. Today, we're talking about the special things you have planned to celebrate the Thanksgiving holiday. I'll be going back home to be with my family. It's been a while, so it promises to be an eventful visit. Our next caller is Daniel. Welcome to WTOK, the airwaves are yours."

"First-time caller, Abby. I enjoy your show. So, here's how the wife and I spend the holidays. We're retired. So, between now and mid-December, we travel to all our children's homes. We have a Thanksgiving meal at each one. Then they all come back home to Boston for Christmas."

"That's the best retirement plan I've ever heard. How many children do you have?"

"Three. One on each coast and one in Chicago, so we spend a lot of time in the air."

"That's marvelous! I'm sure they are so happy for your visits. I bet other listeners are already starting to think about how this idea could work for them. Congratulations on coming up with it first, Daniel! Thanks for your call. Next, we have Cathy. Welcome to WTOK, the airwaves are yours."

"Hi, Abby. I'm here at the gym, listening to your show, and I heard your previous caller talk about how hard his family works to spend meaningful time together. And I thought to myself, my mother wouldn't cross the street for me."

"All families are different, Cathy. I'm sure your mother loves you."

"In her way, I suppose she does. But all the same, I'm, ah, I'm working through, well, voluntary orphanhood, I suppose you could call it."

"Voluntary orphanhood? I think I understand, but could you explain that a little more?"

"Well, my mother and I were never terribly close, but since my father's death about six months ago, the distance has widened. She's gotten more and more judgmental and, just a couple days ago, forced me to choose between her approval and loving a man. When I said I planned to continue my relationship, she told me I was on my own. So, this will be the first Thanksgiving I spend as an orphan."

"Will you be with your boyfriend for the holiday?"

"Yes. His family accepts us. We'll share the day with them."

"They 'accept' you?"

"Oh, I'm Black, he's not."

"Ahh. The lights are going on. Does your mother know your boyfriend?"

"No. We invited her out to dinner to make the introductions, and everything was going pretty well, until we got to the part about loving each other. Then she stormed out. I talked with her the next day but she had little to say. The bottom line is she's adamant that race is a barrier that should never be crossed. With that, she won't speak with him or hear my reasons for loving him."

"That's regrettable. By dismissing him without getting to know him, your mother doesn't give you much choice. The roots of her beliefs could go back years or even generations. They're obviously justified in her mind. Tragically, prejudice over the centuries, almost always white against black, has stifled so much potential, inhibited so much progress. But trying to change her now is the last thing you need to focus on. You need to live the life that gives you happiness. If you've found love, consider yourself richly blessed.

"Your mother's attitude is her choice and her responsibility. We each get to choose. But every choice comes with consequences. Some lead to growth, some to stagnation. In time, she may feel this choice is holding her back. She may reach out to reestablish contact with you. You are still her daughter, after all. If so, hold on to your autonomy while being sensitive to her ego.

"By then, she may have talked with others whom she respects and gotten a different perspective. And her temper may be less volatile. Conversation isn't possible when either party is locked in anger. Once she sees how extraordinary your man is, it will be easy for you to joyfully welcome her back into your life. Make it a celebration in the end. It will be a significant day for both of you. Until then, enjoy your new family. Blossom there."

"I do feel, that for the first time in a long time, I am growing."

"Believe it or not, Cathy, some people never achieve that. Consider yourself twice blessed. All these changes may feel overwhelming. Just keep your eyes facing forward. Enjoy your holidays."

"You do bring clarity to a situation. Thank you."

# 30. Eruption

Abby checks the wall clock. It reads 11:58. "My pleasure. We have just enough time for one more quick call. Hi, Debbie, welcome to WTOK, the airwaves are yours."

Sobbing pours into Abby's earphones and through the station speakers. Abby watches the second hand click around the bottom of the clock's face. "Debbie, are you there? Can you hear me? You've reached out. Connect with me. Debbie?"

"I'm dying."

"You're dying?"

"I can't keep it together. I can't sleep. I can't think. The nightmares and memories bring back the torture. Every night, every day, the torture lives while I'm dying."

"How long have you felt this way?"

"One hundred and seventy-two days."

"Who have you shared this with?"

"I'm too ashamed."

"Now is the first time you've talked about this?"

"I don't know what to do."

Abby views the clock again. 11:59. "Debbie, you're in crisis right now but it won't last forever. You've taken the first critical step. Connecting is the first step. We've connected."

"Please don't hang up."

"We've run out of time. Debbie. Listen. I want you to call me at 555-4932 in twenty minutes. I'll be home by then and we can talk as long as you need to. Did you get that number? 555-4932."

"Twenty minutes?"

"Bundle up in a warm sweater and go for a walk. But call me in twenty minutes. I'll be there."

Donna and Renee attempt to wave a warning to Abby as they watch Linda stride, livid, from her office toward the studio.

"Twenty minutes?"

"555-4932. I'll be there."

Their jumping and flailing finally snag Abby's attention. Too late. The damage is done. Linda yanks the studio door open and emphatically slices her finger across her throat. Twice. Disoriented, Abby abruptly closes the show. "This is LifeLine."

Linda, face red and fists clenched, towers over Abby. Abby's sunken eyes and lifeless hair magnify the weakness she feels seated in Linda's shadow.

"Abigail, what were you thinking?"

"I don't understand."

"You broadcast your home number. Multiple times!"

Abby's face contorts as she struggles to come up with an explanation. She sincerely voices her contrition, "I did, didn't I? I'm really sorry, Linda. Station policy never even crossed my mind. I just knew I was out of time. How could I let her go till Monday?"

Exasperated, Linda shakes her head and sternly points toward her office door. "Gather your things. I need to see you in my office."

118

Abby finishes putting on her coat and snaps her briefcase shut. Linda turns to leave. Abby stops her mid-stride. "I can't, Linda. I told her I'd be home in twenty minutes. It's at least a twenty-five-minute drive. I have to go."

Astonished by Abby's resistance, Linda retorts, "We need to talk."

"It'll have to be Monday. I'll be in by seven." Abby grabs her briefcase and purse and runs from the studio.

Furious, Linda yells after her. "Abigail, you're making a mistake!"

Abby bangs repeatedly on the elevator down button. She sees the car is stuck on the third floor. She checks her watch. 12:04. She disappears down the stairway and into the bleak day.

Outside, the clouds hang heavy. Weather like this turns Debbie's body cold, no matter the temperature, no matter how many sweaters. Gray. Dreary. Gnawing flashes of helplessness and insignificance. "'Go for a walk.' she said, 'twenty minutes.'"

Abby checks her watch. *12:18.* "Seriously? Of all the days to have a moving van blocking an entire lane of traffic!" Quickly weighing the options of sitting in the queue and waiting to merge versus ducking down a side street and taking her chances, she opts for the road less traveled. "I'm coming, Debbie!" Abby follows closely behind the car ahead...

Debbie keeps careful watch of the time. 12:19. "How slowly twenty minutes pass." She unlocks the deadbolt and enters her building, then her apartment, then her room. She times her arrival impeccably. 12:20. She unzips her coat, gathers her thoughts and dials the phone. "5-5-5-4-9-3-2. Busy?"

Debbie depresses and releases the disconnect button and dials again. *5-5-5-4-9-3-2. Busy again?*

…and finds herself on the far side of the stoppage in no time. 12:21.

Again Debbie dials. *5-5-5-4-9-3-2, Busy.* And again. *5-5-5-4-9-3-2, Busy. 5-5-5-4-9-3-2, Busy. 5-5-5-4-9-3-2, Busy. 5-5-5-4-9-3-2, Busy.*

Focusing as best she can on driving, Abby arrives home and parks in front of her apartment. 12:32. She hears the faint sound of her ringing phone as soon as she opens the car door. "Focus. You can do this."

And again. "5-5-5-4-9-3-2, Busy!!"

Abby takes a deep breath and staggers with all her available energy toward the sound. Gasping for air, finally at her stoop, she reaches toward her hip for her purse. "Damn." In desperation, she checks her other hip. "Damn. Damn. Damn."

And again. "5-5-5-4-9-3-2, Busy!!"

12:35. "Damn!" Abby stumbles back to the car and digs her purse out from under discarded packaging. The muted sound of the ringing phone stops. "Damn." While faltering back to her stoop, she rummages through her purse and finds the key. Her hands shake with frustration and hunger as she awkwardly slides it into the lock. 12:36. The phone rings again. Gasping, she twists the key and shoves the door open. The momentum propels her over the sofa as she lunges for the phone. Her heart and lungs race to supply her needs. "Debbie? I'm expecting an important call. I'm hanging up now." She hangs up the phone. It rings immediately.

*5-5-5-4-9-3-2, Busy!*

"Oh, no." Abby answers it. "Hello? I can't talk to you now, honey." She plunges the button. "Damn!" It rings immediately.

"5-5-5-4-9-3-2. It's ringing!"

Abby answers it. "Hello?"
"Hello?"
"Debbie?"
"Yes. Abby?"
Abby's heart pounds in her ears. She releases every muscle and collapses on the floor. She inhales, pauses, exhales, inhales, pauses, exhales, as her breaths and pulse slowly inch back toward her normal. The receiver lies on the floor next to her. "Yes. Did you take a walk?"
"A short one."
Still catching her breath, Abby centers her thoughts as best she can. "Good. That's very good. So you got some fresh air? Maybe saw a sliver of sunshine?"
"Sunshine and fresh air won't fix me, Abby."
"No. You're right. They won't fix you, but you saw that the world is still out there. You've connected with me. You will eventually need to reconnect with the world."
"The world? I can't bear to look at my self. It sickens me to see my own body."
Abby notices the loose skin on her own diminished hand. "Your body is a gift, it contains all your talents and possibilities."

"My body is a curse. Maybe if I were really fat or really skinny, no man would want to get near me."

"Is that what you want?"

"I want to disappear."

"Did a man hurt you?"

"An animal killed me. I used to smile. I haven't focused my eyes in a hundred and seventy-two days. He forced me. I fought him, but he was stronger than I am. I couldn't scream. I felt like I was weighted down with lava in my lungs. He kept saying, 'I love you.' He didn't even know me."

"Debbie, we can talk all night if you want, but eventually, you're going to have to talk to someone who knows more about rape than I do."

"Please don't hang up. Please."

"I will not hang up."


After hours of listening and responding, Abby lies nearly lifeless on the floor, her head on a throw pillow, her ear to the phone. "Little bits of sleep – even if they're interrupted by violent thoughts – will nourish you. They'll tide you through till the night terrors are only memories. I'm sorry, I won't be here. I'll be at my family's home for the holiday. It would be better if you call me. Will you be home tomorrow? Since you'll be face-to-face with your family, maybe this weekend is a good time to tell them. Their support could be crucial. You don't know that for sure. Yes, Debbie, you're going to live. Sleep sounds like a very good idea. So, I'll talk with you on Monday? Remember, what you believe, yes, exactly, makes all the difference. I'll be here, after one. You're welcome. Goodnight, Debbie."

Abby hears silence from the receiver. She pulls the phone toward her and presses the button to retrieve a dial tone. She dials with trembling fingers. "Mom? I am so, so sorry. I know how busy you are. No, I'm still in Boston. I'm fine. It was a work call. I'll explain later. I won't be there till tomorrow. I'm so sorry. I'll see you then. Bye." She hangs up the phone. It rings before she gets halfway to standing. Dangerously starved, she ignores it.

By the dim beam of the streetlight, Abby feels her way to the darkened kitchen and grabs the first box she touches. She opens it, then the plastic pouch and dumps the heavy powder into her palm. Handful-by-handful, she consumes the pancake mix without pausing, despite it nearly choking her. She forces it down with a liter of soda. Next, she chooses a box of cookies and a quart of milk. She walks to the bathroom to relieve her turgid abdomen. Water running, flush. She returns and eats a jar of pickles and a bag of sandwich buns. Another liter of soda follows. Another trip to the bathroom. Water running, flush. She reappears and returns to the table. She removes a carton of ice cream from the freezer and sits at the table, spoon in hand.

# 31. Hurdles

The tub spigot trickles water. An empty purge bottle lies next to Abby's motionless body on the cold tile floor. The incessantly ringing phone startles Abby into consciousness. Fully dressed in yesterday's clothes, she sits up, holding onto the toilet to steady herself. She checks her watch. 9:30. Laboriously, she stands, turns off the spigot, undresses and steps on the scale. One hundred and twenty-three pounds. Her face remains solemn. She runs the shower and steps inside.

Two hundred miles away, the aromas of roasting turkey, simmering gravy, apple and pecan pies and fresh-baked bread announce Thanksgiving's arrival to all who take breath in the Thompson home. After each completed dish, Chloe takes the opportunity to cycle the used bowls and utensils, cutting boards, pots and knives from the counters through the cleansing sink and into the drain. As each load air dries, she tackles another side dish — broccoli casserole, cranberry relish, sweet potatoes.

Reclined in the living room, Mark listens to a book-on-tape while Russell taunts the floundering quarterback of a team he doesn't follow with insults no one but Russell will ever hear. Chloe waits for a break in the nondescript tirade to answer

Russell's question. "I told you she called last night and said work kept her late."

"What about her home obligations? She'll stay there and let you make this meal alone."

"She'll be here as soon as she can. She was very apologetic."

Oblivious to his surroundings, Mark removes his earphones. "Dad, did you ever have a dog? This book is about a big St. Bernard called Cujo. I thought Stephen King wrote thrillers? What's so scary about a big, friendly dog?"

"Don't you have something better to do with your time? Get me another beer."

"Sorry, that was the last one. Mom, how long is Abby staying?"

Russell does a quick empties count. "The last one?"

"Until Sunday afternoon, I think. She said she's off tomorrow and, of course, the weekend. Let's try to get along while she's here."

Russell pounces on this lightly veiled critique, "What's that supposed to mean?"

"I'm just saying the fuses around here have been rather short lately."

"And that's my fault?"

Fearing her efforts have only wound Russell tighter, Chloe demurs. "Forget I mentioned it. When are you going to get your mother?"

"Abby can go. I need to watch the Lions finish mopping up the Chiefs. They're already ahead by ten."

"I could use her help when she gets here."

Mark interjects to ease the mounting tension, "I could go. With Gram in the lead, I could fold up my red-tipped cane on the way home. Course it would take us a while?"

"Stop being rebellious!"

"God, I'm just kidding."

Mark, sensing a building row, takes his cassette player and earphones and seeks higher ground.

Imagining Gram's reaction to the undercurrent of friction, Chloe once again slides her words in edgewise. "This is what I mean. Could we please keep this bickering to a minimum?"

Inhaling to retort, Russell hears the front door close. "Before you take off your coat, go get your grandmother."

Abby drags her luggage to the foot of the stairs, avoiding his attention. "Hi, Dad. Happy Thanksgiving. Hi, Mom! Wow, it smells really good in here."

Chloe yells from the kitchen as she chops, "Hello, sweetheart! How was your drive?"

Abby cautiously makes her way toward the kitchen. "Not bad. Sorry I'm so late." Knowing everything will change forever in the next moment, Abby grasps Chloe's shoulders from behind and gives her bowed head a solemn kiss.

Chloe joyously turns around to embrace her daughter in a long-awaited hug. Instead, she sees an emaciated stranger looking back at her. Her arms instinctively recoil. Her body deflates in horror. "Abby?! What's happened to you?"

"Nothing. I've just lost a little weight."

"Are you sick? Are you, sick?! Are you eating? Surely you're not too busy to eat."

"I'm not too busy. I want to lose my college fat, that's all."

"College fat? How much do you weigh?"

"I don't know."

Aghast, Chloe immediately shifts into solution mode. "Sit down. I'm making you something."

"Mom, it's Thanksgiving. I'll wait for dinner."

Strategizing his next move, Russell interjects. "Abby, your grandmother's waiting."

"I'd better go get Gram."

"You're eating something first."

"When I get back, I promise."

"Abby!"

"I'm going, Dad."

"Stop by the store and get me a six-pack."

Chloe simmers. "All the stores are closed, Russell. It's Thanksgiving."

"The bars are open."

Pushed beyond her limit, she boils over. "For God's sake. Have you seen your daughter?"

With the game in a time-out and his curiosity piqued, Russell enters the kitchen. "What the hell happened to you? You look like something from a freak show."

"I'm going to get Gram." Abby storms out the front door.

"What's the matter with her?"

"She says she's trying to lose her college fat."

"She did that to herself?"

Abby's nerves splinter as she drives. Besides the argument, she dreads arriving. The smell. It's mostly the smell, of old. She pulls open the heavy glass door of Gram's assisted living complex. There it is. Old. The combination of stray urine, disinfectants, cheap detergent and bad breath all confined by poor ventilation and an overtaxed heating system. The particulars change. This time, the hallway grab-bar supports a shuffling man in his effort to keep up with his toddling granddaughter. An assortment of televised voices filters through open doors as the food-trolley attendant stops at the rooms of those not lucky enough to be going out for their holiday feast. But the essence never changes. Old. Abby slows her breath as she approaches room B61. Gram beckons her visitor in when she hears the anticipated, heartening knock at her door. "Hello, Russell."

"Hi Gram."

"Abigail! I was expecting your father. Welcome home! Happy Thanksgiving!"

Abby tentatively enters the oppressive room. She refuses to picture her here, out of the family homestead, away from her flowers and fields. Gram's photographs of family and friends do little to counter the institutional aura of her space. But, they embrace and suddenly the room warms. "Thanks, Gram. He said I could come and get you. I'm so glad to see you! Are you ready?"

"There's no hurry. Your mother can do without you for a few extra minutes."

"Dad wants some beer."

"I know he can do without that."

Abby picks up Gram's coat and takes its place on the meticulously made bed. Gram remains transfixed and attentive as she steadies herself to seated in her vinyl and chrome armchair.

"Talk to me, Abigail. The change in you frightens me."

Abby feels an odd stirring of courage and honesty in the presence of her beloved grandmother. "Please don't tell Mom or Dad, but I'm kinda scared, too. Everything was going all right for a while. It still is but,"

"But what?"

"I can't explain it."

"Are you not eating?"

"I eat. I do eat."

Gram struggles to remember what she's learned from troubled guests on her daytime programming. "You don't keep your food. You throw it up before it can do you any good."

"Any harm."

"Look at yourself, sweetheart. Your throwing up is doing you harm. Why are you hurting yourself?"

"I don't see it that way. I see it as mind over matter."

"Mind over matter? Could you keep your food if you wanted to?"

"If I wanted to."

"If I wanted you to? Your mother's prepared a wonderful Thanksgiving meal. I want you to eat it—and keep it—for me."

"I'll try, Gram. We should go. Dad'll be ballistic."

"Your father's got my blood in him, too. He'll live."

Forced by circumstances to do the unveiling alone, Chloe folds the protective cloth from the table to reveal her cherished white linens, gold-trimmed china, and gold and silver flatware. She smiles. *I love Thanksgiving.* She positions a water goblet at each place-setting and white candlesticks and a vase of fresh flowers in one corner, leaving the center for the pièce de résistance. *Lovely, if I do say so myself.* Chloe returns to the kitchen and arranges the serving dishes in preparation for filling. She gives the gravy another stir and pokes the boiling potatoes with a fork. *Getting there.*

Off his normal meal schedule, Mark enters the kitchen seeking to satisfy his cravings. "I'm hungry. When are we going to eat?"

*Good lord.* "As soon as your sister and grandmother get here."

"Can I have something now?"

*No.* "They should be here any minute. Just wait."

Dejected, he turns to leave.

Chloe calls him back. "Mark?"

"Yeah?"

"I don't want you to say anything about Abby's appearance."

"What's she got, blue hair?"

"She's lost a lot of weight and I don't want you —" Chloe amplifies her voice to overpower the game announcer. " — or your father, giving her a hard time. Do you understand?"

"Yeah, sure. She looks like a twig but you want me to pretend everything's okay. Got it. What a joke. Oh, sorry. Nothing's ever wrong with the Thompsons."

Russell barks his displeasure. "Stop being rebellious!"

"No prob."

As Abby and Gram drive, a gossamer cloth of sadness drapes their conversation. Abby does her best to persuade Gram that she need not worry. Doubtful of her success, she pulls into the driveway, gets out and goes to the passenger side to help Gram out of the car. She pulls a six-pack from atop piles of discarded food and drink packaging in her back seat. The two fragile, invincible women support each other as they approach the door.

"You're going to do this, for me?"

"Yes, Gram."

"I love you, Abigail."

"I love you, Gram."

They exchange knowing glances as Abby opens the door. Russell greets them at the threshold and kisses his mother on the cheek.

"Hi, Mom. Happy Thanksgiving." He takes the beer from Abby.

"Mmmm. It's cold. So, Mom, what do you think of Abby?"

"I think she's lovely."

"I mean the way she looks."

Chloe stomps in exasperation. "Russell!"

"I think she's lovely."

Unsure if he actually reclaimed his alpha status, he returns to his chair, his attention to another game. Chloe softens the mood with a kiss and embrace. "Hi, Mom. Happy Thanksgiving. How are you?"

"Fine, dear. Sorry we're a bit late. I needed Abby to do a few things for me."

"I'm glad she could help. Dinner will be ready soon."

Abby recognizes the weary in her mother's voice, face and shoulders. "What can I do, Mom?"

"Do you feel alright? Can you mash the potatoes?"

"Sure."

Reflecting dozens of annual performances of this precise ballet, the three dancers execute the final steps of feast-preparation in silence. In no time, heaping bowls and platters of steaming food grace the table.

"We're ready."

The extravagance of the Thanksgiving feast changes little of the Thompson dynamic. Mark, who waited out the hullabaloo four steps up the stairway, arrives at his seat at the foot of the table before Chloe finishes her announcement. Russell, feeling inconvenienced by the timing, barks out one last feeble insult before turning off the game and taking his seat at the head of the table. Abby follows Gram to the chair to Russell's left and helps her nudge in, while Chloe lights the candles and sits to Russell's right. Abby takes the remaining seat across from the vased bouquet.

Despite the meaning of the holiday, the atmosphere snaps and crackles above the surface. Gram exploits her role as outsider to neutralize the static charge. Fully aware of the planning and effort her daughter-in-law invested in such an elaborate meal, Gram initiates the shower of praise. "Chloe, you've outdone yourself. Not only does everything look beautiful, it smells delicious."

Riddled by guilt for being so little help, Abby quickly chimes in. "Really, Mom. It smells so amazing."

Mark's appetite gets the better of him. "This is great. I'll have a drumstick."

Russell, feeling undo pressure to acquiesce in applauding, exerts his dominance instead. "Bow your heads. Bless these gifts, Lord, received through Your bounty."

"Amen."

Gram, embarrassed by Russell's lack of social grace, resorts to her chastising tone, "Son, don't you think you owe Chloe a thank you, too?"

"Give me time. I haven't tasted anything yet."

Russell stands up with his buzzing electric knife in hand. Engrossed in strategizing the task before him, he misses even the facial expressions of his family's silent judgment.

*Seriously, what a creep.*

*Why does Gram even try to get through to him?*

*I wonder if his praying is actually taking the Lord's name in vain?*

*That was harsh.*

Five plates, piled high with a patchwork quilt of side dishes, await the center square as Russell carves the bird. Gram catches Abby's eye and nods. Abby nods in return.

Seven days to prepare and thirty-three minutes to deconstruct, the Thompson's Thanksgiving feast moves to memory status. Russell pushes away from the table and pats his distended stomach. "Chloe, that was a fine meal."

"Thank you, Russell."

"Is that better, Mom?"

Gram shakes her head, dismayed by her son. "It's a start. Clear and wash the dishes, then ask me again."

Hoping the tradition had faded from others' memory, Russell reluctantly begins what has become the men's annual execution of housework. "Mark, give me a hand."

Mark begrudgingly stands and joins his father. Abby, acutely aware of the foreign substances moving through her digestive process, fidgets in discomfort. She feels all the weight she so painstakingly lost building up again as she idles. Unable to resist her response, she stands to leave the table. Gram reaches for her hand, begging her back. "Why don't you stay and chat for a moment, Abigail? What's your favorite spot in Boston?"

Abby entwines her fingers with her grandmother's, longing to fulfill her promise. She half-sits back down, willing her attention to focus on Gram. "The Common. It's beautiful in any weather." Her stomach seizes. She feels her throat fill with sour, thick liquid. She re-swallows it in horror. "I'm so sorry, Gram. I'll be right back." Abby darts from the room and runs upstairs.

Chloe rises to follow but Gram calls her back with a word. "Wait."

With tears in her eyes, and helplessness pouring from every pore, Chloe confides her turmoil in hushed tones. "I'm so worried about her."

"You should be, dear. It's an eating disorder. She says she eats, but then needs to throw the food up right away. It's called bulimia."

"What?"

"She's lost control."

"You talked about it?"

The pipes run. The toilet flushes. Abby tiptoes down the stairs and to the doorway. She times her breathing to overhear her story being told.

"Just for a few minutes. It's why we were late. She needs professional help. They say it's as much a mental illness as a physical one. I don't think she should be alone in Boston."

Abby's heard enough. "I know you mean well, Gram, but I'm not staying here. I've got a life in Boston. People there need me."

Love motivates Gram to contest. "You need help, Abigail."

"I'll be fine. If I need them, the doctors at Mass General are better than any around here."

Shocked by the candor of the moment, Chloe does her best to constrain the lightning. "It's all right, darling. You have a few days to think it over."

"I've decided to go back tomorrow. I don't belong here. Can I take you home, Gram?"

Hoping to learn more in private from Gram about her daughter's illness, Chloe edges in. "Mom, you're not ready to leave yet, are you? I'll take you home in a little while after we visit for a bit. The boys are cleaning up so we can sit down in the living room and relax. Abby, you're welcome to join us. I know you said you were up late last night. Would you rather get an early start to bed?"

Abby, exhausted and frustrated, takes the bait unwittingly. "I think I will. It was so helpful to talk with you, Gram. I've missed you. I'll see you again soon." Abby embraces her Gram with all the love she can convey and kisses her gently on the cheek before turning to her mother. "Goodnight, Mom. Thanks again for a wonderful meal. I'm sorry it ended this way." Abby wraps her arms around Chloe. Both women instinctively remain still in their embrace, longing for understanding, a way out, a second chance. No words, just resignation, as they part.

# 32.  Mine Field

The recent upheaval in her sleeping and waking schedule overrides Abby's normal dawn routine. The sun and her family rose hours ago. She has yet to open her eyes since her last wee-hours feeding. The gentle finger-nail-tapping at her door melds into her turbulent dream.

"Abby? Are you awake, darling?" At the sound of a knuckle rapping, she stirs and whimpers. Her mother's familiar voice centers her awareness. "Abby?"

As she shakes off sleep, the rattling of her door knob accompanied by a ferocious knock and her father's growl start her heart pounding. "Abigail, stop being rebellious! Unlock this door, now!"

Abby wearily climbs out of bed and puts on her robe. She unlocks the door and opens it a crack, holding it fast with her foot. "What is it?" Seeing the look on both their faces, she holds the knob behind her back and slides out of her room, closing the door seamlessly behind her.

"Your father and I have been talking."

"Young lady, your mother and I insist that you get help with this eating thing before you to go back to Boston. Your

135

grandmother knows about it from those talk shows she watches. Personally, I think you need to get right with the Lord. I talked to Reverend Jim. He'll see you today at his office."

The mere suggestion blindsides Abby. "Why did you call him?"

Chloe lovingly defends their idea. "You know you two have always had a special bond. He thinks of you as a daughter."

"A daughter?"

Russell reprises his tirade. "Maybe if you'd get right with the Lord you wouldn't be so ready to defile your temple."

Exasperated, Abby fires back. "Is that what you think? I'm defiling my temple?"

"Now honey, we don't want to see you unhappy."

"I think for as smart as you are, you're acting like a pathetic idiot. If you were actually smart or strong or capable, you'd be able to stop vomiting everything you eat."

"Russell, we agreed you'd stay calm."

Abby's fury surfaces. "Calm? He's never calm. He gives no love, no support, no approval. Send me to Reverend Jim? A daughter? I've never been treated like a daughter by you or any man. I'm going home this morning."

Abby goes back in her room and slams the door.

"If you leave without doing as I say, you won't be a daughter to me."

"Russell, you don't mean that."

"I didn't feed and clothe her for twenty-some years to see her flush her life down the toilet."

Russell storms off.

"Abby, please."

With three short words, Russell condemns the family to turmoil. "Let her go!"

"Abby, he doesn't mean it. You know how he gets."

"I do know how he gets!"

"Let me in, darling."

Autumn's chill and holiday visiting keep the streets and highways nearly deserted for Abby's early return to Boston. She relies on the crisp, refreshing air that streams in her open windows to restore serenity. She inhales the aromas of rising campfire tendrils and ripened apples left too long on the ground. Accompanied by a soundtrack of Brahms, the relaxed drive gives her time to process. "Home. That definition certainly changed quickly. Daughter? That one, too. See Reverend Jim? Seriously! Dad's rage was nothing new. Mom's giving in, also, same as always. Stay in Brookfield? I'd rather die."

As she makes the final turn, she watches swirling winds toss and gather tawny skeletons of summer's greenery in heaps and mounds along her street. Squirrels fuss and chatter as they scrounge among the litter for tidbits to last the winter. Grateful for a safe drive, Abby sighs with relief as she parks her car at the curb. "Home."

Her relief fades to concern when she hears the sound of her ringing phone as she approaches her front stoop. She juggles her depleted belongings as she pushes the door open. She drops her parcels at the threshold and slumps down on the sofa. "Ahhhhhh." She reaches for the phone. "Hi, Mom...I'm sorry, who is this? No. You can call the station on Monday between ten and twelve. Goodbye." She hangs up the phone. Before she has time to exhale, it rings again. She picks up the receiver and hangs it up without a word. It rings again. With building frustration, she answers it. "Hello. Call my show on Monday morning. Thank you." Again it rings. "Has this been constant since yesterday? How could all these people have been listening?" Abby picks up the receiver just long enough to disconnect the call. "I'm so sorry." Then lays it silenced on the sofa. "Good Lord."

Determined to mask her guilt for ignoring her callers and to make the most of her hard-won day of solitude—*Painting on the Common, that's the answer.* —she retreats to her bedroom and returns with her satchel of supplies, a board with paper and her easel. She returns from her car to gather a tote of food and drink, and her radio. Then, she's off.

Abby selects a sun-drenched corner of the Common as her vantage point for today's *plein air.* Shadows multiply the branch lines by two until floating mountains of condensed water droplets interfere. She exhales to the rhythm of the breeze. Solitude works wonders. Quiet heals tumult. Painting centers thoughts. Until it does not. Her brush strokes quicken then grind. "Reverend Jim. Reverend? A daughter?!"

The memory she fights so hard to suppress slices its way to the center of her consciousness. She was thirteen. Jealous of her brother's special treatment to relieve his depression, she feigned mania so she, too, could visit Reverend Jim. The day she arrived, his waiting room was unusually quiet, empty. He met her at his doorway and welcomed her into his office, lush with beautiful, leather-bound books filling an entire wall.

"Oh, that smell." The Holy Bible laid open on an ornate, iron stand. Religious artwork adorned the walls—paintings of the Madonna and Child, Mary Magdalene at Jesus' feet, Jesus with the children. "Hah! Jesus with the children!"

He went to each of the windows and pulled the right string to drop the blind, then the left string to tighten it. *I'll never forget that sound. Whoosh, clack, whoosh, clack, whoosh, clack.* Dust snapped into the air and danced through the narrow stripes of sunlight mottling the blue pile carpeting. In the sudden darkness, before her eyes could adjust, he took a seat in one of the leather arm chairs opposite his orderly wooden desk. He motioned for her to sit in the adjacent chair facing him. So small, she had to push herself back in the smooth, taut seat to keep from sliding off.

"Abigail, your father told me that he is concerned about you. I told him I would talk with you to see if I can fix you. I helped your brother, Mark, you know."

"I know."

"I hope you know how beautiful you are."

"You think I'm beautiful?"

"Your beauty is more than skin deep. You're so innocent and pure. It makes me want to…" Placing his hands on either side of her cushion, he slid off his chair and knelt down in front of her. "May I touch you? Look at you?" He slowly unbuttoned her best blouse and put his cold, moist right hand under her T-shirt.

"Reverend Jim, this doesn't seem right."

"I'm not going to hurt you. I only want to feel you on my palm. Your soft breasts. They're so young. I love you, Abigail."

"You love me?"

"You're so beautiful." He moved to the side and pushed his hand down her stomach and into her pants and began to fondle her vagina. She flinched. He held her in place with his left hand. She felt his wedding ring pressing against her collar bone.

"Reverend Jim."

"It's okay, Abigail. This is how I'm going to fix you."

"You love me?"

A barking dog startles Abby back to the present. Its owner whistles as it tears past Abby, knocking over her easel and sending her dried pallet and painting into the air. In the confusion, Abby topples off her stool and lands contorted on the cold, dry ground. She lies there, motionless, fighting the urge to shriek her rage. *I hate the bastard!*

The dog's owner, apologizing the entire length of his crossing, reaches Abby within seconds. "I'm so sorry. He gets so wild out here on the Common. Let me help you get everything back in order." He extends a hand and accepts her weightless grip to aid her to standing. He uprights her stool and easel and replaces the painting. He hands her her brush.

Abby wipes her tears with her sleeve as she centers herself on her stool. She chokes out a "Thank you."

"Again, I am so sorry." The embarrassed offender latches the leash on his dog's collar and walks away with a nagging itch of having heard that voice before.

Alone again, Abby folds in the corners and staples the memory of this sexual assault shut. She wedges it among the nightmares and affronts she chooses not to acknowledge. Control. She forces herself to refocus on the beauty surrounding her until sunset's advance coaxes her to lid her paints and rinse her brushes. She lingers on her stool, decompressing, admiring the fleeting moments of today's crown jewel. Driven by her pestering appetite and the impending darkness, Abby reluctantly gathers the clutter from the space around her and heads for home.

The streetlight casts short shadows of Abby's trips between car and stoop. With a few minutes to spare before her next feeding, she takes a leisurely stroll to the nearby dumpster to hand-deliver today's discards herself. A pang of realization registers deep within as she steals furtive glances through glowing bays and bows. Recalling her parents' harsh parting words, she finds comfort imagining that happiness resides somewhere.

Unable to heave the heavy bag into the bin from ground level, Abby maneuvers herself and her load up on a rusted ledge on the dumpster's side. "Huh? What's that?" From her position above the rim, she notices, reflected by streetlight, aluminum soda cans stuffed into a clear plastic bag. *Who would throw those away? They're worth money.* She tosses her garbage in ahead, then twists and lowers herself over the cold edge and into the bin. The blue reflective glow of a feasting raccoon's eyes startle her as she grabs the treasure. A forceful "Git!" sends the unsatisfied creature clambering over a mountain of bags and on its way. Following its lead, though impeded by near darkness, Abby hoists several garbage bags together to create an incline out. "Hmmm. That was pretty simple."

Back on her block, Abby waits in the shadows for her neighbor's guests to kiss their final kisses, hug their final hugs and wave their final goodbyes. She realizes, from her vantage point outside the streetlight's beam, that her stealth and rummaging put her in the community of other scavengers of the night. "That's sobering."

Finally, the click of the front door latch and the extinguishing of the lamppost light signal her all clear. "That took longer than I expected." *I need food.* Weakened by hunger and feeling untethered in a spinning vortex of churning emotions, Abby mindlessly unlocks her door and deposits her now two bags of recyclables inside. Then, with the simple twist of a knob, she grounds herself and fills her home and spirit with Brahms.

When she opens the refrigerator door—*Damn!* —the sparse shelves suddenly remind her that her vacation preparation included consuming their entire contents, save the mustard and mayonnaise. "Shopping tomorrow, early." Without wasting a precious moment, she fills a large pot with water and dumps in a pound of linguine noodles the second it reaches full boil. Two jars of cold marinara sauce and a box of saltines join the pasta in the Boston sewage system less than an hour later. Control.

Cleansed, showered and dressed for bed, Abby checks the surface of today's painting to make sure every stroke is set and dry. Finding it so, she lifts her mattress and tucks her masterpiece safely beneath. "I'm getting quite a collection."

Exhausted, but too agitated to sleep, she documents today's turning point.

> *November 27, 1981, Dear Diary, What a day! It's only Friday and I'm already home after a disastrous Thanksgiving trip to Brookfield. I had high hopes for a better stay. I should have known. Dad, no from now on he's Russell. If I'm not a daughter to him, he's not a 'dad' to me. Russell went ballistic when I refused to stay there and get help for my "sickness." Send me to Rev. Jim?! That's all stirred up again. He pulled out his "Stop being rebellious!" line. If I were strong or smart or... I'd be able to stop throwing up. He told me I'm no longer a daughter to him. Imagine! Like I ever was. He's probably issued one of his decrees. What a mess! Maybe Mom will call tomorrow. If she's allowed.*

Writing moves her frustration into the universe. Her eyes drift closed as she leans toward relaxation. *Heavenly family, thank you for the knowledge that you will never abandon me. In your mercy, please catch me if I fall. Amen.*

Abby grabs her recyclables and bulging coupon file as she runs out the door. Getting to the store as it opens is particularly critical on weekends, far too many people to wheel around otherwise. Excited to have so many extras, Abby makes a quick stop at the recycling station to turn her aluminum cans into cash. Then, aware of the murmuring in her wake, "Mommy, why is that man so skinny?" "Shhhh. That's a woman. She can hear you." she makes a quick pass up and down each aisle until her cart brims with multiples of this week's specials: apple pies, pumpkin pies, dinner rolls, sweet potatoes, white potatoes,

142

carrots, walnuts, ginger ale, electrolyte drinks, pudding packs, yogurt, dried mashed potatoes, bags of stuffing, cranberry sauce, flour, pumpkin pie filling, brownie mix, graham crackers, coffee creamer, butter, milk, bags of frozen berries, corn and beans, and leftover turkey breasts. She walks past three check-out lines before coming to the one she chooses. She willingly stands in line for her regular cashier. Abby knows he will stay quiet. He will barely look up. He will stare blankly as he discounts the stream of coupons. He will accept quarters, dimes, nickels and pennies. He is worth the wait.

Abby packs her groceries into the trunk just as the sun makes its return over the earth's edge. Tucked in behind the building, still shrouded in darkness, Abby notices a dumpster on her way out of the parking lot. "Hmmmm." She puts her car in reverse and backs it into the alley and out of view. Looking both ways, she surreptitiously gets out of her car, runs to the dumpster, quickly climbs up the ledge, and looks in. "Hah!" She carefully lowers herself from the ledge and returns to her car where she empties one of her grocery bags. "Perfect."

She nimbly makes another trip up the ledge and smoothly over the cold, metal side and, with pride in her heart, she reclaims "one, two, three, four, five, how many are there?" bags of carrots. Only then she notices the bin is nearly empty. With last night's lesson fresh in her memory, she knows getting out will take stacking every remaining box and bag. She races against the sun in its quest to rise above the building and flood the alley with revealing light. She finally collects enough of a mound to make her way over the edge and down to safety, carrots in tow. "Plan better next time." *Next time?*

Abby watches "60 Minutes" sitting beside her disassembled phone. Four days later and it still rings within minutes of being hung up. She tests it when loneliness sets in. The calls originate from children and adults. Some stone cold sober; others, not so much. But no call from home.

Abby readies for bed and opens her journal.

> *November 29, 1981, Dear Diary, Well, the weekend is over and Mom hasn't called. Maybe she tried to call but was stopped by Russell. She may have tried and got a busy signal. Every time I hang it up it rings, so I just had to take it off the hook. She may not have tried at all. No matter which, my life has changed. Time will tell whether for better or worse. So be it. I had every right to stand up for myself. I'll make my way without him. I will miss mom. I really will miss mom. And Gram. Big day tomorrow. An early rise. I hope Linda calmed down over the holiday.*

With that, Abby clicks off the lamp, curls into a cozy position under the covers and joins her hands. *Heavenly Father, Goddess Mother, I have always turned to you for help. I may need to stop by more often now that I've lost my family. Please keep my mind clear tomorrow when I meet with Linda. And please, catch me if I fall. Amen.*

# 33. Mud Crawl

The approaching winter's frigid bite permeates the dark apartment. Abby feels it on her moist skin as she towels off after her steaming shower. She feels it under her skin, as foreboding taints her unusually early Monday morning preparation. Not even Brahms calms her today. Faced with the reality of facing Linda, she reluctantly accepts that no prayer can save her from some consequence for her actions, "Not after that knife-across-the-throat thing."

Still wrapped in a towel, Abby enters her bedroom and stands before the mirror. Shivering, she drops the towel—*Getting there.*—and quickly slides her panties up her thinning legs and over her defined hip bones. She hooks and spins her bra into place, adjusting the straps in the hollows beside her shoulders. Her size 8 pants and size 6 blouse hang as limply on her as on their hangers.

As she combs her cropped hair into place, she does her best to allay her worst fears by conversing with herself in the mirror. "'Abigail, it's strict company policy not to give out home numbers on the air.' 'You're quite right, Linda. My inexperience really showed. I'll be more careful next time.'" Abby slides into her denim jacket and a hat. "I'll be conciliatory. I'll be forgiven." On her way out of the apartment, she resists the temptation, for the hundredth time, to hang up her phone. "Please, catch me if I fall."

The unusual circumstances of her commute take Abby out of her head and into the moment. "Geez, this traffic is nerve-wracking." She inches along, careful to keep her eyes on the road while she supplements her breakfast with a few granola bars and juice. Her routine, though off by three hours, follows like clockwork. Park the car, run up the steps and into the lobby, avoid Renee's gaze, duck into the restroom, cleanse quietly, rinse and wipe, enter the office. "Okay, stay humble and apologetic. You'll be fine."

An uncharacteristic still and quiet drapes the room. Renee, her face and energy absent of all joy, looks up at Abby through bloodshot eyes. "She's waiting for you."

Renee's forlorn tone abruptly silences Abby's hopeful thoughts. "Thanks." Trying to regain some serenity, Abby recalls Linda's 'confidence builder' and her offer to help in a pinch, anything to stop her gut from seizing as she makes the seemingly endless trek to Linda's door. Terrified to hear the worst, she hesitates, for what, to every pair, of transfixed eyes, seems like, years, before, knocking.

Linda's reply snaps the tension. "Come in."

"Good morning, Linda."

"Let's take a walk."

As they near her desk, Renee abruptly fakes focus and pantomimes busy. Linda, with her head and attitude fixed for confrontation, leads Abby, ashen and trembling, out the door. "I'll be back in half an hour."

"Yes, ma'am."

The frigid, crisp air of November's last morning keeps the vendors of Quincy Market moving at a seasonally-adjusted pace just to stay warm. Booths rise to standing and dollies roll to carry crates of the latest catch and the final offerings of farmers' fields. Abby, wishing she had chosen her winter coat, remains slightly in Linda's wake as she weaves her way among the merchants' comings and goings.

Linda's voice arrives on a current of the wafting air. "What you did was against station policy. You do understand how our entire enterprise depends on the exploitation of extremes. Extremely funny, extremely sad, extremely distraught. You gave out your number. That dilutes the extreme into mediocre."

Abby struggles to catch up. "I do understand, but, did you hear her? She was in crisis."

"Had you not talked to her on your own time, which I must presume you did, she would still be in crisis today, ready to enthrall another enraptured audience.'

"Or maybe she'd be dead."

"Young people don't kill themselves."

Abby, wide-eyed and dumbfounded by Linda's harshness, feels her knees buckle and her head swoon. *Who is this person? How did I not know how callous she is?* With nowhere else to turn, she falters toward Linda to steady herself.

Linda cringes to feel Abby's birdlike grip on her arm. Grateful that her prepared speech has neared its end, she sternly loosens Abby's hold and continues. "Be that as it may, for the sake of our owners, I have no choice but to let you go."

*What the hell?* "You're firing me?"

"I also have a written request for an unlisted phone number for you. All it needs is your signature."

*A what?*

Linda removes a pen and paper from her purse and forces them into Abby's frozen hands. Abby, stunned in equal parts by despair and outrage, reluctantly accepts the pen and scribbles her signature on the form as best she can. Linda takes both from her and shoves them back into her purse. "You're good at what you do, Abby. The station will miss you. But yes, I've got a replacement for your show today. You don't need to come back."

"But I've got…"

"Your last paycheck will be mailed to you. Goodbye, Abigail." Linda turns on her heels and disappears among the confusion of the market.

Back at WTOK, Renee swallows hard as Linda steps off the elevator—alone. She notices Linda's focus turning in her direction and averts her stare too late to avoid visual connection. *Shit.*

Locked in her turbulent gaze, Renee watches as Linda approaches decisively, still noticeably enraged by the situation. "Did Steve call for me?"

"No, Ms. Warner. No messages."

"Call him. And keep calling him. Put him through to me when you reach him."

Linda paces defiantly behind her desk to diffuse her frustration. Disheveled and disoriented, Steve, the late-night call-in host, wipes the sleep from his eyes with the back of his hand as he gulps down his essential second dose of nature's stimulant and sucks the smoke from a filterless cig. "Sure, Ms. Warner, I'll do it. But, I've never actually heard LifeLine. It's on when I'm in the sack."

Linda snaps despite her desperation, "It's not rocket science. She doesn't even have a format. People can talk about anything and they do. Just sound interested. You'll be fine."

# PART TWO

# 34. Low Dive

Abby, frozen in shock, struggles desperately to recover enough to locate a place tc sit down. "What just happened?"

"Hey, buddy? Ya mind gettin' out of the way? Hey buddy! Hey!"

Abby turns to see a cart overflowing with lobsters-on-ice inches from her back. Her eyes meet its owner's. "Ya mind?"

"Oh, I'm so sorry. I..."

Abby shakes off her hypothermic stupor. Feeling more alone than ever, she snugs her collar around her neck and wanders away to start her journey back to true anonymity.

Quaking, Abby maneuvers her key into the lock. The combination of bone-splitting cold and gut-gnawing hunger reduces her to Russell's prediction, "pathetic." She sucks in the blast of warm air that starts her face and hands tingling. She stumbles to the sink and runs warm water over her frosty fingers to ignite the thawing fire. Her breathing trembles with shivers that denote more than mere chill. "What now?" Her imagined solutions derail mid-way across many smoldering bridges. "I know. Els."

She goes into the kitchen and lifts a green and white magnet from the freezer door. She takes the released paper with her. She dials. A mechanized voice delivers a crushing message. "The number you have reached, 617-555-0300, is not in service. Please check the number and dial again. There is no further information available about 617-555 03..." Abby dials again. "The number you..." She hangs up the receiver, crumples the faded, pink memo and tosses it toward her garbage can. "Els."

It's been nearly two hours, but the shock of this morning's ordeal, combined with the lingering chill from Quincy Market, still sends erratic tremors through Abby's fragile frame. Now a sobering question adds to her instability. "Where's Els?" Ellen's message occupied the front of Abby's refrigerator for months, resurfacing when bills and to-do lists rotated off. Every sighting stirred something, but not deeply enough. Now, with nowhere else to turn, her mind races into survival mode. She needs to think. She grabs a box of sugared donuts and retreats into bed to conserve heat and replenish energy.

Restless, Abby's eyes lock on her clock's display. She watches the numbers advance. Finally. 9:58. She extends her arm from under the covers and switches on the radio. She flips the toggle to AM and tunes the dial to WTOK.

"Okay, guys. That's all the time we have. Thanks for tuning in. Come back tomorrow when the topic will be how to bag the really big game on Ready. Aim. Fire. Up next is LifeLine with, ah, guest host Steve Winston."

"Steve Winston?" Abby listens intently as the LifeLine theme plays through her tinny speakers.

"Who's Steve Winston?"

Despite the cold air penetrating the room from the wall of poorly glazed windows and his years of call-in-host experience, perspiration beads on Steve's upper lip and brow. He anxiously wipes his face with his sleeve. Gordon signals "on air." Steve flips the mic live and feigns excitement.

"Helloooo LifeLine listeners! I'm Steve Winston. Welcome to today's show. I'm sitting in today for LifeLine's, ahh, former host, Abigail Thompson."

Gordon waves to grab Steve's attention and points to the flashing phone bank.

"Oh, all our lines are lit up. Let's see who's on the line. Hello, this is LifeLine."

"Hi."

"Hi."

"Who are you? Where's Abby?"

"Ah, I'm Steve Winston. Abiga… Abby took another job. No hard feelings."

"That's bogus. Nothin' against you, man. But that Abby is a real charmer."

"What's on your mind?"

"They shoulda countered with double da money."

"Okay then. I'll pass that on. Our next caller is Janice. Hello, Janice."

"Are you telling me Abby isn't coming back?"

"Yep. She's taken another—"

"She just up and left?"

"Aaaah, not sure what happened."

"She didn't seem like the kind of person who would chase money."

"Yah, not sure why she left. Got something you wanna talk about?"

"I agree with your last caller. WTOK made a bad mistake. Good-bye."

Smacked with the realization that every call for the next two hours will likely mimic those of the past two minutes, Steve's nervous expression turns to bewilderment. He looks at Gordon for feedback of any kind. Gordon shrugs in resignation. "Okay, thanks for your call. I'll let 'em know. Our next caller is Sam. Hello?"

Hearing her show violated, exasperation tinged with sadness rises from deep within. Abby flips the switch back to FM and tunes in inspiration. Her classical masters ease her disquiet and lull her to an uneasy sleep.

Abby awakens with a start. Her eyes struggle to adjust. "What time is it?" She checks her watch. "Four o'clock?" She takes a deep inhale that fills her lungs to capacity. The troublesome thoughts that confounded sleep now transform into her unwelcome reality. All alternatives fall away, save one. *Free food is free food.* Exhale. She draws her covers back, twists her temperamental body to put her feet on the floor and makes her way to the kitchen. "One step at a time."

While mapping out the most efficient course to visit the viable dumpsters in her vicinity, Abby satisfies her appetite starting with turkey, pumpkin pie filling and stale dinner rolls. Several purges and feedings later, with the sun bidding farewell, she grabs some garbage bags and heads for her car.

Perceived necessity drives Abby to enter and excavate the discard bins of select groceries, pharmacies and restaurants along her route. In one she finds packages of raw ground beef, not pink as she knows it should be, but— *Beggars can't be choosers.* In another she finds a bag full of Thanksgiving cards. "I must know someone who would use these." Deli pizza slices, in their box, still radiate warmth. "Such waste."

Under cover of darkness, Abby carries her finds indoors. She stores the cards in a box then consumes the pizza while the beef sizzles in a skillet. *Free food is free food.* "If I do this every day, I'll probably just need a part-time job to make ends meet."

Before the week ends, Abby's hunter-gatherer strategy evolves toward perfection. Because her priority is salvaging edible food, she times her route carefully, realizing the overnight deep freeze preserves some items but ruins others. And, despite the awkwardness of extricating herself from deep dumpsters carrying bulging trash bags, she no longer competes with four-legged scavengers, sorting through bags under, at best, dim streetlights. She now does her triaging at home, to avoid prolonged time in the cold and the obvious risks of injury and infection.

These lessons, however, do not lessen the physical drain. Exhausted by a week of grueling foraging, Abby dims her headlights as she pulls her car up to her sidewalk—casting muted beams over the windblown, street-facing boot prints in the waves of snow that bear witness to her wee-hours departure. Her neighbors, shuttered and tucked, lie unaware of the struggle between gravity and bones happening right outside their curtains. Abby's lungs ache and the vapor of her breath condenses as she lugs the initial two unwieldy bags toward her stoop. She loses her grip on one and yanks it along instead. Another lesson learned. *Dragging beats carrying.* "Ha! I wonder what the couple next door will make of these imprints." Three trips later, she forces the door to her apartment open against the already gathered refuse and garbage bags. Clouds of snow billow in. She heaves her current find onto the pile, then closes and latches the door behind her. "It's going to be a long night." She retreats to the kitchen, returns with a balancing act of packaged cheese and crackers and sets them aside in case tonight's pickings disappoint.

They do not. Once again, the store managers' over-projection of Thanksgiving demand provides for her bounty. More week-old pies and pumpkin rolls, preserved in the sub-freezing nighttime temperatures, need only to thaw to be devoured. "Gram's recipe for relish will make quick use of these shriveled cranberries and pomegranates. Wrinkled sweet potatoes and soft Brussels sprouts will be okay once I roast or sauté them. And all this will go beautifully with the turkey breast and mashed potatoes. Tomorrow will be Thanksgiving number four."

After a restless night, Abby resists rising. Childhood memories of being on Thanksgiving-kitchen-duty kept her mind racing until well past her normal sleep time. To make matters worse, the warmth of her covers, snug against her chin, hinders even the thought of exposing her skin to the chill in the air. She rolls over, denying the bands of daylight reflecting off her bedroom walls. She lingers just beyond the reach of wakefulness, returning to visions of being at her grandmother's elbow. Watching. Attentive. Despite the congealing scene, no amount of mental relaxation or force resurrects the recipe for her grandmother's cranberry relish. Consciousness arrives with a solution. *Mom will have it. I'll just have to call home to get it. That's as good an excuse as any.*

Abby slides out of bed, slides into her robe and picks up the phone. "Hi Mark. What are you up to? Is Mom there? Do you know when she'll be back? Okay, well give her this number, 617-555-37... Mark? What do you mean Dad's coming? You're not allowed? Mark? Mark?" *Seriously?* Abby shakes her head as the finality of her father's edict settles in. "Seriously?"

Mourning another Thompson tradition unceremoniously discarded, Abby drags new traditions into being. She creates original dishes that will easily satisfy, as long as it matters. She sits down at her table and bows her head. "Thank you, God for the meal before me. It feels a little like manna from Heaven, so my gratitude is deep. May it give me strength to do your will, whatever and whenever that may be. Amen." Her taste buds reward her ingenuity. Her ingenuity rewards her taste buds. Within minutes, the fruits of her labor float away. She settles down to rest before heading back out for the night's scavenging. Her journal gets a brief visit before sleep steals her away.

> December 5, 1981 Dear Diary, Mark and Mom aren't allowed to talk to me. Things are looking dire. Still unemployed, but at least I have a way to get free food. It's not the safest or respectable. But. I will have to start my job search soon. Nobody tosses rent money in the dumpster.

# 35. Net Ladder

Sixteen days in, Abby establishes a rhythm to her new routine. Nighttime raids, hauling and sorting. Daytime binges, purging and weighing. Today, her mood shifts toward positive as the smooth snow magnifies and reflects the morning sun's rays to fill the kitchen with golden light. Rinsed pots and skillets air dry in the rack beside the sink. Rolled drawstring potato sacks accumulate in a corner. Three wishbones hang to dry. Water gushes from the bathtub spigot. The hard-won contents of Abby's stomach disappear, along with minute traces of her dental enamel, into the Boston sewage system. While she lounges, waiting to satisfy her growing appetite, she tunes in to WTOK to satisfy her curiosity.

"We're back to take your calls. Next up is Joan. Hi Joan, is there a story you wanna share? Hello? Hello? Thanks for your call? We're wrappin' up another week of LifeLine. We've got a few open lines. The number is 555-WTOK. This is host Steve Winston. We're talkin' to folks about their human-ness and openin' your thoughts to us. We have a call from, Dale. Hello, Dale."

"I got a hot tip. Get Abby back."

"Thanks for your call."

Abby shakes her head. "How much longer can he keep this up? Then again, how much longer can I?"

With Christmas fast approaching, sparkling holiday lights outline the eaves and doorways of every home on the street, save Abby's. Her priorities, both of time and money, necessarily stray from the norm. Without a job, sheer survival now takes center stage around the clock. She manages to incorporate the Christmas season into her life nonetheless. Carols, arranged in classical style, reverberate against the ceiling and walls of her crowded apartment. She sings along while her reclaimed dinner warms. No time to dance.

Nearly obscured by the crescendo of handbells pealing "O Holy Night," she detects a faint knocking sound. She freezes. Despite her practice of not answering, the neighbor's son never assumes a 'no' when it comes to shoveling her sidewalk. Another knock. And another. Abby's curiosity draws her to the curtain where a slight tug in the right direction creates a clear view of the light beam on her front porch. Congregating snowflakes accumulate on her visitor's head.

"Linda?!" Flustered, Abby grabs her coat and opens the door a fraction. "Hello, Linda. What do you want?"

"Hello Abigail. I'm sorry to disturb you at home. I wanted to talk to you in person."

Thrilled to use a line she's rehearsed *ad nauseam*, Abby coolly retorts, "You had to talk to me in person, you mean, since you forced me to unlist my number."

"I apologize for that. May I come in?"

Abby slides her arms into her coat as she slides her body between the door and the jamb. She raises her hood to cast an effective shadow over her exposed face. "It's not a good time. We can talk out here."

"Fine. Okay. Well, the station owners asked me, told me, to persuade you to come back. Frankly, your slot was pulling its weight and now it's virtually dead airtime. Ninety percent of the callers are still wondering when you'll be back. We can't even put them on the air. We considered terminating the show altogether, but fear a station boycott. I'm prepared to offer you a sizable raise. I hope it will smooth over any hard feelings."

"I've imagined this happening thousands of times. You fired me to save your almighty profits. Now you're here to buy my forgiveness—same reason. Thrown away, like garbage, then dragged back when it suits you."

"I can, I do, understand if your answer is 'no.'"

"Oh, I'll do the show again, but this time on my terms."

"What exactly are your terms?"

# 36. Rope Bridge

White pine garland, embellished with glistening red and gold ornaments, crisscrosses the front of Renee's desk. Her desk-top dancing Santa slowly undulates to an indiscernible melody of mostly sleigh bells and ho-ho-ho's. The festive paraphernalia does little to mask the tension tucked into every nook and cranny of the WTOK studio. No one realizes that all eyes follow the second hand on the wall clock as it rounds the bend past seven, eight, nine, ten, eleven.

Alone in the booth, Gordon crosses himself and throws the ON AIR switch. As if by magic, Abby's voice fills the space.

"Good morning, Boston! It's wonderful to be back. This is Abby Thompson, your host for LifeLine."

Gordon's face beams. He rises to his feet and claps his hands, punching the air with his fist. "It worked!" A communal sigh underlays spontaneous applause as it erupts in the studio. For the first time in sixteen broadcasts, every phone line flashes red.

"We've got some catching up to do. Our number here is 555-WTOK."

Abby glows. Her voice ascends to its confident timbre. Her "terms" put her here, connecting to her audience from the privacy of her own home, from the seclusion of her own refuge. So, from her sofa, surrounded by pillows of dull black plastic, with a speakerphone on her lap, Abby revives LifeLine. "Nothing short of wild horses could pull me away again. So, let's get started. Welcome to LifeLine. With whom am I speaking?"

"This is Peggy. I knew they'd bring you back. We missed you."

"I missed all of you, too. Do you have a story to share?"

"Heard your voice, had to call."

"Well, Peggy, I'm thankful that you took the time. I wish you a holiday that exceeds your expectations."

"Thanks, Abby. I'm so glad you're back."

"I am, too. Take care."

Abby shifts her weight uncomfortably from one ilium to the other. "So, all of a sudden, we're closing out 1981. Some of us will be going through the holidays alone for the first time. I'd like to hear from listeners who've made the holidays joyful, despite the solitude. Welcome to LifeLine, with whom am I speaking?"

"Hi, Abby. This is Robbie. My mum died two years ago after a long fight with diabetes. She needed to spend her last several months in a nursing home. It was over Christmas, so I took a little tree in and we decorated it together. The people there, the other residents, were pretty cool. They'd stop in and see it on their way to eat or just walking by. Since she died, the last two Christmases, I've gone back there. Most of the folks I knew are gone, but a few are still there and the new people seem kinda happy for a visit, even from a stranger.

"See, I drag a tree into the place, and all the old folks decorate it. We put on some old recordings. At first, it made me feel like I was doing them a favor. But it didn't take long to figure out, they were doing something for me. Being around them, especially at

Christmas, helped me get through one of the roughest parts of losing my mum."

"That's an amazing story, Robbie. You found a wonderful way to honor your mom and help fill the emptiness her passing left behind. It's a great example of the way giving transforms into receiving when love is involved. This time of year, especially, can remind us of that. Your call may inspire other listeners to be giving in their loss. I know my Gram is my favorite person on the planet. She's always been in my corner. It's going to be a very sad day for me when she passes away. I hope I figure out a way to grieve her that is so healing. Thanks so much for sharing, Robbie. Hello, welcome to LifeLine, with whom am I speaking?"

# 37. Free Climb

The cold, turbulent days of winter corrode the thinning veneer of Abby's patience. Nighttime scavenging during blizzard conditions, gnaws away at her body and soul. She relies on the two hours she dedicates to LifeLine to reverse the damage inflicted by the remaining twenty-two.

Abby situates herself among her clutter and prepares for the unexpected. "Hello, Boston, Welcome to LifeLine, the radio program directed by you. I'm your host, Abby Thompson. I have to admit, recent days are starting to take their toll on me. I'm doing my best to focus on spring's arrival, which, according to the groundhog, is less than six weeks away. What other good news do you have to cheer us all up? Our first caller is Tim. Welcome to LifeLine, the airwaves are yours."

"Hi, Abby, my good news is, I got a new job. You probably don't remember me, I called in a couple months ago 'cause my old job was makin' me crazy. I couldn't sleep and I was blowin' up at all the wrong people. You told me I should 'find my joy.' It sounded goofy, I mean, what's joy got to do with work? But I knew what you meant, so I started lookin' around. Been at the new job for about five weeks. The pay's actually about the same, but the people just want to work. No backstabbin', no hazing. We all kinda like what we do. So we just put in our eight hours, and the jobs get done. Anyway, that's my good news. And, thanks for the push."

"Wow, Tim, that is great news! I'm glad it worked out so well for you. I hope you continue to feel good about the move. Thanks for sharing.

"So many people think of change as a terrifying thing. And, because of that, they stay in awful situations. Some even put the responsibility on God… 'If God wanted me to be somewhere else, why am I here?' Or, worse yet, 'God wants me to suffer, this is my cross to bear.' I think, if human parents, albeit good human parents, would do anything in their power to smooth the path for their children, why wouldn't the ultimate Abba? Why wouldn't God bless each of us with the talents and desires we need to make the most of our time here, and give us joy in the process?

"I believe finding joy is not only the better option for our own good, it's a pretty clear indication that we are tapping our full potential to do good for others. And that's when the society, the world's great tapestry, gets stronger, because our strand gets stronger.

"But, you have to be willing to give up what you have. And that can be scary and a real challenge when bills need to be paid. Fortunately, misery is a great motivator. So eventually, it's probably worth giving change a thought. Ok, we have Cathy up next? Hello, Cathy, Welcome to LifeLine."

"Hi, Abby! I also have some good news to share because of your advice. Right before Thanksgiving, I called because my mother had stepped away from me over a relationship I was intent on pursuing. Well, I'm here to report that my relationship is going very well and I couldn't be happier."

"That's wonderful! You found your joy! Has your mother reached out to you? Has all that been resolved?"

"No, she hasn't. I'm not expecting her to any time soon. But, I'm still open to it. Hopefully, one day she'll see how limiting her mindset is and she'll be ready to get to know my boyfriend. So, thank you, Abby. You gave me a new perspective to consider. We both appreciate it."

"You're welcome. Maybe the next time I ask for good-news calls, you'll phone to say that you've worked it out. Thanks for your call. Wow, two great stories. I'm feeling better already."

"Who's up next? Hello, welcome to LifeLine, the airwaves are yours."

"Hello, Abby. This is Maria. This isn't exactly good news, but it is how I get through the doldrums of February. I start my mental health spring cleaning. I'm not a big fan of housework, but I have found value in taking an honest look at the emotional weight I lug around and clearing out the useless stuff. It could be a little thing that starts out like a pebble in my shoe. Before long, the energy I devote to it has me limping, so I put it in my pocket. I give it more energy and it ends up flung over my back, until it outgrows the pack and it moves to my arms. And I realize, I'm carrying this giant boulder around, voluntarily, and for no good reason.

"It might be a hurtful conversation I keep replaying. It may be a relationship that was once meaningful, but now crowds out new possibilities. So, once a year, I figure out what's weighing on me, I put it down and let it go. It takes practice. I've had to train myself not to look back, not to pick it up again. But it's amazing how freeing it is."

"Maria, I've never heard it described so clearly. We just keep carrying around useless negative energy that keeps us from being free to move about the world in a productive way. I guess it's never too early to start our mental health spring cleaning. I hope lots of people are listening and taking notes. Our February just got brighter. Thanks, Maria. Who's up next? The airwaves are yours."

"Hi Abby, this is Lee. I don't fly very often, but a couple times, my plane's taken off during a dark, dismal day that, if it weren't for the excitement of the trip, would have gotten me really down. But then, after some scary turbulence, we broke through the clouds and I saw that the skies are blue up there. It was a powerful realization. It became a musical mantra for me. 'It's blue above the clouds, the sun is shining above the clouds, there's no rain there, no pain there and it's blue above the clouds.' So, when I start to feel pressed down by mean people, or scary times or even long stretches of depressing weather, I try to remember it's better very close by, I just can't see it at the moment, and I just have to be patient and work toward staying positive."

"Hah! Lee, I've never flown, so I've missed out on that powerful aha moment. I will need to keep that in mind. 'It's blue above the clouds.' Thank you for sharing that. What other ideas are out there waiting to be shared?"

# 38. Chalking

The anticipated telltale putt-putt-putt of the postal vehicle, carried on the fragrant mid-May breeze through her open window, coaxes Abby from her task of organizing today's grocery haul. Manufacturers' coupons arrive today. She grabs a tote bag and waits for the sound to fade toward the next block before opening her door and looking both ways. Her weekly devotion to scarfing up all the circulars saves her money. Her weekly devotion to scarfing up all the circulars feeds her obsession. The balance tilts away from sanity.

She rushes to the mail station and loads the pile of colorful leaflets into her bag. A diagonal line crossing her mail slot surprises her. "Who sent me something?" She contorts her body to peer into the dark crevice for a glimpse of some hint about the sender's identity. She sees her mother's handwriting has crossed out her Brookfield address and scrolled her Boston address over it. "Hmm."

She walks back to her apartment and returns with the key to unlock the mystery. "Brookfield High School?" She opens the envelope. "An invitation to our fifth reunion?" *Wow. It's been five years.* Abby mindlessly reads the invitation's particulars while returning home. "September third," *1982, 5:30 to 10:30 p.m.,* "White Oak Country Club. Dinner and dancing. Come catch up with the BHS gang!" *The gang.*

She closes the door behind her and fights to recall where in her labyrinth apartment she last saw her high school yearbook. She lifts the cereal boxes in front of her entertainment center by fives to check its shelf. "No." She shoves aside the stack of cake mix boxes and icing containers to open the closet. "No. Where is it?" *My bedroom?* She struggles to lift two two-liter bottles of soda at once to move the mountain that blocks her file drawers. "Yes. Here it is."

She pulls the book from a collection of Brookfield High memorabilia and clears a space on her bed to sit and leaf through the pages of her past. "Els." A picture of her "gang," her and Ellen, snapped by a roaming Photography Club member at homecoming, sends shudders to her core. She looks at her reflection in the mirror. "Els."

Suddenly, Abby remembers a forgotten link to her past. "Where is my old...?" *It must be in that drawer, too.* Abby sits down on a box packed with random greeting cards to search. She removes her commencement program and Class of 1977 cap and tassel, her diploma folder and photo album, the faded centerpiece from homecoming and a fragile envelope of concert ticket stubs. Wedged in between the rolled-up Happy 16th Birthday sign and her homemade tie-dyed T-shirt she finds it.

She draws her finger down the minuscule tabs of each alphabet letter until she comes to K. 'Kincaid. Ellen Kincaid. That's right! 5080." She takes the book and the jogged memory of her best friend's number with her to the living room and dials her phone. "Hello, Mrs. Kincaid. This is Abby, Abby Thompson. I'm fine, how are you? Boston's very nice. How is Phillip? That's good. I'm calling to see if you have Ellen's phone number. I seem to have misplaced it. You do? Great." Abby quickly adds the number to the K page for safe keeping. "Thanks so much! Take care."

Abby depresses the receiver button to disconnect the call. She lets it rise. The dial tone hums. She lingers, eyes unfocused and imagination racing. An impatient mechanical voice snaps her mind's meandering. "If you would like to make a call, please hang up and try again. If you need help, hang up and dial the operator." She nods, affirming her decision. She depresses the button to engage the dial tone. She dials the number to engage her friend. "Hi, Els? It's Ab."

"Abby? Is that you? Oh my gosh, it's so good to hear your voice! I thought I might never hear from you again!"

"Oh, Els, it's great to hear your voice, too. I'm so sorry about that. I had your message on my fridge all these months, but every chance I had to call, the timing seemed bad, too late or too early. When I finally did call last November, the number was disconnected. How are you? Where's the 412 area code? In Massachusetts?"

"I'm sorry we didn't connect sooner, too. No, I'm in southwestern Pennsylvania. Pittsburgh, to be exact. I got engaged, Abby."

"What? Engaged? When?"

"Last October. My fiancé, Ted, was offered a great job with a university here. It made sense to move. How did you get my new number?"

"I still had the little phone book I won at your tenth birthday party. It has your family's number. I called your mom. Thankfully, she hadn't moved."

"Great minds. I called your parents' a few months ago, but your mom said the number she had was disconnected and she didn't have a new one. Is everything okay?"

"Actually, no. No. A lot is not okay."

"What? No! Start at the beginning."

"Let's talk about your good news first. Tell me about Ted."

Abby paces in place, anchored to her living room by the range of her speakerphone. "So today, when I got the invitation to our five-year reunion, I dug out my yearbook and saw that picture Kyle took of us at homecoming. I think it's the first time in a year that I honestly saw my actual reflection in a mirror."

"What do you mean?"

"I look at myself in a full length mirror every day. Sometimes multiple times a day. Front and back. I could blame it on how slowly my weight dropped. But, I still see myself as fat. My grandmother insists it's also a mental illness. Maybe she's right. But, when I compared my face to the face in the photo, I couldn't deny it any longer. Lately, I lie in bed and think how innocently it started. The day I made the choice to alter my body. Just a bit. To be the consummate professional—smart, independent, slim. Just a few pounds."

The fragile rhythm of Abby's voice breaks. Her emotions swell the void beneath her ribs. Tears pool in her eyes, then cascade down her angular cheeks, and blend with the stains on her soiled T-shirt. "I felt in control of something. My image was finally up to me. No one could shake me. By the time I realized that my body was on automatic pilot, I was in free fall. When I started, I just wouldn't eat for days. Then I got so hungry I'd eat everything in sight. The horror of all that food in my body. Purging was easy enough. I heard other girls in the apartment talking about it. Finger down the throat and... Easy. The glamour of having a fashion-magazine body, of being self-sufficient, of being perfect." Abby lifts her head to gaze into the mirror. *Of being perfect.*

169

"So, all year? Your body has depended on virtually nothing for an entire year to stay alive?"

"Yes."

"Wait, how much do you weigh?"

"Not much."

"You said earlier you were in control."

"I was." Honesty finds its footing. "I thought I was."

"What happened? Have you tried to stop?"

"Lately, well actually, since before last Thanksgiving, my body just rejects the food. I have tried to keep it down, but it won't stay. That's what I mean by autopilot. But it's more complicated than that. You're not going to believe this, but I've been at this so long I see myself as a one hundred and eight-pound, compulsive, obsessive outcast. It's a sick identity, but it is an identity."

"A hundred and eight pounds? Abby? A hundred and eight? What about your radio show? You're still doing that? Isn't that an identity?"

"For two hours a day I feel sane. It's a power thing, too. Can I be rational at least for others?"

"Does your boss know? Anyone from work?"

"My boss's mind's on other things. I do my best to keep it from all of them. It's why I insisted on working from home. How can their personal advice host be this ill?"

"Well, now that I know, I want to do something."

"Els, really, I appreciate that, but I think I'm beyond help. In all honesty, I almost didn't call. I don't want you to be dragged into fighting a hopeless battle."

"It doesn't have to be hopeless. I have another friend who went through this. Her family pulled out all the stops."

"My family is useless. Russell is convinced, if I turned to God, I could get well. He blames my weakness for all of it. If I were 'perfect,' like he is, none of this would have happened. It was awful. The last time I saw him. Last Thanksgiving. My mother tried to reason with him, but, in the end, as always, his word was edict. I swore to myself he won't be right about this. I'd show him. Since then, he's forbidden my mother to even acknowledge me, let alone accept my calls. I'm 'dead to him.'"

"But, Abby, that means you don't get better. That's a horrible price to pay. What about support groups, Overeaters Anonymous, therapy?"

Abby dries her face and straightens her back. She detects a faint, defensive impulse scratching its way to the surface, nagging for expression. She suppresses it, instead, choosing acquiescence to bring Ellen's attempt to fix her to a swift end. "You're right, of course. I do need to get help. Connect. It's the advice I give most often."

"It's great advice."

Abby's stomach twinges. She checks her watch. The hours-long consequence of her urgent desire to unburden to her trusted friend pushes past her feeding comfort zone. "I'd better eat or I'll pass out."

"It's killing me to think of you so drained."

"I'll be alright. Really. I'm so grateful for you."

"I'm grateful for you, too. Let's talk more often. Maybe once a week?"

"That would be great. How about on Sundays? Around 10? I've disavowed organized religion ever since I realized my trusted pastor made a habit of sexually assaulting me."

"What? He did what?"

Immediately regretting opening the conversation wider, Abby deflects. "Yep, I was too young to understand at the time. But, in time. Nasty business."

"Wow! We have so much to talk about, but I'll let you go so you can eat."

"Okay, goodbye for now, Els. Love you."

"Goodbye for now, Abby. I love you, too."

Having unloaded two crushing secrets, she strides even lighter than her one hundred and eight pounds. "Els." She draws back the curtains and invites in the sunshine. She welcomes classical musicians into her space to play Chopin just for her. She selects her favorite food, oatmeal cookies, from the stack of sweets and takes them with her into the kitchen to prepare her meal. "Seven days until we talk again. Now, feeding time."

Abby pauses mid-stride. Her brow knits and her head twists and tilts, just a bit. She realizes that at some point, like a whisper in the wind, she lost the joy of eating. Neither does glamour or subtlety remain in her food preparation. Raw meat gets browned. Raw vegetables get steamed. Packaged dry goods go down as is. Fruit and canned goods, too, as is. "When did that happen?"

Inspired by the wakened memory of Brookfield, she reaches back five years to the times in her mother's kitchen and her recipe for baked macaroni and cheese, a recipe she committed to memory for the comfort it promised. She finds and assembles the ingredients. She fills a pot with water and sets the fire beneath it on high. Lid. She cuts a chunk of butter from the stick and heats it to melt in a saucepan on the stove. She measures out and adds the flour, salt and ground mustard. Then stirs in the cool, white milk and watches it thicken the way it did a lifetime ago. In goes the grated cheddar, melting as it's swirled, it turns the slowly bubbling brew a familiar hue of bright, sunny yellow. Elbow macaroni dumped in the boiling water excites the molecules to overflowing. Simmer. Preheat. Al dente. Drain. Casserole. Combine. Breadcrumbs. Cheese. Paprika. Bake. Dance. "Els." Pray. Eat. Purge. Some things do not change. Some things cannot change.

# 39. Duck Pond

Hoots of laughter echo off the weathered, brick facades of the store fronts lining the trendiest street in Boston. Cathy's bright, floral dress spins out as she twirls under Drew's arm while onlooking children point and giggle. She loosens her grip and exchanges his hand for a lamp post and twirls, "Singin'-in-the-Rain" style until Drew clutches her again and pulls her in for a hug. "Hey, I was enjoying that! Where are we going, anyway?"

"I told you, it's a surprise."

"Now, Drew, you know I'm not a giant fan of surprises."

"I know."

They walk cheerfully, swinging their joined hands between them. Drew slows their stride and stops in front of a dimpled plate glass window with "O'Sullivan's Dazzling Delights" etched across it.

Cathy looks up to read the marquee. "Is this my surprise?"

"Yes." Drew chuckles. "It's a minor surprise to spare you a major surprise. You made me the happiest man on the planet when you said 'yes,' but as I told you, I'd like you to choose your own engagement ring. I've been all over town and I think you'll find one in here that melts your heart as totally as you melt mine." Drew wraps his arm around Cathy's waist and turns the brass knob to open the door, sending a dangling array of sterling silver bells jingling.

A smiling shopkeeper welcomes them with a bright, "Hello, how are you today, Mr. Aldrich?" and shows them to the estate jewelry case.

Cathy spins on her toes and gloats. "Mr. Aldrich. And I'll soon be Mrs. Aldrich!" She leans over the display and points to a shimmering ring that calls her name. "That one's very pretty."

# 40. Aftershocks

A rattling box fan secured in the window forces thick, suffocating air across the room. Abby's nearly naked body drapes over the sofa. Each breath presses her exposed ribs against her glistening skin. She twists the hair at the nape of her neck to allow the perspiration gathered there to evaporate in the moving currents. A nudge from somewhere deep inside urges her to pluck out a few strands. *Why not?* "The weather forecast calls for more high humidity for Memorial Day weekend in our fair city. As you head out after our show, I hope you find a fun way to stay comfortable. But before that, we have time for another call or two. Hello, you're on LifeLine."

"Hello, Abby. This is Debbie."

Abby bolts up, recognizing the voice. "Debbie?"

"Yes. We spoke last Thanksgiving."

"Of course. How are you?"

"I'm okay. But I'm not sure how I'm going to make it through. Next week. It will be a year."

"A year. What help have you gotten?"

"Well, I went to therapy like you suggested. And I found a support group. That probably helped the most. You were right, my parents couldn't have been better. They still make sure I keep up with my visits and keep talking. After a lot of painful work, I took my body back. I'm able to sleep most nights without nightmares."

"All of that is great progress. It sounds like you are ready to get out into the world more."

"I have been, actually. I go with friends, not alone, but I do go outside."

"Reestablishing feelings of safety and being able to trust your instincts again are signs of tremendous progress. Keep yourself occupied with friends and family next week. Do an activity that you always enjoyed."

"I've always loved green spaces, parks. Maybe a walk?"

"That sounds wonderful. Don't be alone. Stay connected. We do lots of things in secret that we'd never do in public."

"You've been terrific."

"You're a terrific woman, Debbie."

"Thanks, Abby."

"Well friends, that's all the time we have today. Please join me again tomorrow at ten a.m., when WTOK is your LifeLine. Stay cool, Boston."

Abby carefully eases her fingers between her phone and her bare thighs to break the moist adhesion. She massages the burning imprint until the edges and the pain fade. Another show over. She gathers the dozen or so hairs she piled neatly at her side and rolls them in a ball.

As if by rote, Abby rises and slowly makes her way to the kitchen. Her knees buckle. She reaches out to the door jamb to steady herself. Two and a quarter hours have passed since she last rinsed her mouth. Less than two hours between feedings is her new normal. The vicious cycle, that dictates the order and timing of her life, condensed against her will. She knows, with her reserves diminished to near zero, ingesting morsels every hundred and twenty minutes, even for mere moments, provides crucial sustenance. She drops the hair ball into the garbage and harvests the fresh components of her meal from her refrigerator shelves. She supplements with a box of cookies and packages of sandwich buns.

Once bloated, she makes her way to the cold, ceramic funnel. Drinking water triggers the reflex that lies at the vortex of her life. She wipes her chafed lips and looks at her watch. She will kneel here again in one hundred and eighteen minutes. Abby instantly starts the next race against her compulsion. Deducting the time required to prepare and consume her meal, she calculates she must accomplish the errand for this two-hour cycle —drive to the grocery store, select and buy today's limit of sale items, drive back home and unload—in under seventy-eight minutes.

Her frequent ventures down the mega-grocer's aisles prepare her well as she walks her cart directly to the shelves and cases for each item on her list, each item in her bursting coupon folder. Her customary clerk braces for the challenge of appearing nonchalant as he rings up the purchases of a fading human. As always, her heart-of-an-angel bagger limits each satchel's contents to less than ten pounds—manageable, even if it requires more trips between car and threshold. The haunting appearance of Abby's skeletal face and body lends a grotesque irony to her battered but sincere expression of gratitude. "Thank you for your kindness."

Hiding his frustration, the clerk nods a cheery, "You're welcome," certain, if she had said just a few words more, he could finally have placed her voice.

Abby struggles to control the headstrong cart on the uneven asphalt of the parking lot. She maneuvers her grip from the handle to the front and pulls it alongside the trunk of her car. As always, she fixes her attention on the task at hand, careful to avoid getting snagged in the stares or remarks of passing adults or, especially, children. Their comments, though innocent, cut deep.

Finally home, her energy waning, Abby lingers in her car, waiting for the neighborhood children to retreat indoors for their daily naps. She is nothing if not intentional with her scheduling. Within moments, curtains billow closed and blinds roll lower providing virtual privacy in the open air. Free to start unloading, Abby appreciates her packer's kind discipline more and more with each two-bag trip between car and entryway. By the tenth, her available energy crosses into the red zone. Her seventy-eight-minute allowance expires. Time to feed and start the next two-hour cycle. Back to the kitchen.

# 41. Approach

Abby's denim shorts and gray tank top hang limply on her boney frame. She slides a ball cap over her now patchy scalp, the consequence of her most recent compulsion. Despite the sweltering heat, she heads out the door. She has no choice. Summer weather ushered in changes to Abby's nightly obsession to intercede on behalf of discarded food, clothing, housewares and heirlooms. Nocturnal creatures, like she, evolved to take shelter in the heat of the day, and avoid the shooing nature of selfish discarders. But, items left to endure scorching heat rot or melt or shatter. Better to brave the elements, extreme or no, to rescue the tossed-away. So, what keeps the faint-of-heart in swimming pools, air conditioning and forest burrows now drives Abby to scavenge twice daily. To make the rounds twice daily. To crawl into bins and dumpsters and drag home anything with perceived value, twice daily.

Her tenacity rewards her illness. Clothing, medications, vases, afghans, packaged meat and cheese, photo albums, yogurt, flatware, shoes, shovels, table lamps, vegetables, bed linens, table linens, bath linens, dinnerware, fruits, drills, Valentine hearts, Easter baskets, Christmas wrapping, greeting cards for Mother's

Day, Father's Day, birthday, wedding, new baby, graduation, friendship, sympathy, new job. She scavenges and reclaims and suffers the ache of intrinsic oneness with the devalued and discarded. Vicious.

As she retraces her route to unload, physically and emotionally drained, Abby relies on the air blowing through her car windows to disperse the rank odors of rot and decay. Stopped at a traffic light, she gags as the fog of malodor stagnates and assaults her sinuses. Moving again, she lowers the sun visor and slides the screen to expose the hidden mirror. Glancing at her gaunt reflection and the ripped and rippling bags behind her, she concedes, "Maybe you're right, Ellen. Maybe I... But Russell... No, I'll connect. I'll find a doctor." She replaces the screen, flips the visor back up and continues home.

# 42. Rewrites

Doing her best to recall her late-night composition, Betty quietly starts and stops and starts again to hum a disjointed melody as she distributes the contents of an oversized laundry basket among her family's dressers and closets. Going from room to room, she experiments adding bits of her poetry as a refrain. "That could work."

Joey follows behind, spinning the rubber band on the propeller of his toy airplane. "What could work, Mommy?"

"You know how I like to sing along with the radio, right?"

Joey nods with his entire body.

"Well, I'm writing my own songs, like the ones on the radio. Mine are just for me, though, so they can be just the way I want them." She takes the empty basket downstairs. Joey hops down the steps behind her and beats her to the piano bench with seconds to spare. "Are you gonna write songs now?"

"I'm gonna try."

Betty, present yet oblivious, sits in rapt concentration at her new-to-her piano plinking down single keys and jotting down the notes on handmade scored paper. Lost in creativity, she neglects Joey a minute too long. Within seconds, a beam of blazing afternoon sunlight makes glitter from flecks of dust that dance in the turbulence he stirs as he races around from room to room.

"Hey, Mommy, look! I can make the propeller spin even faster just by running super fast! Mommy, look!"

Betty turns away from her task and watches Joey make one spirited lap around the first floor. "That's fine, Joey. You should be so proud. You know, Ben will be back from his friend's soon. Why don't you build something to show him when he gets here?"

Joey, always eager to shine in his big brother's eyes, skids to a stop and takes a seat on the floor amid an impressive pile of interlocking blocks. He calmly builds an elaborate structure as he hums along with Betty's melody. Betty glances in his direction and smiles. "Oh my, Joey. Yes, that's very nice. You are so good at building."

"Thanks, Mommy. You are so good at making songs."

"Thank you, my love."

# 43. Sloper

Before entering, Abby takes a long, sobering look at her reflection in the lobby's plate glass window. She scans it top to bottom—her sculpted cheekbones, sunken eyes, rotting teeth and skeletal limbs. "He won't need to do any tests to figure out what's wrong with me, that's for sure." She shakes her head in dismay. "Well, what you see…" The heavy door taxes her strength as she struggles to open it wide enough to wedge herself inside. An escaping gush of cold air takes her breath away. She rubs her arms to neutralize the chill.

Her eyes, weary from last night's stress-driven insomnia, focus on the office directory. *Greater Metropolitan Mental Health Associates, Dr. Simon, 314.* She presses the elevator button. Relieved to be alone, she waits impatiently, hoping it stays that way. The elevator door opens. *Empty. Good.* She drops her head to avoid seeing herself again in the car's mirrored walls and imagines instead, for the umpteenth time, how the next hour may alter what's left of her life.

The car slows. It stops. The light behind "3" goes dark. The door opens. She lingers. The door's retraction mechanism engages. She reluctantly steps between the moving panels. They bump, rattle and retract again. She takes a deep breath and steps out. "Okay, God, catch me if I fall."

*314.* Abby places her hand on the door knob. "I don't know, Els. I hope this is worth it." She turns the knob and enters a bright, sunlit room furnished with floor plants, wall art, upholstered chairs and end tables. *Hmmm. My place used to look like this.* Her anxiety churns. *Being here early is not an advantage.*

Intent on calming her nerves, Abby scans the magazine covers in the rack. They boast the secrets to happiness, sexual attraction and tighter abs. She jests mockingly, "Maybe I just need to subscribe to a couple of these." She selects one and sits down, ready to learn the benefits of Dutch-oven cooking when the inner door opens. Two men emerge, their conversation halts instantly as she comes into view. She returns the magazine to its place.

"Okay, that was a good visit. I'll see you next week at the same time. Hello, you must be Abigail. I'm Dr. Simon."

For the next fifty-five minutes, Abby answers every question fully and honestly.

"Age?" He jots a number

"Siblings?" He jots three words.

"Birth order?" He jots another word.

"Parents?" He scribbles illegibly.

"Upbringing?" He listens intently.

"Childhood joys?" He frowns.

"Childhood traumas?" He bites his lip.

"Adult joys?" He smiles.

"Adult traumas?" He registers surprise.

"When did it start?" He marks a date.

"Why did it start?" He nods his head.

"How does it manifest?" His face grows grave.

"What supports do you have?" He grimaces.

"What help have you gotten?" He sighs.

"What help do you want?" He shakes his head.

"Do you want to get better?" He shrugs his shoulders.

"Then, why are you here?" He reads her expression.

Her face speaks volumes. *I don't know.*

"Do you want medication?" He writes a prescription.

Abby saves it for later. *You never know.*

# 44. Mantel

Abby waits by the phone jotting the start of today's journal entry.

*November 14, 1982. Dear Diary, The weather is cold and staying cold. That's not good. Getting in and out of the dumpsters is so much trickier. Overnight I found an entire pizza except for two pieces! The drug store threw out all their leftover Halloween candy. In perfectly sealed bags. Thrown away! Ellen calls today.*

Thanks to her pen's fine point and her steady hand, she squeezes a third line of minuscule printing between the ones before and the guideline on the page. Waste not, want not. At its best, her commitment to recall and record ensures an enduring daily account of particularly fortunate finds and poignant insights. At their most authentic, entries generally devolve into a one-sided tirade used to vent her debilitating anger and rant against injustice and evil. This daily, emotional, cleansing ritual continues despite her weekly therapy sessions and having Ellen as a human sounding board. Abby has more to say after one day than can cram into two hours and ten minutes a week.

Nonetheless, her calls with Ellen serve a purpose for both friends. For Abby, conversing with a trustworthy person, who willingly absolves her of her deepest darkness, feels like confession. Devoting two hours every week to conversation with Abby provides Ellen a new context for her life. Both prepare to talk about everything. No subject is taboo, none off limits.

Abby sets her journal aside and answers the ringing phone. She starts their conversation with a light demeanor. "Hi Ellen! How was your week?"

"Not too bad. How was yours?"

"You know, same as always. How are your wedding plans progressing?"

"Slowly, but we're making decisions. Your birthday's almost here."

"Yes, it is. I don't plan to celebrate."

"Hmmm. Any interesting callers on LifeLine?"

Within minutes, however, the subject of Abby's disease diverts the carefree flow and she once again lifts the impenetrable shroud to reveal how completely her illness overwhelms every aspect of her life. "I added another dumpster to my route."

"Oh my God, another one?"

"Yes. That makes ten. My range keeps getting wider. I don't know how to keep from searching. I lie awake at night knowing something of value might find its way from a dumpster-I-don't-check to an inaccessible dump and out of reach. I have no choice. I try to resist, but my mind won't settle until I agree to add the next one."

"But what about in a couple weeks, when the weather turns deadly again? That will keep you in, right? What if you convince yourself that being out in the weather could kill you, even if it's not actually treacherous?"

Filled with frustration and remorse, Abby exposes a sobering truth. "No. The weather doesn't make any difference. I go out when it's stagnant air and ninety-nine degrees and in blizzards with wind chills below zero. My life is always at risk, but the voices and my obsession never rest, never concede. Anything. Ever."

"What does your doctor say? Do you tell him all of this?"

"Like I've told you before, I'm in there for at most ten minutes. He asks me about my weight and whether I want to get better. I could record my answers and just send the cassette instead of going. And then, once a month, he writes me a refill for my prescription."

"What about the meds? They don't help at all?"

"I'm not taking them."

"Still? Don't you want this to end?"

"Els, if they work, which who's to say, but if they work, my taking them won't salvage the food and valuables from the dumpsters. If I don't save them, who will? Nobody."

"But…?"

"Nobody. And I need all the food I find, and the food I buy. My body spontaneously vomits within minutes of swallowing. It's been doing that for more than a year. I have no choice but to eat at least every two hours."

By the conversation's end, Abby confirms that regardless of any potential peril, she will always succumb to her illness, day after night after day after night, season after season, with no light at the end of the narrowing tunnel. As Ellen listens, she imagines the bars of Abby's prison as flesh and bone. She hangs up, as always, feeling horrified and impotent. Desperate, she makes a decision.

"Hello, Mrs. Thompson? Hi. This is Ellen Kincaid, Abby's friend from elementary school. I'm fine. How are you? I can barely hear you. Oh, okay. You don't have to say anything. I'll just talk. I'm calling about Abby. She and I have been talking every week for the past several months. She isn't doing very well and, oh, please don't cry. I'm sorry to upset you. I know it's none of my business, but I think she would really benefit from hearing your voice.

"She mentioned that Mr. Thompson has some rule about her, but her birthday's coming up. Surely he wouldn't stop you from calling to wish her a happy birthday. Do you have something to write on? Her new number is 617-555-1593. In case you ever need it, my mom's number is 203-555-5080. She'll know how to reach me. Okay. Bye. Thank you."

Shaking, Chloe silently hangs up the phone and tucks the shred of paper into her apron pocket. Fighting back tears, she inhales and exhales at a slow and shallow pace. *Abby.* She remains in the kitchen waiting for her breath, hands and eyes to return to their steady state of resignation. Twelve months of practice makes perfect. Her eyes dart as her thoughts form and dissolve. *Now what? He hasn't stopped my praying for her. He doesn't know I do. How can I make a long-distance phone call? He pays the bill.* Chloe touches her forehead, her heart, left shoulder and right. "God, help me."

"What did you say?" Russell appears like a shadow from nowhere. "Who was on the phone? What's the matter?"

Chloe turns away, wets a dishcloth and nervously wipes the pristine countertop of nothing at all. "Nothing's the matter."

"Who was on the phone?"

Chloe releases the cloth and braces herself on the counter with both hands. *Breathe.* She draws in the strength her thousands of prayers have begged for. *Do it.* She pivots in defiance, her lip quivering. "It was Ellen Kincaid. Our daughter's best friend. She said Abby isn't well. And asked me to call her."

Instantly Russell's brow furrows, his chin presses his mouth into a grimace, his eyes narrow. "What's the rule in this house? She is not to be mentioned. Of course she's sick. She left here sick!" He shakes his head as blood shunts to his face and carotid artery. "No. You will not call her. She's on her own."

"Abby, Abby, Abigail, Abby is still my daughter even if you are too cruel and weak to accept her! I will call her, so help me God!" Chloe dodges around Russell to reach her car keys. She flees the driveway leaving Russell sputtering sounds of outrage at her car's rear window.

# 45. Crack

Back to arm wrestling the elements, Abby snugs her front door tightly against the weather stripping and locks it. She exhales an audible sigh of exhaustion. "November 19." Off comes her hat, coat, sweater and sweatshirt. With each item's removal, the haunting effects of her lifestyle glare all the more. The severity of her weight loss would compete with thinning hair and dental decay as most disturbing were anyone privy to see. Her fidget-driven trichotillomania, that began with tugging out the well-hidden strands at the nape of her neck, morphed without permission to obsessively pinching hair from limbs and face. Dousing her teeth in stomach acid up to twelve times a day disintegrated their protective enamel months ago, leaving darkened teeth to mar her smile.

But neither her appearance nor their underlying illnesses alter her compulsive behaviors. She kneels on a pillow among this morning's groceries and divides them according to section. She loads them back into bags to carry them to their final destination. Flour with flour in the bedroom near the corner. Canned peaches with canned peaches in the bedroom under the window. Soda with soda in the bedroom at the bed's foot. Rice with rice in the bedroom between the dresser and laundry basket. She places the last folded bag on the pile. She checks her clock. 9:18. "Just enough time to feed."

Abby carries today's dairy items to the kitchen and wedges them into the already packed refrigerator. She heaves a fresh gallon of milk from the top shelf and, struggling, barely manages to reach the table before losing her grip. Her eyes turn to the varied selection of boxed cake mixes piled high in front of the closet. She runs her hand down the height and deliberately wiggles a box of devil's food from the middle of the stack, careful to ease those above down to refill the gap. She wedges her fingers between the layers of sealed cardboard, rips the plastic-film inner pouch and pours its contents into a bowl. She stirs in enough milk to make a smooth batter. "Happy birthday, to me." She consumes the cold, gooey mixture by the spoonful then presses her fingertips against the bowl's sides to scrape up the last remaining smears.

Abby completes her purging and weighing rituals without notice, let alone fanfare. "Happy birthday." She rinses and wipes her dry, split lips and takes her place on the sofa, the speakerphone on her lap. The second hand rounds the clock face. Ten o'clock.

"Hello, Boston! Welcome to LifeLine, the call-in show that offers you the opportunity to share your humanity—the extraordinary, the mundane and everything in between. I'm your host, Abby Thompson. Let's see who we have on the line. Welcome to LifeLine, the airwaves are yours."

"Hello, Abby."

Abby inhales sharply and sits motionless, staring at nothing. Her heart quakes in her chest, blood pounds in her ears. She swallows hard and slowly struggles back to reality. "Hello?" She takes another sharp, deep breath. "Mom?"

"Hello Abigail. I just wanted to wish you a happy birthday. I love you."

Abby unwittingly grasps at the air to capture the dispersing sound waves in her hands. "I love you, too."

Chloe's voice falters. "Have a great day, sweetheart. I miss you."

The call disconnects.

"I miss... Mom? Are you there? Mom?" Abby pauses to gather her composure to no avail. Her head falls, stretching her skeletal neck and torso over her knees. She remains collapsed moments before remembering her show. She pushes herself back to sitting and wipes her eyes and nose with her shirt sleeve. "Well, everyone, that was my mother, Chloe. Let's, let's see who else we have calling in. Welcome to LifeLine, the airwaves are yours."

"Happy birthday, Abby! This is Carl. I hope the people who love you are planning to celebrate you in a great way."

"Thank you, Carl. That's very kind of you. Is there another reason for your call?"

Despite two hours of back-to-back wishes for happiness, Abby sets the phone aside drained of any positive emotion. Unanswerable questions torture her turbulent thoughts. "Why didn't she stay on longer? Why did she call at all?" Her growling stomach reminds her that her need for nourishment supersedes dwelling on unsolicited enigmas a moment longer.

She slogs to the kitchen, opens the refrigerator and removes three sandwiches she scavenged from the dumpster at the school the day before. "Smashed a bit," *but otherwise palatable?* She lifts the top slice of the first. "Limp lettuce but no mold." She takes a sniff. *No rancid mayonnaise.* She got to them just in time. "Bless this food, dear God, may it give me the strength to be of service to the world."

While she chews her first bite, she polishes a resurrected apple on her sleeve. She swallows and chomps through the shiny green peel into the crisp and juicy fruit. "Owww!" She runs her tongue around the inside of her mouth and draws blood on a razor-sharp edge where her lower incisor used to be. She spits the fractured piece into her hand and rolls it between her fingers before throwing it away. She shakes her head in resignation. "I guess it was only a matter of time." She cuts up the remaining apple and devours it with her molars. "Where there's a will." Still, every bite sends a bolt of nerve pain high into her jaw. "It seems my days of painless feeding are over." In need of more to fill her belly, she softens the contents of a bag of potato chips and a box of cookies in milk before spooning the tepid, soggy mush into her mouth. She winces as she swallows. "That should be enough."

Enslaved by her dreaded routine, Abby goes to the sink and fills the empty soda bottle with water from the spigot. She makes her way to the bathroom and leans over the empty toilet instantly bringing her meal back to her mouth. Her tongue pressed low, the contents flow unimpeded over her cracked tooth and into the first stop in the sewage system. She refills her void with water and vomits again. Then repeats this effective, perfected method of cleansing the horror of food from her mind and body. Then again. And again. And the expelled water runs clear. She wipes her lips and releases a troubled and honest sigh.

She lifts her dampened shirt off her body and over her head. Her pale, limp breasts hang deflated over the slats of her ribs. She pushes her oversized sweatpants and panties over her protruding pelvic bones and down to her ankles, exposing her curved spine that bulges in equal intervals without flesh to smooth the indentations on the vertebrae. She leans on the sink and steps out deliberately, safely. Her legs, lacking nearly all muscle from her bulging knees down, prop up her skin and torso against gravity. She faces front, then back, in the mirror. She steps on the scale and impatiently watches its needle waver—93, 95, 93, 95, 94, 94. "94."

Abby picks up her clothing and walks naked to her bedroom. She digs through a pile of soiled garments on her floor and selects a pair that do not wreak of rot. Once dressed, she layers on her sweatshirt, sweater, coat and hat and grabs her collection of thirty-gallon garbage bags before unlocking her front door. Her phone rings the moment the fresh, outdoor air bursts into her lungs. "Who could that be?" She begrudgingly closes and latches the door, then empties her hands and sits knees-to-chest on the rug in front of her sofa. "Hello? Ellen?"

"Hello, Abigail."

Abby's breath catches. "Mom? Is that you?"

A vocal quiver underscores Chloe's restrained excitement. "Yes, dear, it's me. Happy birthday."

"Thank you." Abby's mind races to sort out an onslaught of questions. "But how did you get this number?"

"Your friend, Ellen, called. She gave it to me. She thought it would be a good idea if we talked. She's a good friend."

"She is a good friend, but why are you calling?"

"Because I miss you." Chloe's voice breaks. "And you're my daughter. I'm sorry about this morning. I wasn't sure I'd be able to make this call and I wanted to at least wish you a happy birthday. I'm calling from Gram's phone since, well, you know how your father is."

"Gram's phone? Is she there? Wait, he still won't let you talk to me? Do you know how ridiculous this is?"

"I know, darling, but calling from here will work out fine. Gram is here, of course. She'd like to wish you a happy birthday, too. I'll put her on."

Abby braces herself to hear the sound of her grandmother's voice for the first time in twelve months.

"Abigail?"

Abby grabs a pillow from her sofa and squeezes it to her chest. Tears stream down her face. "Gram? Oh, Gram, I've missed you so much. How are you?"

"I'm feeling better. Healing anyway. Which, they say, is about as good as it gets at my age."

Caught by surprise, Abby wipes her face and directs all her attention to making sense of Gram's words. "Healing? From what?"

Gram defuses in a relaxed tone. "Oh, Abby, it's not worth mentioning. How are you?"

"No, Gram, healing from what? What happened?"

"Well, they found a lump on my lymph node that turned out to be cancer."

Stunned by the news, Abby's tears flow again. "Cancer?! Oh, Gram. Why didn't anyone tell me?"

Again Gram minimizes. "Well, sweetheart, we didn't know how. Neither your mother nor I had your number. They cut it out and believe they got it all. I have to trust them, I guess. The incision is healing well. Now I'll just have to see what the next few months hold."

"Cancer? I want to see you. Where are you?"

"I'm still in the same place, just a different room with more care. I have my very own nurse."

"I'll come tomorrow, okay?"

"I'd love to see you. We all miss you, Abby."

"I miss you too, Gram."

"I'll put your mother back on."

Chloe sniffles as she retakes the receiver. "Sorry about not calling you about Gram. I really didn't know how to reach you. I tried so many times to call after you left last Thanksgiving. Your line was always busy. Then the recording said your number was disconnected."

"You could have called the station. And I should have called Gram long ago. I just didn't have any good news to report."

"You and I both made mistakes. Thankfully, the doctors think Gram has a good chance to recover from this. I spend a lot of time here visiting. It gets me out of the house and we enjoy each other's company."

"I told Gram I will see her tomorrow. Can you make sure Russell isn't there between noon and three?"

"Russell? Oh, no worries about that. Dad hardly ever visits. He says these places depress him."

"Fine. How's Mark?"

"He's coming along. Sometimes I think he's going to be fine. Other times I fear that he will never really fit in. Oh, he confided in me that he's decided he's a homosexual. Your dad won't tolerate that, so needless to say, he's not been told."

"Mark's a homosexual?"

Abby struggles to stand and frantically paces. "What? That's gotta be so difficult for him. Do you think you can arrange for me to see him or at least talk with him? Only if he's interested, of course."

"He doesn't spend much time at home, either. Things have not gotten better here since you left. Your father's temper always simmers right at the surface."

"I'm sorry to hear that, though I'm not surprised. His anger seems to fill most of his available space."

Chloe takes an audible breath. "Abigail, how are you? How is your eating? Any better? Have you put any weight back on?"

Abby sits down on the floor, wrapping her arms around her knees again. "No, not really. I'm still the way I was last year."

"What can I do? Can I give your number to Reverend Jim?"

Abby rolls her eyes in irritation. "No. Don't call him. There's really nothing you can do. I can't even do anything. Ellen suggested OA but I haven't gone yet. I've gone to a psychiatrist a few times."

"Did that seem to help at all?"

"Not really. He just gives me some pills that I don't take. Mom, I'd better go. You caught me just as I was about to go out."

Desperate to finally salvage their connection, Chloe pleads, "May I call again? Now that I have your number?"

Surprised by the offer, Abby carefully weighs the risks and benefits of reconciliation. "I don't spend too much time in my apartment, but you're welcome to call, and if I can answer, I will."

Relief softens Chloe's despair. "That sounds like a good plan. I do miss you, Abby. I understand we let you down, your father and I, but we — I do love you."

"I love you, too, Mom. I just can't be exposed to his toxicity. His demand for perfection feels like an emotional straight jacket. I choose not to listen to him searching for reasons to criticize and belittle me, and everyone for that matter."

"I understand. I'll call again soon. I love you."

"I love you, too."

Abby hangs up the phone as her eyes glaze over. She feels cemented to the floor, the weight she no longer has, dragging her down. Her head bows in anguish. Releasing a year's worth of dammed disappointment and rage transforms her modicum of confidence into a torrent of emotion. Her tears swell past her strength into her vulnerability and over her weakness. "I love you, too, Mom. I love you, too."

When her tears finally subside, she wipes her face and pulls a folded cloth from her pocket to clear her sinuses. Her fragile calm inches back. She twists and uses the sofa to push herself up to standing. Still shaken but compelled, she resumes her trip out the door, garbage bags in hand. Abby checks her watch. *I'll have to move faster.*

Pulling away from the curb, she makes a determined beeline for the community dumpster at the end of her block. A week ago she noticed a "SOLD" sticker placed across the "For Sale" sign in the front yard of a house a few doors away. From the obituary, she knows the owner was in her 80's, increasing the likelihood that treasures will be among the discards. Impatient relatives, who dispose of all but the obviously valuable, unwittingly contributed many of the heirlooms Abby holds so dear. She has high hopes for some journal-worthy finds.

She pulls her car alongside the rusted, blue bin, heartened by the cardboard boxes in view above its rim. With agility borne of hundreds of practice runs, she scales the side and overlooks the bounty. She shakes her head in disgust. "Wow." *How indifferent must you be to just throw all this away?* She manages to lift a floor lamp over the edge and set it safely on the ground. She sets a box of kitchen utensils on the bin's corner, exits, retrieves it and carries it to her car.

She climbs back in and undoes the braided flaps of a heavy box after righting it. "Oh, my! How beautiful are these?" She takes one white china plate with a platinum edge from the box, flips it over to read the inscription and realizes its quality. *How am I going to get all of these out of here?* She wedges her hands under it, budging the box, but barely. *There's no other way.*

She carefully balances the first plate securely on the corner of the bin. She climbs out and cautiously reaches up to lift it safely away and puts it on the ground. Back in. Another plate to the corner of the bin. Out again. Onto the ground. Back in. She repeats these tedious steps until all twelve place settings of five pieces each and the six servings pieces are rescued. With sweat gathering between her body and clothing layers, she tosses the empty box out over the bin's side and makes her final exit.

She nestles the box securely in the back seat of her car and painstakingly carries the fragile pieces, two-at-a-time, to the box and situates them deliberately according to size. She squeezes her feeble hand down into the crux of the seat and feels for the seat belt latch. She rotates it into position and pulls the belt around the box and buckles it snugly into place. "Happy birthday to me! Journal-worthy, for sure." As if attending to a beloved child, her gaze revisits the reflection of her exceptional find in the rearview mirror as she continues the remainder of her route.

# 46. Chimney

Nauseated by the omnipresent odor of old, Abby follows the wall signs pointing down unfamiliar corridors that finally bring her within sight of the nurses' station in the medical-support wing of Gram's residential center. She reluctantly takes a deep, calming breath as she approaches. "Okay, I can do this." She speaks to the crown of the nurse's head. "Hi, I'm here to visit my grandmother, Elizabeth Thompson. Can you please tell me how to get to her room?"

In one seamless motion, the nurse raises her head and drops her jaw. Abby flushes brilliant red. The nurse runs her professional gaze over the person before her and assigns a diagnosis before her brain realizes a question was posed. "I'm sorry, may I help you?"

"Yes, hello, I'm here to visit Elizabeth Thompson. Can you please direct me to her room?"

"Um, sure. Lizzy's room is 105, third on the left just past the bend in the hallway. If she's not there, she may be in the common room. That's right at the bend."

"Thank you." *Lizzy? Since when does Gram go by Lizzy?* Abby admires the decorative cardboard turkeys and cornucopias as she gently raps on the door ajar. Her ears tuned-in, she waits for permission to enter.

"Yes?"

The familiarity of the voice suctions Abby's breath away. Her emotions instantly rise to the surface. "Gram?"

"Come in, Abigail!"

Abby straightens her spine, wraps her scarf around her bony neck and enters the room. As her wet, reddened eyes lock with Gram's, she realizes the futility of devoting last night's sleep time to preparing for this emotional tempest. All control cascades away.

At first sight, Gram's eyes widen in shock and horror. She sees through the five layers of clothing and enviable posture, and clasps her hands over her nose and mouth as "Holy Mother of God," blurts from her heart and through her lips. Her prayer rises like incense as she reaches toward Abby and grasps her frail outstretched hands. "My darling, Abigail, what's happened to you?"

Abby collapses into an embrace more welcomed than any she's ever known. "Oh, Gram. I'm so lost."

With no language to suffice, the two tortured, vulnerable women allow fearful silence to speak for them. Legions of angels answer Gram's stratus cloud of prayers and instill the loving pair with trust. In time, their weeping ends. Weak with hunger and hollowed by reality, Abby pulls away and finds agony still present in her beloved grandmother's face. Compelled to ease Gram's anguish, Abby fumbles to explain, to admit her torment. "I found some old pictures. I hadn't realized, I know it's hard to believe—until I saw those pictures."

"You must keep at it, Abigail. Let someone help you. My life is almost over, but yours is so new. Don't let pride kill you."

"I know in my heart you're right. I just can't seem to get my head to take the first step. It's stronger than I am, Gram."

"You've given it that power. Impose the power of Abigail Thompson. It can't be stronger than my Abby."

"I love you so much, Gram."

"I love you, Abigail. Will you join us for Thanksgiving next week? I'm sure your mother and brother would be happy to see you."

"Gram, you know I can't show up there. I can never go back. That part of my life is over. Mom would never stop crying, Russell would never stop yelling, and you would be caught in the middle, again. No, I won't be going back. I needed to see you. I don't need to see them."

As their visit comes to an end, Gram reaches for Abby's hand and squeezes it tightly.

"Oh, Abigail, I don't want you to leave. I'm afraid I'll never see you again."

Abby strokes Gram's hand with as much sincerity as her heart can generate. "You're going to get better and so am I. In the spring. I'll come back as soon as the weather breaks. Promise. But I can call you more often in the meantime, if that would be okay?"

"That would be grand."

Abby manages a troubled smile. "It will be grand."

Abby replays her visit with Gram on a loop all the way home, during meal preparation and purging, while cleaning up and showering. She recalls it once again at journaling time. Her penned words have no thread of hope woven even loosely through them.

> *November 20, 1982, I made my visit to see Gram today. The drive was grueling. It's three and a half hours each way. My body doesn't do well sitting still that long. I was stupid to think I could prepare*

*myself for her reaction. She couldn't hide it like she did last year. But no wonder. I look like a skeleton, even with my five layers of clothes. It hurt so much to disappoint her. She's the one with cancer and the only one she was worried about was me. I told her I'd be back. It was the second promise I made to her that I can't keep.*

Despite Gram's faith in her, and her own words to the contrary, she is dreadfully confident that her path has only one direction.

*She thinks I can get better if I just will it to be so. But I know there is no turning back. Not now. That window closed as soon as I made defying Russell's arrogance my highest priority. I'm terribly afraid the next time we see each other will be in Heaven.*

With emotion welling up, she closes her book and blesses herself. The weight of the day coerces her to recline. Her neck releases as her head sinks into the pillow, her fingers interlink and her hands press into folding. Through her sadness she prays, "Mother God, please bless Elizabeth with your peace. Gently guide her toward her heavenly reward. Please bless us both in our despair. And in your grace, please, catch me if I fall. Amen."

Shallow breaths and Beethoven accompany her to sleep.

# 47. Pumped

Abby pushes away from the table. She lifts what remains of her body off the chair and walks to the refrigerator. For the sixth time today, she takes her prized Christmas card from its place behind a green and white magnet and reads it, shaking her head in resignation. "No, Els," *it wouldn't be better at home.* With downcast eyes, she returns her keepsake to its place of honor.

For the sixth time today, she follows the worn path to the bathroom and kneels over the commode. Her bloat releases as reflex. She silently uses and reuses her purge bottle till the liquid she vomits runs clear. She grabs hold of the bowl to steady herself to standing and depresses the toilet handle. At once, she feels the rug beneath her feet turn wet and cold. "Oh, no. Not again!" She grabs a towel from the bar and sops up as much water as it will hold. The pool around the toilet replenishes faster than she can wring. Floor-bound packaging suctions the gathering liquid upward creating irregular, waterlogged shadows on its sides. "Damn."

She opens the medicine cabinet and removes a rumpled business card tucked behind her collection of prescription bottles. She takes it to the phone and dials. "Hi. Lou? It's Abby. Hi. I hate to bother you so late, but my toilet's leaking again. No, you know it can't wait till morning. Maybe, but you get as much out of this arrangement as I do. Two hours? Then I'm going out, but I should be back before you get here. Thanks." Abby hangs up and returns to the bathroom. She wrings out the heavy, drenched towel in the sink then tucks it against the base of the toilet. "Good enough."

Abby pulls back the curtain to check her outdoor thermometer. "Twenty-five degrees—and windy." Without body fat, she depends on layering to keep warm. Anything below freezing means at least three. On go woolen stockings, long underwear and jeans, a turtleneck and sweatshirt. "Do I need boots?" She grabs a few garbage bags from the kitchen on her way to check how much snow accumulated since her last venture outside. A leaning drift tumbles onto her mat the moment she opens the door. "Boots." She slides her feet into woolen socks then her well-worn mudruckers. Her dressing ritual, born of reason, maintained by compulsion, follows. She wraps her colorful scarf three times around her neck and tucks the fringed ends into her collar. Long-wristed gloves emerge through the cuffs of her coat. Zip. Her fleece-lined hood reinforces her two-layer hat. Tie. "Ready."

By the time Abby finishes brushing the snow from her rear window, her windshield is covered again. She dusts the wayward flakes from her seat and starts the engine. "Wipers, do your thing." The beauty of snow falling through streetlights lends an air of bittersweet nostalgia to her route. *Ice skating at East Park Rink with Ellen. Watching the snow fall through the beams of light against the night sky as I fumbled around the oval. She spent more time picking me up than skating. How much fun we had! Every Friday night. Those were the only times I felt free, out of the house and free. So long ago. Did it ever really happen?* Abby pulls into the first cul-de-sac and pushes the car door open against the howling wind.

Within moments of her entering, a lumpy bag rolls over the edge of the dumpster and lands with a thud on a cushioning drift. Abby's snow-covered hood and shoulders appear. Her turn to exit. Hands on rim, twist, right leg over rim, lift and twist, left leg over rim, lower body, right boot on the ledge, left boot on…, searching for the ledge, searching for the ledge. "Where is it?!" The melting snow beneath her gloves refreezes against the frigid iron. Her already numb hands loose their grip. Her precarious footing falters sending her down, scraping her face on the ledge her boot failed to find. "Owww!"

Abby lies motionless in a heap as blood from her injured cheek oozes down her face and onto the crushed snow. As it cools, the red pool disappears beneath new layers of glistening crystals. Mustering all her strength, she painstakingly pushes her contorted torso upright, hoping the cold keeps the otherwise-certain bruises from forming. She winces in pain. Finally seated, Abby brushes the snow from her hood and coat. Then, holding her bleeding cheek with her gloved hand, she drags the bag back to her car with the other. "I hope this is worth it."

Having squandered precious time, Abby half-heartedly checks and raids the remaining dumpsters on her route. For better or worse, she finds little of value among the pre-holiday pickings. Exhausted, and dangerously cold and wet, she returns home with mere moments to spare.

Abby drags her finds inside, then goes directly to the medicine cabinet to clean and dress her wound. Her wet clothes selfishly hold their chill. She shivers, deeply. *You can't undress. He'll be here any minute.* A knock at her door confirms her expectations and interrupts her progress. She quickly daubs her face with iodine and, peeking through a break in the curtains, verifies

Lou's arrival. "You can do this." She steels herself for an inquisition and opens the door. "Hi, Lou. Thanks for making time."

Lou steps inside and drops his heavy toolbox in disbelief. "Hey! Wow! You look terrible! I mean, what'd you do to yourself? What's on your face?"

"It's iodine. I fell accidentally and cut it. I was just cleaning it when you knocked."

"What happened to your hair? Your eyebrows? Are your eyelashes gone, too?"

"Lou, you're here to fix my toilet."

"Right. You know the pipes are gonna keep corroding as long as you keep throwing up stomach acid."

"Then they're going to keep corroding."

Lou remembers his side of the bargain and instinctively projects his most convincing machismo with a wink. "Lucky for me we have our little" —he adds a subtle head wag for effect— "arrangement."

A conflicted combination of resignation and embarrassment flushes Abby's face. Before she can lead him to the bedroom, Lou's attention drifts past Abby's depleted being and onto her bursting surroundings. "Whoa! You must have twice as much stuff as the last time I was here. What are you gonna do with all this junk?"

"It has nothing to do with you. I know people who could use it. I just need you to fix my toilet."

A ghoulish grin emerges on Lou's face. "Got it. Ya know, I'm happy to be at your service if you service me."

"Fine, as long as what you see and do here stays a secret, I'll 'service' you. Again. But this stays between us. I don't want my landlord at my door. I can't afford to be evicted. I could never move all my belongings."

"No kiddin'. You'd be outta here so fast it would make your bald little head spin."

"Can we just get this over with?"

Lou takes his toolbox in the bathroom. "What the hell? Where do you shower? You've got junk everywhere."

Abby yells from the bedroom. "I use the sink."

Lou joins her, his belt already unbuckled. He drops his baggy pants to the floor. He sits on the bed with his spindly legs spread wide. He spits on his hand and lubricates himself. Abby takes hold of his penis and, without looking in his direction, brings him to orgasm. While he retracts, she washes her hands and wets a cloth. She hands it to him. He cleans up the remnants of his cum and re-dresses without a word. Abby responds in kind, her eyes unfocused and fixed straight ahead. Her heart pounding. It's the price she pays.

# 48. Crimp

Good morning, Boston. Welcome back to LifeLine, the call-in program directed by you. We're talking about whatever is on your mind, from the mundane to the extraordinary. Now that the holidays are behind us, and 1983's in full swing, how about sharing your favorite winter recreation spots. For sledding, tubing, skating or skiing. Where are you heading to make the most of the frigid temps? Welcome to LifeLine, the airwaves are yours."

"Good morning, Abby! I'm Carol. I'm really not a fan of winter. I broke my leg a couple years ago and ever since even walking on slippery sidewalks makes me nervous. So instead of going out, I make hundreds of paper snowflakes and on a clear-roads day, I take them down to the children's hospital to decorate their rooms and hallways. While I'm there to drop them off, I go to the waiting room, and any kid who wants to can make a few for their own room. It's not much, but it's my winter activity."

"I just love this show. I get so many good ideas. I bet the kids really appreciate that! The staff, too. There's something about paper snowflakes gently floating in any little breeze that makes them so pleasing. Thanks for sharing, Carol."

"Who do we have next? Welcome to LifeLine, the airwaves are yours."

"Hi Abby. It's Richard. When I was a kid, my family always enjoyed going around New England on the weekends to all the winter festivals. I've learned how to do snow sculptures, so now as an adult, I take part in some of the competitions. I've even started teaching my son and daughter the tricks of the trade. It's so zen—they are so beautiful when they're done, but then the work just melts away."

"Well, Richard, I've lived in the Northeast all my life and I've never been to a winter festival. Now I know how I'll spend next weekend. So, is the snow natural or manmade?"

"The best is obviously wet, natural snow. It holds together really well. But, if a festival is planned and there's not enough to go around, the organizers have to make it. Either way, it's still a great exercise to remember the transience of life."

"Interesting. Beauty and a moral, that makes it quite a powerful and unusual art form. I hope you have all the wet, natural snow you need to create many masterpieces. Thanks for your call! Let's see what great ideas our next caller has. Welcome to LifeLine, the airwaves are yours."

"Sorry, Abby, I don't have any ideas about winter. I'm in serious trouble and I don't know what to do."

Abby recognizes her brother's voice. "Okay, what can you share about it?"

"I didn't hurt anyone, so don't worry about that. I just don't see my life working out, or how to make this go away. I've always felt different, but now I know what's wrong with me."

"What do you think is wrong with you?"

"I figured out a couple months ago why I've never liked girls. I'm a fag. All those feelings men are supposed to have when women are around? I have them when men are around. My father always rants about people like me and how God hates them and they're sinners and they're all going to Hell. I didn't understand how he knew who God hated, but he said it so many times, I believed him. Now, it turns out, I'm one of those 'degenerates,' those 'abominations.' Hate-able from start to finish. I can never tell my father. My mother knows but promised not to tell because she knows how he gets. I don't see a way out of this."

Silence. Abby desperately searches for the words she rehearsed in case her invitation to Mark, through Chloe, emboldened his trust. Snippets resurface. Within seconds she realizes, now two months later, how naive and frightful a reply it was, especially to broadcast to her LifeLine audience. With pressure building to say something meaningful, she needs to quickly reimagine an answer to resonate not only with her brother, but with others experiencing similar self-loathing. The silence breaks.

"First, I don't believe God hates anyone. I believe the opposite, as a matter of fact, that God loves us all, exactly the way we were created, exactly as we are. But you're right, for some reason some people think it's their right to curse and dehumanize homosexuals or anyone whose looks or lives differ from their own. It's no wonder so many people live in pain and despair with the threat of that hatred and violence hanging over them. Do you still live in your parents' house?"

"No, I moved out. It was time. Not just because of this."

"Have you met any other men that you can talk with about how they're getting through their days and nights without giving in to depression and guilt?"

"No. I'm afraid if I say it out loud I'll never be able to take it back. What if I just forget the truth and just fake being normal?"

"You used the word 'just' twice in that sentence. There is no 'just' when it comes to suppressing your sexuality, something so fundamental to being alive. But, you are not alone. There are many men and women who are hiding this most basic truth from most of their world. They, like all of us, are looking for a way to feel accepted and loved. Your father doesn't need to know—ever, well, certainly not until you're ready and feel supported elsewhere. But I think you need to find that support. Maybe if we hang up and let other callers get through you'll get some good advice."

"Okay, Abby. That sounds like a good idea. Get connected. Thank you."

"You're welcome. Thanks for your call. Okay, Boston. Here's what I want you to do. If you have ideas about where our last caller can be himself in a safe space, here or maybe in New York City, please send them to my attention at WTOK. The address is in the phone book. And thanks in advance.

"Okay, who do we have next?"

"Hi Abby, I'm Jessica. The guy who just hung up sounds like he's in a lot of pain. I know so many kids like that. If I was God, I would get rid of pain. I don't know why God allows it."

Hearing a younger voice, Abby switches gears. She welcomes the chance to share her ideas with an inquiring teen. "Well, Jessica. That sounds like a different kind of world. One without pain. Do you think that if we didn't feel pain that harm would go away?"

"I don't know what you mean exactly. But, if we didn't feel pain, I think we'd be happier."

"In some ways, I suppose we would. But, in other ways, we'd be in big trouble. Think about this: What if you were helping to make dinner and you picked up a skillet that you didn't know was hot. If pain didn't exist, you wouldn't know to put it down as fast as you could. You might just hold it until your hand burned very badly."

"Oh, that's true."

Abby pauses to let the concept percolate through her listeners' consciousness. "Yes, and if you were in a relationship that wasn't good for you, didn't allow you to be free to explore your talents or made you feel small and weak, and there was no pain, you might not speak up or you might stay in that relationship much longer than you should.

"I believe pain is a way for the world to tell you something is wrong. Without pain we might not notice ourselves being harmed. So I actually thank God for pain. It has helped motivate me to search for a better path several times. And even if I don't choose a less painful path right away, pain is always there to remind me that I have options."

"I never thought of it that way, Abby."

"And while we're on the subject of pain, pain is the one outcome you can count on if you risk loving someone. The universal price of loving is sorrow, for someone, no matter what. That's not a reason to avoid loving, by any means. You can't experience the highs in life unless you're willing to risk the lows. But, it's a reminder that when you are going through the pain of loving, you are one of billions of loving people who have gone before you and who will follow. You are not alone and you will get through it."

"Wow, you gave me a lot to think about."

"I hope not too much, Jessica. Okay, that's all the time we have for today. I'm Abby Thompson saying please enjoy the rest of your day and join us again tomorrow morning, here at WTOK, for LifeLine from ten until twelve."

Abby disconnects the call. She lingers longer than usual among the stacks and piles and refuse bags that define her life and her space. "If only I had me to turn to when I was young. What a waste."

# 49. Jug

Hi, Gram! How are you? So that's it? You're all healed? Great! I'm the same. Maybe a pound, or two. Winter is more difficult since it's so much harder to keep warm, even with layers of clothes and coats. I do. Yes, the stores are close enough. I usually wait for the streets to be plowed. Guess who called my radio program. Mark! He didn't say it was him, but of course. I think he mostly wanted to hear what I thought about his sexuality. Russell is failing him, too. Mom mentioned it to me during that first conversation before Thanksgiving, so I'd given it some thought. But when the time came to answer him, I pictured Russell standing over him bellowing, and I just couldn't tell him he had a right to make it public and be proud of who he is. But, I did ask my listeners to send in ideas of where he could go to be safe and talk with other men. He'll have to leave Brookfield, I'm sure. But there must be places in New York City. Hopefully he'll get some useful information. How is Mom doing? She keeps saying that. Encourage her not to. I wouldn't have time to spend with her anyway."

# 50. Top Out

Glorious sunshine streams through the open windows of Abby's apartment, casting a honey glow deep into the crevices of her treasure trove. Abby greets this welcomed visitor with words she longs to hear, "Hello, beautiful!" Summer's arrival kindles the ember of hope she kept alive throughout the dark, unrelenting winter and the struggling, dank spring. Now the mournful coos of courting doves provide the rhythm line for the spirited, improvised rifts of a pair of mockingbirds. Abby's hummed rendition of "The Magic Flute" rounds out the *a cappella* quintet with a flourish. Abby relishes any day that offers more than insurmountable challenges. Today dangles possibilities.

First, Abby's callers had bubbled over with ideas of how to enjoy so gorgeous a day. Then, Mark called her home to thank her for all the ideas LifeLine listeners gave him. And to top it off, when she came out of the laundromat, Abby had found a coupon under her windshield wiper for half-off a Y membership. Focusing on these positives, Abby does her best to tamp down the anxiety snapping at her nerves and convoluting her digestive tract. The thought of interacting in person with anyone besides familiar check-out clerks, even if it means access to a cool pool and a return to hot showers, terrifies her.

Abby overturns the last pot into her dish drain and dries her hands. She checks her watch and does the math. "Seventy-six minutes and counting. Enough procrastinating." She hurriedly grabs her satchel and slides the coupon for the Y into its outer pocket. "Half off, it's worth it."

As she drives, memories of summers in Brookfield pop open and dilute her escalating worries. Her father gloating when his membership at the White Oak Country Club came through. Her discomfort lying on a chaise lounge, poolside, wearing a full-cover swimsuit with sneering boys walking by. The lunch-table stories shared by her classmates of the fun their families had at the neighborhood YMCA. The gnawing jealousy she felt wishing "fun" could be part of her summer. She imagines how different her life might be, had she grown up more naturally, less isolated.

"Starting today, it's my turn to decide."

Abby parks her car and pulls her sleeves down to cover her arms. She situates her ball cap snug over her ears. Her shirt tail disguises her concave waist and protruding hips. She fills her lungs and extends her posture on the exhale. "I can do this."

Her entrance eludes the attention of the guide at the welcome desk herding a motley crew of young and old. Abby approaches and consciously maintains her stance, working hard to appear larger. The guide's voice rings weary but firm. "Okay folks, if you can just follow me, we'll finish up our tour." Following the gaze of the distracted teens in the group, the guide pivots to see Abby cross the lobby. His face blanches. "Hi. Welcome to the YMCA. How can I help you?"

"Hello. I'd like to start a membership. Someone left your coupon on my windshield."

"Great. We're almost done with the tour. Why don't you join in? I can sign you up when we get back."

"Hmmmm. How long will it take?"

"Fifteen, maybe twenty minutes max. We're visiting the pool, gym and weight room. What's your name?"

Abby checks her watch and makes a quick calculation and decision. "Okay, I'll tag along. I'm Elizabeth, Elizabeth Thompson."

"Nice to meet you, Elizabeth."

Anonymity.

Abby senses silent scrutiny from the children in the group. Without context, they take refuge at their parents' sides seemingly fearful their nightmares have ventured to daylight. An older gentleman, gregarious to a fault, welcomes Abby with a suffocating hug. "Hi, my name's Stuart. Nice to meet you, Elizabeth. My wife's name was Elizabeth. Called her Lizzie."

Abby shrinks in his embrace and wiggles free. "Hello, Stuart." She takes a step back to see his weathered smile and gray tufts of unruly hair flowing over his shoulders.

"It's been years since I was at a Y. Now that my Lizzie is safe in Heaven, I've gotta get back to taking care of myself. How about you? You don't seem to have a weight problem."

"I'm joining to swim. To cool off once the summer heats up."

"How about that? I'm a swimmer, too. Maybe I'll see you in the pool sometime."

"Maybe."

The group listens to all the benefits they may now enjoy as they wind through stenches of humid chlorine, ripe sweat and stale air. Strokers, dribblers and lifters cast inquisitive glances Abby's way and wonder how a person gets so thin. Abby diverts her gaze to avoid validating their curiosity. She checks her watch, again.

The guide notices her agitation. "Okay folks, that's our tour. On behalf of the Boston YMCA, thank you for joining. Elizabeth, can you follow me back to the lobby?"

"Ah, sure. I'm in a bit of a hurry. I have that coupon and cash for my first payment."

"Great, that'll speed things up. My name is Leo, by the way."

"Nice to meet you, Leo."

The group dissipates and meanders off toward their destinations while Abby and Leo approach the front desk. As he searches for a blank membership form, Leo mulls quietly. His empathy breaks the silence. "I had a younger sister with an eating disorder. She's gone now."

Abby absorbs his loss. "I'm so sorry to hear that. I wondered. You didn't have the normal reaction when you saw me. You looked sad instead of, well, disgusted."

"I know how terrible my sister felt, all the time. I didn't want you to feel bad about coming here."

"Thank you for that."

Abby hands over the cash. "Elizabeth Thompson, seventy Bramble Court, Mattapan, Massachusetts, zero, two, one, two, six. I've always heard good things about the Y. I'm glad to finally be a member. I really do have to leave, though. It's time for my meal."

"Of course. I get it."

"Thank you, Leo. You made this a better experience than I thought possible."

"I'm happy I had the chance. I'll see you later."

Abby tucks her membership card in her wallet and walks to her car with an ease not felt in months. *Connection. So that's what it feels like.*

# 51. Limelight

Harry surveys his buoyant family from behind. Pride in Betty and their children pulls his shoulders back and lifts his chin. *Wow. Who could have seen this coming?* In the lead, Betty and Ben approach the glass door and pause until the other jabberers catch up. Harry reaches around the crowd and edges open the gateway to another life. He winks at Betty. "OMNI Recording Studio. Wow! You're really doing this. You should be so proud." He ushers her in with a nod. "After you."

Betty, heart thumping in her gums, swallows hard to suppress her nervousness. "I'll be proud once it's over if I haven't made a fool of myself." She mindlessly takes the hand reaching into her grasp.

Joey tugs her along. "We're gonna be great, Mom!"

Sandy and Ben tussle through the doorway before Harry glares them into behaving. The hubbub of the studio gives Betty's heart rate an unwelcome boost. Harry notices her breaths getting shallow. "Okay, everyone, give Mom a good luck kiss and hug. Next time you do, she'll be a star." Ben looks toward his mother and dutifully accepts his imprint of lipstick on the forehead. Sandy takes hers on the cheek. Their faces read embarrassed. The warmth of their embrace, tenderness.

"Thanks for all you did to make this happen. Spending time with Joey so I could work meant everything. I couldn't have done it without you both."

"It's okay, Mom. We enjoyed it."

Betty pushes her shoulder bag to the side and lifts Joey up to kiss him on his nose. He glows with satisfaction. "And you, we could be a duo, you know my songs so well."

Joey pulls at her heartstrings with pleading in his eyes. "I could sing with you, Mom."

"Not today, sweetheart, but maybe someday." She kisses him again.

With Joey still snug in Betty's arms, Harry gathers everyone together in a family hug. Betty turns and kisses him gently on his lips. Their joyful tears mingle. "And honey, thank you for listening and sacrificing so my dream could get this far. I know it wasn't easy."

Harry feels his heart swell to near bursting. His chest expands to prove it. He kisses her tenderly and reluctantly releases his hold.

Betty kneels down to give Joey his freedom. He returns the favor with a hug and kiss. "Don't worry, Joey! We'll sing together soon. Promise." Betty gazes into the eyes of her loving family. She absorbs and consolidates their positive energy and uses it to center her breathing. She pulls the studio door open. "Okay. I hope you all like what you hear. Here I go!"

"Good luck, Mom!"

"Good luck, Betty."

Harry corrals the children, single file, into the recording booth. Their eyes dart from one surface to another taking in all the knobs, switches and lights. Harry realizes how serious his role just became. "Okay, kids, don't touch anything." The director graciously ushers them to their seats, situating Joey up front.

All eyes follow Betty as she introduces herself to the musicians in the studio. Harry sits captivated, watching Betty's nervousness melt away bit by bit with every greeting. A warm glow emanates around her. She laughs. With a wave of gratification showing through, she reaches into her bag and hands each a binder—the pianist, drummer, bassist and reed player. Her posture responds. Her aura expands. *They're gonna play my music!*

Harry sees the feature missing from her face all this time. Her authentic smile. *Welcome back, Betty, my love.*

Betty opens her binder and places it on the stand. Hands shaking, she adjusts her earphones and steps up to the microphone. *Find your joy. You can do this.* She looks through the plate glass and smiles at the smiles smiling back at her. *You can do this.* She turns her face toward the director. A magic nod. He takes his place at the controls. "Are you all set? Let's hear how you sound."

Betty counts out the rhythm. The drummer and bassist adopt it. The saxophone melts in. The keys introduce the harmony. Betty soars. And Joey, from his place front and center, sings along with his mom.

# 52. Accolades

Abby spends her early morning resisting the impulse to start her day. Still reclined, her crisp sheets lie loosely over her naked body. She flaps them periodically to give her perspiration some semblance of a breeze. July 4. Independence Day. She feels radiant heat building as the invading sun casts its earliest beams though every available opening in her window covering. *It's going to be a scorcher.*

She wonders if nature's fever will also descend on Brookfield, where her mother likely stands in the kitchen, chopping the celery and onions and boiling the red-skinned potatoes for Gram's famous German potato salad. The tipping of that memory-domino triggers another of Chloe's tangy barbecue sauce drowning racks of spare ribs, marinating-in-wait for grilling. As it falls, the next memory transports the sauce's flavor close enough to taste. *Mom.*

Caught in an inadvertent avalanche of dredged recollections, she visualizes Mark on corn-shucking duty—and rinse duty for the seven cans that gave up their contents for Chloe's seven-variety baked bean casserole. *Mark.*

She pictures Russell staking three dozen small American flags along both sides of their front walk — and hoisting the giant Stars and Stripes on their 20-foot flagpole — then saluting it, smartly, as it gently flutters in the breeze — then laying out the display of fireworks and sparklers for the after-dark festivities — before reclining with a beer to proudly survey his domain. *Russell.*

The last memory to tumble, she wonders who's doing her jobs of setting up the badminton net in the backyard, making the lemonade and cutting the watermelon. *It's been so long. I wonder if they even miss me.*

She flaps her sheet again. As it lightly settles, cooler for a moment, she reflects on her clearly failed plan to replace painful memories with better ones. She might have taken the day off and gone to the parade downtown. But her compulsive routine demanded otherwise. She needed to adhere to it instead. *LifeLine!* She checks her clock. 8:35. She throws her sheet back and rotates out of bed.

Fed and cleansed, Abby sits spread eagle on the sofa with her box fan blowing warm but evaporating air directly at her perspiring body. She musters her strained enthusiasm and connects with her audience. "Welcome to LifeLine. Happy July Fourth. I'm sure many of our regular listeners are hard at work putting last-minute preparations in place for their holiday celebrations. Or maybe some of you are enjoying the festivities along the parade route. If you have time to pick up the phone, I'd be happy to hear about your plans for the rest of the day."

"Hello Abby, this is Sarah. Happy Fourth! We've got a family cookout planned for later this afternoon. The heat wave may make that less enjoyable than usual, but hopefully it will cool down enough to enjoy the Pops' concert and of course, the fireworks tonight."

"That sounds like a stellar way to celebrate. All the highlights. Any special recipes that come out for the holiday?"

"We host a potluck, so we never know what will be on the table. We'll have burgers and hotdogs on the grill, and watermelon with coconut flakes and blueberries for a cool dessert, but the rest comes from our guests."

"Sounds delicious. A red, white and blue dessert. Potlucks are so much fun. When everybody brings their favorite recipes, how can you go wrong? Have a great time. Thanks for sharing. Let's see who we have on the line. Welcome to LifeLine, the airwaves are yours."

Each caller, one after the other, ups the ante with the description of their holiday decorations, activities and summer fare. Abby does her best to resist inching from admiration to jealousy. *Maybe this wasn't the best topic to choose.* When the accounts turn to the details of gathering friends and family, her struggle intensifies. She realizes, in the most sobering way, she will never evolve from her bittersweet role as observer—intimately connected but distant—surrounded by an isolating reality that excludes her in every way that truly matters. With the end of the barrage in sight, Abby presses on. "If you're just tuning in, Happy Fourth of July! We've heard lots of great plans already. We have time for one last call. Who's up next? Welcome to LifeLine, the airwaves are yours."

"Hi, Abby. I'm Betty. Our plans sound a lot like the callers' before me. We'll be heading out for our picnic at a neighborhood park with another family. All our kids love fireworks, so that's how we'll end the day. My main reason for calling is to say 'thank you.' My husband called your show almost two years ago because he was afraid he had lost me. I can see now how distant I was, in so many ways. I thought I was doing a good job of keeping my inner voice concealed. I guess he could still read that

I was all twisted up. You told him I needed to 'find my joy.' The second I heard it, the tension in my soul unwound. Like letting go of one of those toy planes with the rubber band at the propeller. I've heard you give that advice since, and every time I do, I think, 'I sure hope the person takes it to heart.' My husband and I took it to heart, and last week I actually recorded my own songs in an actual studio. I am absolutely sure that your conversation with Harry made it possible. I, we all, my husband and three children, owe you so much."

Relieved for the spontaneous change of subject, Abby perks up. "Betty, I am so happy for you! I've wondered how that all turned out. You surpassed all my imaginings. Will your recordings be for sale?"

"Haha, no, they were just for me. But it was a dream come true, to hear them played by real musicians and to sing my words along with them. The thrill hasn't dulled and I doubt that it will any time soon."

"Well, I hope you change your mind and decide to share your music with a wider audience. So many times, hearing a song, even if it's a sad song, can be reassuring because it proves that other people made it through tragedy, or lost love, or heartache and even had enough energy left over to write about it."

"You know, you're right! That same thing occurred to me over the years. Thanks, Abby. I guess 'never say never.'"

"Yes, Never assume a 'no.'"

"Well, friends, another Lifeline has come to a close. We'll meet up again tomorrow from ten until twelve. I hope you all have a safe and fun holiday. Drink lots of fluids. Eat some corn on the cob for me! Take care, Boston."

Abby places the phone on the sofa and eases to standing. "Finally, time for my picnic meal!" Within minutes, eight hotdogs, sliced end to end and flattened, sizzle in a skillet.

Mounds of creamy potato salad and coleslaw mingle their oozing juices on her dish. An assortment of condiments stand ready for the sizzling to end. Abby cuts the braised frankfurters into miniature pieces and spoons them into waiting buns. On goes the relish, mustard and ketchup. "Happy Independence Day to me!"

With her meal and its undoing complete, Abby gathers extra garbage bags and heads out into the suffocating heat. She moves through the wall of dry, hot air that collides with her lightly clothed body like the exhaust from a roaring blast furnace. Despite the soaring temperatures, she succumbs to her compulsion to stop and rummage through the contents of each bin on her route. With temperatures hovering near one hundred degrees, she knows any discarded food has decayed beyond salvation. Feeling dizzy and drained from worsening dehydration, she invests less time than usual scouring for other treasures. Her life-threatening efforts go unrewarded. She returns home, with nothing to show for her risk-taking, dangerously close to shutting down.

Recognizing the symptoms, Abby immediately guzzles two quarts of replenishing beverage to combat her dehydration, vertigo and confusion. Within minutes, her condition improves, until her reflex to regurgitate undermines her remedy. Still weakened, she forgoes starting her next meal. "Just a little nap."

# 53. Breaststroke

As is her custom, Abby times her daylight scavenging returns with precision. She has recently found that her privacy at three o'clock is all but assured since few but she voluntarily endure Boston's blazing zenith sun during mid-July. With sweat running down her temples and the center of her chest, she unloads today's limited take unobserved save for the enviable cardinal flitting water out of the birdbath across the street and the squirrel chattering loudly from a branch above.

Once indoors, she unties each bag, unleashing its trapped air like a putrid burp. The scavenged rag rug in the living room, Abby's triage center, reeks of soured juices and popped eggs, casualties of her past wars with the imperfect Trojan horses she wrestles into her home. The window fan swirls the heavy odors into an olfactory cacophony, one she notices only for the first few moments.

After nineteen months of sorting the good, the better and the lost, Abby proudly moves quickly and methodically through the process. In light of its vulnerability to spoilage, she consumes all edible, retrieved food immediately or at the latest, within a day. Waste not, want not. All non-food items fall into two categories:

229

those to donate to thrift stores and those to give as gifts. Both groups take up temporary residence in one encroaching pile or another, although invariably, out of sight, out of mind wreaks havoc on the pass-through of either.

Abby has good reason to celebrate her hard-won efficiency. Every moment she saves throughout the day and night translates into more Y-time. By combining her incremental savings, she manages to squeeze in at least two visits during the week and one on the weekend. Her motivation is clear and simple. Time at the Y uplifts her otherwise soul-crushing routine.

First, she secretly gloats over her spontaneous ingenuity each time she responds to the name Elizabeth. Identity freedom. Second, she revels in the ecstasy of being completely supported by water — even cold water — then showering in a scalding spray. Physical freedom. And while at the outset she purposely planned her visits to avoid the attention of Stuart, the hugger, her aversion to him has lessened into feelings just shy of tolerance. Connection freedom.

Abby wipes her mouth and washes her hands. She slips her dried swimsuit from the shower rod and into her tote. She tosses in her towel, a couple bags of cookies and an empty soda bottle. Ready.

Abby exits the warm locker room into the cold, chlorine-laden atmosphere of the pool, wearing a bathing cap to discourage snickers and to retain some of her precious body heat. Still, her skin stubbornly reacts to the unwelcome change in temperature in a futile effort to stay warm. Futile. Undeterred, she neatly rolls her locker key into her tri-folded towel then places the parcel on the bench at the perimeter.

With halting breaths, she slides into the chilly water as the lifeguard blows her shrill whistle for adult swim. Abby's suit balloons away from her body until, once soaked, it clings.

Parents with toddlers in arms and resentful pre-teens plod to the ladders. They thwap their dripping bodies to the bleachers and wrap themselves in towels and attention eager to watch the exposé before them. They follow Abby's every stroke as she paddles length after labored length, sure the enormous one-piece she wears will float off eventually to reveal the rest of her skeletal physique. She pays them no mind. Swimming. Freedom.

Abby stops to catch her breath as Stuart appears in the doorway of the men's locker room. She wipes the dripping water from her eyes and waves a hello. He meets her at the side of the pool and turns his charms in her direction. "Back again? You're sure making the most of your new membership."

"I really had no idea how relaxing swimming could be. And it's so hot outside, it's the perfect way to spend an hour or so."

"I live just a couple blocks from here. If you're interested, I'd be happy if you'd come for a visit, maybe not today, but sometime."

"Maybe."

Stuart resists taking "maybe" for a final answer. "Lizzie used to love this really dark chocolate from Germany. I always keep a bar around to remind me of her. I think you'd like it. And I still have her collection of Hummels."

Abby struggles to counter her aversion to companionship. "Maybe. Not today, but maybe."

Stuart pivots and climbs down the ladder and into Abby's personal space. He struggles to express his need for companionship. "I just got some lemonade, the good stuff, made with real lemons."

Abby chuckles at his determination. "Haha, the good stuff? I have to be back home in less than an hour, so I don't think a visit will work today."

Stuart takes her hand and pulls her toward the ladder. "We can go now. I don't need to swim. I just came hoping you'd be here."

Abby feels boxed in but concedes nonetheless. She checks the clock. "Okay, but I can only stay for a little while. I do have to be home in forty-eight minutes."

"That's precise."

"Yes, it is."

Stuart unlocks his apartment's door and pushes it open. He steps aside and motions Abby in. She inhales the familiar odor of old that hangs in the still air. Gram.

Stuart disappears to the kitchen and returns with two dripping tumblers of lemonade over ice and a plate with a broken chocolate bar. "Lemonade?"

Abby startles herself for forgetting about purging. "No, thank you. Is that the fancy chocolate?"

Stuart winks and nods with pride. "Lizzie's favorite. Try a piece."

Abby lets a tiny morsel melt on her tongue and massages every molecule of flavor from it. "You're right. It is very dark. I like it that way."

"Oh, good. Well, you're always welcome to visit. Let me show you Lizzie's Hummels."

Abby reluctantly follows Stuart into the bedroom. Three shelves display an assortment of statuettes of children in clothes of muted colors engaged in various wholesome activities, from whistling to feeding birds. Abby turns her back to Stuart to admire their delicately painted facial expressions and suddenly feels his hands on her non-existent breasts. He moans and massages the skin around her nipples.

Frozen in place, she protests. "Stuart, what are you doing? I didn't come here for this."

Flustered but not dissuaded, Stuart imposes his advantage. "I know, Elizabeth, I'm just so lonely. I miss my Lizzie. Can I please just touch you? You can touch me, too."

Abby feels an unfamiliar stirring between her legs that sends shock waves through her. *What's that?*

Stuart slides his hands down Abby's waist and over the ridges of her hip bones. He massages between her legs with one hand while stroking himself with the other. His moaning intensifies and reaches a climax as an expanding patch of ejaculate darkens his pants. "Oh, Lizzie, I missed you so much."

"I'm not Lizzie, Stuart. I'm Elizabeth."

"Maybe every once in a while you can be my Lizzie?"

"I'm not sure I…"

"Not often, just sometimes."

"Maybe."

# 54. Treading

Hi Gram! How are you? I'm glad you're still feeling okay. Have you moved back into your old wing? I hope it's soon. I'm really enjoying the autumn, too. It's been really gorgeous here. Really gorgeous! I don't remember the trees ever looking so colorful. Do you get out into the sunshine much? Yep, that's the best. I try to get out every day, too. I've made some nice paintings in the Common. I'm heading up the coast next weekend to find a harbor to paint. Yes, I'm finally ready to move on from trees and beaches. I'm still enjoying it. ... I've gotten to know him better. He's still a little bit creepy and a little bit funny. Who knew we'd be friends? He's just an old man. Right. I never really felt like I fit in. But the Y is different. I guess we're all just normal people there. Speaking of not fitting in, how's Mark? Has he found anyone to be friends with, to help him get out more? Really? Obviously, it will need to be a trustworthy person. They'll have to be his eyes, like I was, after all. Great! Into places where he's understood? ... Yes. Always. LifeLine people are very diverse. It's got to be the best job on the planet, at least for me. It's the best part of my day. Yep, okay, enjoy your meal. Tell Mom and Mark I said 'hi' and that I send my love when you see them next. Oh, please discourage Mom from visiting me. She keeps bringing it up. I keep telling her it would really be bad for both of us. Okay. Thanks. Love you, Gram."

# 55. Crampon

Abby smiles as she gently stirs a steaming mug of hot chocolate, careful to keep the bobbing marshmallow from escaping over the rim. She holds it to one side with her spoon to take a sip. Still too scalding. Making a blessing of her predicament, she dunks the softening, white puff under, then sucks off the gooey, melted layer before sending it back below the surface for another soak. Such frivolity rarely occurs on a normal day. Today is not normal. Abby tunes her radio to AM to hear this hour's weather report. The announcer repeats the day's refrain of travel advisories issued up and down the East Coast with rain, sleet and snow dropping in waves. He closes with the emergency services' official statement warning non-essential vehicles to "stay off roads and highways so emergency vehicles can do their work and rescue stranded motorists."

For better or worse, the forecast twelve hours ago left Abby a window to satisfy her gathering obsession. She leaned against the premonitory wind as it buffeted her ventures between car and dumpster and magnified her struggles to wrestle bags and retrieved items into her car. But the falling precipitation did not turn the roads treacherous until her return. Accumulating sleet twice raised her tire treads above the asphalt. She felt her rear wheels swerve and fishtail. She held her breath and fought the urge to brake. The second time, as her car bounced off a curb and slid to a stop, she considered trudging back, acutely aware of the dangers of ice-driving. One minute in the howling, stinging squall sent her back inside her car. Weighing the imminent risk of hypothermia against the likelihood of a deadly collision at five miles per hour, she resigned to inch the mile back home instead. Her reward for safely returning home—repeated refills of hot beverages—has flowed ever since. Her bag of marshmallows lies half-empty beside her.

Abby pulls her window curtain aside and checks the accumulation. *Still falling.* She returns to her sofa and picks up the ringing phone. "Welcome to LifeLine. I'm your host Abby Thompson. For two hours each weekday, we talk about anything that's on your mind. The extraordinary, the mundane and everything in between. Today, the weather is extraordinary. It is nasty out there, my friends. I hope you and everyone you know are hunkered down safe in your homes during this spectacular storm. My folks live just over the Connecticut line where two feet of snow dropped in a matter of hours. I heard Logan shut down because of white-out conditions. All of New England is paralyzed, not to mention the East Coast. I've got a feeling March 15, 1984, will be remembered as an Ides of March for the record books. Let's open the phone lines and hear how you are all getting through this challenge. Welcome to LifeLine, the airwaves are yours."

"Hi Abby. Evan here. I'm holed up in my house with the wife and kids. We're getting pelted by freezing rain. The streets gotta be a mess. On my way to work, I just made it past a snow plow in a ditch. Musta lost visibility and just drove off the road. I turned around and headed back. I just know we're gonna hear about someone dying because they got stuck out in this or had a bad accident. What a waste. I'm glad it's not gonna be me. I'm stayin' in till it's over."

"Thanks for your call, Evan. I couldn't agree with you more. It's best to just wait it out. Losing traction for a few seconds on a patch of ice—that could be gone in less than an hour—can be the difference between seeing tomorrow and not. I'll admit, memories of freak accidents stay with me. Probably because they remind me how vulnerable we all are. But I find I still drift into complacency. Then a storm like today's, with the potential for real harm, reminds me that there are no guarantees. No day, no minute should be taken for granted or squandered. We need to live every day like it's our last. Because, you never know.

"Like you, when I hear about a person dying, by accident or due to illness, or suicide, before they have a chance to experience what we consider life's milestones, of course I'm indignant about how unfair it is. And it is. From any perspective, it's tragic, heart-wrenching and wildly unjust. But I have come to believe that the value of those lives does not diminish because they didn't stretch into old age. We mourn our loss and rightly so. And it's deep and painful and long-lasting. But we do those marvelous souls a disservice if we see them only as ones who were cheated by life, instead of those who managed to squeeze a full lifetime's worth of meaning from a mere fragment. And what's more, and this may not sit well with some of our listeners, but I believe souls come back again and again, to inch up the empathy ladder with every new life lived, every set of relationships experienced. So we get many, many chances to fulfill our potential to be fully loving, caring people.

"We've got another caller. Hello, the airwaves are yours."

"Hi Abby. I'm Marge. I can tell you of a little boy in my town who was diagnosed with a brain tumor when he was just three years old. He needed surgery, but the family had a high co-pay. Word got around, and before you knew it, everyone in our little town got to work raising money to help them out. Kids had bake sales and car washes. Adults had raffles and did odd jobs for a donation. We even organized an art auction. It really brought the community together. The day he came home from the hospital the entire route was lined with people clapping and waving 'Get Well!' signs. It was just amazing."

Marge pauses, clears her throat, pauses again, and continues. "When he died—the funeral procession went on and on and on. I have to believe—that the energy all those people, young and old, poured into our community—for the sake of that little boy— changed something deep inside. He had barely learned to talk, but his short life inspired great empathy and generosity. How could a person see the pain in his parents' eyes and not decide then and there to treat their own children better? Everyone better? So, yes, I agree, age does not decide. And I'd be really happy to know that his soul gets to come back and live again."

"Marge, what a heartbreaking and inspiring story. Such a testimonial to the power of love. I have a feeling your sharing it will inspire others to call, that there are many more stories of the profound impact all lives can have. Thank you so much for calling. Stay safe out there. Who is our next caller? The airwaves are yours."

"Hello, I'm Toni. I was married to a wonderful man named Art..."

# 56. Brush

The eastern horizon glows as Abby wiggles the legs of her stool deep enough in the sand to steady it within arm's reach of her anchored easel. The warm, steady breeze billowing off the ocean brings the aroma of salt sea air and seaweed swirling around her miniature encampment. Seagulls, eyeing her eating, clammer above—sensitized to the weak wills of pestered humans. Today's *plein-air* subject, The Highland Light, flashes its warning toward the Atlantic as it has from Truro for nearly two hundred years. Abby smiles, picturing countless artists before her plunking themselves before this very beacon, expecting, hoping, to capture its essence in a novel way. *If it's good enough for Edward Hopper, it's good enough for me.* She purges her meal into a plastic bag and turns her artist's vision upon her surroundings.

With the sun's rays at her back, she clips her prepared board to the easel and moistens her paints. A diluted wash of the palest blue sets the tone. Glance and stroke. Glance and stroke. Abby forfeited her night's sleep to capture this light—the first of a crystal clear June morning—before the flow of tourists and tour guides would obscure the vertical lines of this historic landmark's tower and keeper's house. She alternates between observation and representation, observation and representation, oblivious to the cares of the encroaching world.

Tucking such adventures into her obsessively structured schedule requires determination, planning and energy. The last of which, for Abby, diminishes by the day and the hour. She knows every outing could be her last. She makes the most of each. Abby willingly shoehorned today's activities within the confines of her strict two-hour cycles. Bracketed by periodic scavengings and feedings, and two hundred-mile drives, she distills just three and a half hours of easel time to paint this iconic scene, from her commitment of nine.

As the morning unfolds, the famous lighthouse lures wandering early risers from the surrounding walkways and dunes. Before long, a crowd gathers around Abby, drawn originally by her stick-figure appearance, but held fast by sheer fascination. They watch in awe as her carefree brush strokes recreate the vista before them. She maintains her focus, determined not to let her discomfort with the attention interfere with her art. But, edging closer to her next feeding, she knows she needs an escape plan. *I'll just stand up.* Adhering to her schedule, she calmly stands and closes her paints and opens her cooler. The crowd slowly takes the hint. Two hours later, she steps away from her finished painting. "Not too bad, for a novice."

The sun beats down on Abby's shoulders as she deposits the bulk of her final meal in the waiting plastic bag, careful to time her purging between the stares of curious beachcombers. She packs her food containers and packaging back into the cooler; her paints, easel, stool and painting back into the car. Knowing this may be her last trip to the Cape, she bids a solemn farewell to the crashing waves and sparkling sand. *Thank you, God, for this day.*

# 57. Abseil

The panes of Abby's kitchen windows whistle, turned instrumental by the buffeting of a ferocious October hurricane edging up the East Coast. Her lights flicker. She tightens the tie of her velour robe against the chill. Moving by muscle memory, this cycle's meal materializes. Abby rips open and dumps two bags of frozen corn into a pot. She impatiently turns the flame below it to high. Lid. She pulls the first slice of bread from the loaf's packaging and smears it with chunky peanut butter. The tiny nuggets dig into the bread's soft surface. She folds it in half and opens her gaping mouth. Her tongue rises to mash it against her gums as she chews it into a soft putty. She forces it down. She alternates slices of cold bread and spoonfuls of scalding corn as her abdomen refills. The ringing phone interrupts her rhythm. She holds her breath and presses the speaker button.

"Hello?"

"Hello, Abby?"

"Mom, what's happened?"

"Hello, sweetheart. How are you?"

"I'm the same. What's happened?"

"I'm so sorry to have to tell you this way, but your grandmother died about an hour ago. She slipped into a coma overnight. The morphine kept most of her pain away. She's finally at peace."

Abby's throat seizes, "Died? Morphine? But, I just talked with her last weekend. She didn't say things had gotten worse."

"That's her way. You know that. Always minimizing when it comes to her health. I think you learned that from her."

Abby fights to speak through her shock and sorrow. "I can't believe I didn't get to say 'goodbye.' I mean. To really say 'goodbye.' Oh, Mom, I'm so sorry for you, too. I know how close you got over the last couple years. How are you?"

"I'm very sad. And lonely. Already. She became a mother to me. I'd come to depend on her. But I'll be okay. You understand, I saw her everyday. I saw her get thin and frail, and lose her ability to care for herself. She was able to keep those changes from you since you only talked on the phone. Her voice never changed, I guess. But I think she was ready."

"I didn't know she lost so much weight. Oh, Gram."

"She loved you. She asked me to make sure you knew that."

"I know that. I love her, too."

"Her funeral will be lovely. Dad's found a choir and string quartet to play at the service. And her casket is beautiful. Truly."

"Really, now he acts concerned? He can't be bothered to visit her when she's living down the block or even show her respect? But, whatever!"

"Visitation at the funeral home will be on Friday morning. The funeral is Friday afternoon. When will you be home?"

Having spent two years anticipating this eventuality, Abby relies on her rehearsed words and tone to convey deep sorrow mixed with non-committal excuses. "You know I want to be there, but I'm not sure if I can make it."

"Darling, this is your grandmother. Surely she meant enough to you."

"She meant the world to me. You know that. I'll ask, but I may not be able to get off work." Abby feels her meal rising through her esophagus. "Mom, I've got to go. If I can't be there, at least I talked to Gram a couple times a week. She knows how much I love her."

"Well, I hope you can make it."

"I'll do my best. I've got to go."

# 58. Bivouac

Abby's head rests on the thick lamb's wool sheath covering her steering wheel. Wrapped in a blanket to counter October's chill, her solemn gaze locks on the nearly deserted funeral home across the street. Memories ebb and flow of the many times she walked past this expansive white edifice on her way to and from school. Now it earns a far deeper significance. Now, her head bows and her stomach turns to imagine the funeral director, behind the blind in the only glowing window, preparing what remains of Gram for curious gawkers.

"Thank God Mom and Mark know I want a closed casket. No embalming, no caked makeup, nobody standing over me saying, 'My, doesn't she look natural?' Or, most probably, 'Wow, what happened to her?'" Her bitterness simmers. "But then again, Gram told all of us she wanted to be cremated."

Imagining the ceremonial pomp Russell arranged for Gram's funeral, her resentment boils over. *As if hiring a full choir and a string quartet will make up for his disrespect. As if putting her body in a gaudy coffin will pardon him for worrying more about his comfort than visiting her. No matter how much money he throws at it now, nothing can change that he abandoned his own mother for years while she wasted away.*

Exhaustion battles her indignation, luring Abby's breaths to slow, her eyelids to droop. Forcing herself to stay awake, keeping vigil for her Gram, she recalls the lie she told Chloe, that she worked today and must work tomorrow. Her plan to keep her distance serves her purpose. Although she feels a wave of satisfaction imagining embarrassing Russell on his regalia day, she knows her own suffering would erupt if the Thompson clan witnessed her condition. "I am never going to a hospital." *Besides, why would I want to be there? In a crowded room with an empty body? No one loved Gram as much as I do. No one was as close to her as I am. You always made time for me. It felt so easy to talk with you about things that really mattered. I love you, Gram. I love you, too, Abigail.* "I do miss you, Gram." *I am with you, Abigail.*

Suddenly, the window darkens. The change breaks Abby's distraction and cuts to her heart. She imagines the director lowering the casket lid, leaving behind just another cold, vacant body ready for viewing. "Oh, Gram. You're done." A torrent of stifled sadness spontaneously wells up from deep within, drowning every pocket of control. Each word she speaks inters in a wave of grief. "You were… the only one… in my family… who loved… me unconditionally… now… you're gone." Uncontrollable weeping drains what remains of her energy. Through her tears, she watches a crooked figure pull the exterior door shut and walk away. "Oh, Gram." Dangerously starved and with no reason to stay, Abby reluctantly twists the key in the ignition. Still weeping, she signals east, toward a parking lot she trusts as safe.

She snugs her car in the far corner adjacent to the surrounding woods. Masked in the shadows, she turns off the engine and reaches for one of the coolers she packed with sandwiches and pasta salad. Her tortured gorging feels different in this setting, in the open air, but it ends the same. The high weeds beside her car conceal the regurgitated contents of her stomach. Exhaustion battles her anguish. Exhaustion finally wins.

The clapping brakes of a downshifting container truck shock Abby awake. "Whaaa?" She eases open one puffy, encrusted eyelid just enough, then rubs them both to release the few lashes that remain affixed. "Still dark. Good. Oh, my neck!" She painstakingly unwinds her pretzeled backbone and digs through the empty packaging on the seat beside her to find her watch. 6:13. "Plenty of time to feed."

Filled and emptied, Abby mindlessly gathers the clutter surrounding her and squeezes it into bags. She takes a cleansing breath and wipes her tears. "Well, Gram, today's the day. It's time to go." Despite her best efforts, raw sorrow saturates her drive to the church. Hands trembling, she methodically circles the perimeter and carefully selects a discrete parking spot with a clear view of the attendees' arrivals. She tucks her blanket around her fragile frame and cries herself toward sleep.

The sound of a revving engine infiltrates Abby's oblivion. "Oh no!" She sits erect and looks around. "It's over?" An orange funeral flag on a magnetized pole flaps above the roof of each car in the lot. Six pallbearers slide the ornate casket into the cavern of the hearse. Leading the exiting crowd, Russell supports the weight of his sobbing wife, guiding both her and Mark to their idling limousine.

Abby frantically consumes the last of her chilled food. She races to finish before the stream of mourners, heads bowed and gaits melancholy, weave to their flagged cars. Her intake touches bottom and exits into a nearby refuse bin. She rinses her mouth and wipes her lips. Slowly, like a dance never rehearsed, the procession of a dozen vehicles with glowing headlights and blinking flashers forms. She watches, engine running, as the motioning traffic officer waves the last privileged driver through the red light. Abby waits impatiently for the light to change as the procession rolls out of view. Stymied by time's passing, she struggles to remember the hearse's most likely route to the cemetery. The light turns green. She breathes a sigh and pulls into traffic. She leaves her flashers off.

Sunshine glints off the trembling leaves of auburn and gold as Abby arrives and scans the surrounding hillside for a gathered crowd. Spying it, she parks her car in the shadow of a mausoleum, a location that offers her a concealed, though clear view of the gravesite. Her tears surface at the sight of Gram's casket suspended above a gaping rectangle in the earth.

A garbled murmur emanates over the breeze as the minister snaps his wrist and sends droplets of water from his gold wand over the oak box and the woven blanket of roses atop. Her breathing quivers and catches as she relinquishes control watching the remains of her grandmother lowered ceremoniously below ground. Blurred by tears, she watches each of those gathered toss a memorial flower out of sight, then turn away and drive off. Back to their lives.

As silence and stillness returns to her surroundings, Abby makes her way to the hallowed site. She stands, hands folded, and solemnly recites the final blessing from funerals past, "Eternal rest grant unto her, Oh Lord. And let perpetual light shine upon her. May her soul and the souls of all the faithfully departed rest in peace. Amen. Goodbye, Gram. I'll see you again, soon."

# 59. Belayer

Imbalanced further by Gram's death, Abby falters into a new abyss. Her sorrow draws the remaining hope from her soul, leaving it to deflate like a lost balloon, shriveled and limp, with no resemblance to its former glory. In the absence of their frequent calls, Abby struggles to summon comfort by connecting with Gram through the ether. She finds little. Without the use of Gram's phone for long distance calls, Chloe, too, slowly drifts away. Even Mark's post-funeral commitment to stay connected fades over the ensuing weeks. So, in time, Abby restores Ellen as her singular connection to the saner world. Challenged by limited good news, their weekly conversations quickly grow dark and edge darker. Abby still cares about the mundane aspects of Ellen's life. She always asks. But, Ellen understands Abby's longing to rage without consequence, so she defers and listens.

She listens to descriptions of the detested waste Abby witnesses multiple times along her twice-daily dumpster route. From the unopened lunches with milk money still intact, to outdated holiday items still in their festive cellophane and bows. From restaurant leftovers or expired ingredients, to grocer's bruised produce and two-day-old baked goods. From meant-to-recycle aluminum cans to the entire contents of an 80-year-old's estate. Ellen listens and sees that each and every item that Abby yanks over the rusted edge of society's dustbins was deemed valueless, not worth the inconvenience of putting it to use, except by Abby.

Ellen listens to stories of fighting extreme weather; of wayward shopping carts, broken boxes and rain-soaked bags that complicate further Abby's compulsion to rescue the discards of others; and of the mounting risks posed to her well-being by the insect-riddled, waist-high-and-rising towers of her collecteds. Ellen listens and develops new insight into the absolute dominance of her obsession.

Ellen listens to descriptions of Abby's physical changes. Reports of her weight loss were a given for a while. Though, once Abby reaches gossamer skin laying on porous bones, the curve mostly levels out. She hears descriptions of the darkening crescents under Abby's shallow and sinking eyes. How her spine and hip bones protrude from her back like knots on twisted trees. How vomiting gastric acid dozens of times a day dissolved her teeth to rotten stubs, making all but softened foods inedible. How hair loss, a natural consequence of starvation, like the end of her menstrual cycle, is helped along by her compulsive pulling of every budding strand from every itchy follicle on her scalp, face and body. How she is cold all the time, from the first chill of autumn to the last fog of spring. How her bruises and lacerations stubbornly resist healing. How her bony feet and ankles swell. Ellen listens and feels Abby's morbid dread of prolonged self-destruction.

Ellen listens to descriptions of how Abby manages her life. How her therapy visits are just long enough to be billed for both the time and the obligatory pharmaceuticals that she stockpiles in her bathroom for an early escape from her living hell. How going to the Y to swim a few times a week and revel in their restorative, blazing hot showers, does far more to improve her mood than admitting her eccentricities to any "damn shrink." How she barters sex like a commodity to avoid eviction and to motivate what passes for companionship. How she represses her memories of sexual assaults. How she will never let Russell win. And how, despite her plight, she holds fast to a genuine love for God, and her belief that goodness and kindness reign supreme and will one day deliver them both to a place of endless light. Ellen listens and struggles to fathom how faith withstands such darkness.

Most frequently of all, Ellen listens to Abby's continuous agony, knowing that tomorrow—and every day on her life's perpetual treadmill—will bring the same loathsome realizations and follow the same horrifying rituals, a lifetime guarantee of a future that rivals any damnation scenario the best fire-and-brimstone pastor can fathom. Ellen listens and grasps the depth of Abby's hopelessness.

Abby speaks. Powerless against Abby's defiance and obstinance, Ellen listens.

# 60. Short Runout

Impenetrable storm clouds blacken the sky from horizon to horizon. Jagged bolts of lightning shatter and sizzle. Abby holds her breath, anticipating the evolving rumbles of tumultuous thunder. "One, two, three, four, five. Wow. Very close." She waits captive in her car watching critical minutes vaporize like the sheeting rain on the searing asphalt. "I can't wait any longer." Abby grabs the groceries within reach and makes a run for her front door.

Within seconds, the unrelenting downpour drenches her to the bone and her parcels to oblivion. The soaked bags rip apart, spilling their contents into puddles of water and mud. Compelled by another strike of lightning, she sacrifices the lost causes as they melt, roll or saturate at her feet. With her dignity at a nadir, Abby relinquishes, *Even I'm appalled by me. I can't do this!* "I give up!" She manages the key and steps dripping onto her door mat. She checks her clock. 9:47. "I'll never make it."

Abby tears open a snack bag and consumes the contents while she stirs the fruit from the bottom of a container of yogurt. The ingested food virtually bounces out. Vomited water cleanses the residue. She checks the clock again. 9:58. Abby centers herself with deep breaths. She positions herself amid the rubble in what was once her living room and answers the phone on the third ring. "Hello, Boston. Welcome to LifeLine. I'm your host, Abigail Thompson. This is the show where you set the direction. I'm counting on you, our listeners, to get us started today. Hello, you're on LifeLine, the airwaves are yours." Abby continues to breathe deeply to center herself.

"Hello, Abby. This is Veronica. Maybe it's the dismal weather we've been having. Maybe, I don't know. Maybe I'm just being selfish, but I can't seem to move on from my husband's death. It's been more than a year. My friends were great, very helpful. They listened when I needed to cry or talk. But now, since the anniversary, I get the feeling, well—they think I should be over it and move on. I'm still so stuck. I miss him so much."

Abby feels raw sorrow ablaze in her chest. She forces her stinging tears inward, her quivering voice outward. "Veronica, grieving is intensely personal and relational. The pain you're feeling is unique to you and your husband. Which is understandable, since no one else had your relationship with your husband."

Memories of Gram crash in tumultuous waves over her. "Only you know how central he was to your life, how you confided in each other, laughed together, quarreled together, planned together. All of the days and nights you shared. No one but you has those memories, those feelings. So it should not surprise you that your friends, despite their love, do not understand.

"Most grieving goes through predictable stages, but the length and order of those stages varies for every individual, every situation. No two people grieve the same, because no two people are the same, no two relationships are the same. Don't rush yourself. Feel what you need to feel. If your friends are less than willing to continue as your source of comfort, there are support groups where you may find more empathy than judgment.

"You will eventually look back on your marriage with less sadness and more gratitude. Try talking to your husband. Share what you would have shared were he still with you. Listen for his reply. You may be strengthened by him from afar."

Abby relaxes, having spent all she has to offer.

"Oh, Abby. I'm so glad I called. I don't know how you understand so many different struggles. Thank you for your ideas. So much."

"You're welcome, Veronica. Just be patient with yourself. You will heal. Who do we have next? Welcome to LifeLine, the airwaves are yours."

"Hi Abby, William here. The caller that just hung up, she needs to just keep doin' what's she's doin'. Heck, it took me a year before I could get a full night's sleep after my old man died. Kept thinking of all the stuff we'd never do. He was young. I looked up to him. Counted on him. He got cancer and sure, he took the chemo and radiation they told him to, but he still died. I thought he'd beat it. I was so angry he died so young while old people were shuffling around, complaining about everything.

"I kept forgetting. I'd pick up the phone and start dialing and then remember. That was tough. I guess we get used to things being a certain way. It takes doing things different, over and over, before the old ways fade. I bet it took me two years not to get a pit in my stomach when I thought of him. To just nod and go on with my day. Of course, then I felt like I let him down, for moving on. I'd say it took me three years to get back to normal. To the point where the memories didn't mess me up. Till I could laugh without feeling guilty. Yah, so, yah. Be patient. It'll happen."

"Well, William, that is really good news for all of us. Being in a dark place can start to feel like struggling in quicksand. The more you try to get out, the deeper you go. It's reassuring to hear your story. I'm grateful you took the time to call in and share. These are really important conversations we're having today. Who's up next? Welcome to LifeLine, the airwaves are yours."

"Hi Abby, this is Yvette. I'm terrified for my daughter. Stay here, you're talking to Abby. I feel like soon I could be watching her die. She's only thirteen and she thinks she's fat. Can you please talk with her? She's right here. Here. Take the phone. Tell Abby what you told me."

Abby preemptively braces herself for another traumatic exchange. "Sure. Hello?"

"Hi Abby, I can't believe my mother's making me do this. Fine. My girlfriends are all beautiful and skinny. They look just like the models in magazines. They say they can eat anything they want. They just throw up after they pig out. I just want to be like them and for them to like me. My parents threatened to ground me forever if I even try to puke."

Abby's professional demeanor vaporizes as her agitation erupts. "Listen to me. To every word. Those models are fantasies. They don't really exist, anywhere. They are tucked and implanted together, then their photos are airbrushed until every bit of their humanity is erased. They are not real.

"Do exactly as I say. Look at yourself in the mirror, front and back, and smile with genuine, heartfelt approval. Thank God that you are exactly the shape you are. Go to your parents and hug them. Thank them for their love. They love you enough to risk making you hate them. That's love. And even if you lose their love somehow, never, never forget that you are loved—if by no one else, always by God, unconditionally, just the way you are. Tell your friends that you love them, and that I said they should get help from their parents or a doctor to stop controlling their weight by purging. They will die if they don't accept the help of loved ones. And it's the worst kind of death. Do you understand? Love yourself. Help your friends."

"Thank you, Abby. She went into her room, but I could hear your voice on her radio. I hope you got through to her. I'm terrified to think of losing her."

Abby fights with every cell of her body to convey the extreme gravity of the danger. "Yvette, don't give up. Stay with her. Help her understand that starving and purging are the worst ways to lose weight. Reach out to her friends' parents. They may not know. It's a habit that can be hidden easily until it's too late to reverse. It starts out innocently and seems so easy and risk-free. But once it becomes automatic, it's like trying to stop a speeding train. There's a moment when a stone on the track is enough to keep an engine in place. But once it starts rolling, well. You understand. Stay with her. Contact her friends' parents."

"I will, Abby. Thank you again."

"Okay, we're going to take a break. But we will be back in three minutes."

Abby's trembling hand hangs up the phone. She looks around her. "It's the worst kind of death."

# 61. Edging

Abby sets three amber prescription containers on the pile of laundry beside her. She watches the minute hand click into position. Her head drops, dragged down by the weight of her world. Anticipation of her Sunday morning phone call got her this far. She makes a note of the date. "June 9, 1985," *four years to the day since I last saw Ellen.* The ringing phone provides a step back from a sharp edge.

"Right on time."

"Hi, Abby! How are you this nearly summer Sunday?"

"Hi, Els. I've been better, but honestly, I can't remember when."

"That doesn't sound good. What's happened?"

"I've decided. I am ready to end this. There is nothing in my life worth living for."

Nonplussed, Ellen struggles to respond. Her thoughts toss wildly in her brain, ejecting a stumbling cliché over her tongue. "Oh, Abby, I don't know what to say."

"You don't have to say anything, Els. You know I'm right. I'm already in Hell. If I end up there for eternity, I'm no worse off."

"Abby, if you end up in Hell there's no hope for the rest of us."

"Russell says I'm defiling my temple. I'm sure that's a mortal sin."

"Your dad's a horrible person. Everything I know about him tells me he has no place judging anyone, let alone you. Love is the measuring stick. You have loved and shown love to so many people in so many ways. I'm sure God considers you an angel."

"Then why am I still here? I've prayed every night since my Gram died to join her, and I'm still here."

"I think that could mean God isn't done with you yet."

"Well, I'm done with me. I've saved more than enough pills from my otherwise worthless shrink visits to go to sleep and not wake up. It would be peaceful and this would be over."

"I understand that. I can't imagine living one day the way you live every day. I can't imagine having no control over actions that I hated doing. I can't imagine, I don't want to think about, how waking up in the morning feels to you."

"I hate every time my eyes open and I see that I am still here. In this body, in this jungle of garbage and horror. I scream. I just want it to be over."

The line goes silent. In the pause, Abby feels her best friend's building desperation, her mind racing, filtering and arranging all the possible words into something with meaning.

Finally, Ellen acknowledges the thoughts Abby withholds in agony. "I know you want me to give you permission to end it. You don't need my permission, Abby, but I feel like you want it. I feel so terrible that I can't just give you that blessing. I wish I could, but I can't. Because if I believed that taking your own life was okay, I would have to believe that God forgot about you. And I'm not willing to believe that of God, or of you. You are too precious to forget. You are the conscience of this misguided society.

"Whether you like it or not, you see its underbelly, all the ugly flaws and gaping holes in the stories we tell ourselves. You see how much potential we squander when we assign value to each other and ourselves based on what our soul's container looks like. How we fight to own, then coldly discard. How the toxicity of holding onto secrets can crush us, and how releasing them can bind us together. You are so precious to me, how precious must you be to God? How precious are you to the people who call into your show every day? Where would they be without you?"

"I've given them all I have to give. It's been four years! I know you love me, Els, but you really have no idea, none at all, how it feels existing this way. No one would believe how I live."

"You're right, of course you're right. Hearing about it from hundreds of miles away is nothing compared to living it. But what if I tell your story, Abby? I will do my best to tell your story."

"How will it end? How will my story end? It will not end well, Els. I can tell you. It will not end well." Silence again shrouds their connection as the meaning of those words sinks in. "I don't know if you will get an answer the next time you call, Els. I can't promise I'll be here. But know that I love you. I thank you for your friendship all these years." Abby's eyes overflow with tears. "I've got to go. Goodbye Ellen." Abby holds her finger above the disconnect button sensing the quiet desperation pouring into her ears as Ellen's tears empty out every ounce of love she has to give.

"Oh Abby. If I never hear your voice again, please wait for me when you see me coming. Please promise I'll see you in Heaven, that you'll be there when I arrive, waiting for me."

"I promise. I'll be there. With arms wide open, right next to your dad. We'll both be there to welcome you."

Ellen's voice barely percolates through her anguish. "I love you, Abigail."

Drenched in sadness and terror, Abby relinquishes what's left. "I love you, too, Ellen."

Abby lets the receiver drop onto the phone and picks up the amber containers. She struggles to standing and carefully weaves her way toward the bathroom between the encroaching canyon walls of her hoarder's stash. Still weeping, she pauses at her stereo to bring Mozart into her space. Her feet, swollen and sore, express no rhythm. Her eyes, with neither brows nor lashes, express no joy. Her hands, brittle and pale, hold the option she ruminates over every moment. She reluctantly places them back among twenty-nine others in a box under the sink. "Okay Els, not today."

# 62. Regeneration

Children squeal and chase. Parents smile and follow. Lovers, young and old, meander, lull or slumber. From their shaded picnic blanket, Debbie and Jeremy watch them all against the lazy backdrop of willows gently weeping new-green cascades of feathery boughs into the pond below. Each and every celebrates the return of warmth and life to Boston Public Garden. Debbie breathes it all in and erupts in gratitude, "What a spectacular day, and what a perfect way to enjoy it. It was so nice of you to call. I might have missed it."

Jeremy nearly bubbles over, "Debbie, are you kidding? I'm glad you said 'yes.'"

"Abby always says to do something you love to replace the energy of bad memories. I can hardly believe that four years ago I wanted to die. There was darkness in every direction. I felt so totally alone."

"I saw so much agony etched on your face. I wanted to swoop in and carry you away from it all."

"I wouldn't have let you. My scar tissue went so deep. Then Megan mentioned Abby's show. I didn't know why you cared.

I'm glad you did. I'll never forget, Abby said, 'What you believe makes all the difference.' It really does."

"I know. Your bravery won out. And now look at you. You're amazing."

"I'm going to call LifeLine tomorrow to let Abby know how far I've come. How about we add a swan boat ride to my new memories. Maybe a spin on the carousel. Game?"

"Of course!"

# 63. New Life

Another sunrise. Another twenty-four hours to face the tedium. The ghastly tedium. Still raw from her thwarted turn toward finalizing her death, Abby gazes deep into her decision to put the amber bottles back. She shares with her journal.

> June 10, 1985, Dear Diary, I'm still here. My body still devours food for no reason. I just wanted it to be over. To end. Then I talked with Ellen. She wouldn't say it was okay. Did I expect her to? She doesn't understand the half of it. If she could see me, see where I live, the way I live. I don't think she'd let an animal live this way. She says god isn't done with me yet. What more can I give?

Robotically, Abby closes her journal and goes to her kitchen to feed her perpetual hunger. She goes to her bathroom to relieve her perpetual discomfort. She wipes her chin. The clock reads 9:58. She reclines, limp, on the sofa and places the phone alongside. Her voice lies unusually flat.

"Welcome to LifeLine, the radio program directed by you. I'm your host Abby Thompson. I'm so grateful that the weather has turned warm again. Let's see where our conversation takes us today. First up is Debbie. Welcome to LifeLine, the airwaves are yours."

"Hi Abby. It's been three years since we talked."

Abby sits up. Her soul engages. "Debbie? Of course, how are you?"

"I'm so much better! You were so right. I can smile again! I just went to Boston Garden yesterday to replace old memories with new ones, again. Four years ago I wanted to die. You saved me from that end. I owe you all the joy I'm feeling. Thank you for being there for me, and for all of us."

"You're welcome, Debbie, but the glory rests in you. You needed to find your center again and trust again. I may have encouraged you to believe in yourself, but you needed to do the work. I'm so grateful that you called to let me know. It means so much."

"What you believe..."

"Makes all the difference. I'm smiling from ear to ear."

"Also, I want you to know that I've been helping out on a crisis hotline. Working to help survivors of trauma when they feel like their lives are lost. I can't tell you how many times I've borrowed your go-to standards. I have a feeling your messages are spreading way beyond LifeLine."

"Well, that's wonderful. We can all do our part. Most of us are not called to notoriety or greatness. But we all have a role to play, a strand in the tapestry to strengthen. It's important to do what you can do. And if you can smile while you're doing it, so much the better. Find your joy."

"Find your joy. Exactly."

"Thanks for calling, Debbie. The idea of 'doing what you can do' has the potential to move a community forward. Finding a way to contribute builds self-esteem and reinforces the foundations of community. Sometimes we question our value, because we feel like we're not educated enough, or handsome or pretty enough, or our speech isn't easily understood or pleasant to listen to. But, those, and other superficial standards, are judgments that we, as a society, need to admit have no bearing on a person's true and lasting value. Judgments based on appearance, or social standing, or religion, or who we love, or heritage only diminish a society. They never enrich it. I'm happy to know that some of our conversations are making an impact beyond their airing. Okay, back to the phone lines. Who's next?"

# 64. Ring Toss

Under the rising August sun, the youngest guests hold their ears against the whistle's sharp, blaring exhale. The remainder watch the pier worker toss the last of the heavy mooring ropes onto the deck of the floating celebration as the captain edges it away from Long Wharf. The party officially begins. With seagulls high overhead and a flautist calling them to gather, Cathy and Drew's friends and family murmur quietly as they file into the rows of white folding chairs and take their seats.

A spontaneous hush welcomes the flautist as she softly accompanies Drew's parents down the center aisle. Drew, head held high and beaming, stands with his best man next to the ceremony's officiate. Cathy's maid of honor, carrying a cascading bouquet of bobbling daisies and draping ivy, signals to cue the processional. Despite her excitement, she obediently manages to step, halt, step, halt the length of the crash. Once she reaches her destination, the adoring crowd stands and turns to see Cathy, accompanied by her uncle, appear in stunning radiance. Transfigured by her joy, Cathy acknowledges each guest with a loving nod and a sincere "thank you" as she intentionally takes in every moment of this once-in-a-lifetime occasion. Her uncle warmly places her hand in that of her fiancé, kisses her gently and steps away.

The officiate takes her place. "Dearest friends and family, we are gathered here on this magnificent morning to witness Cathy Morgan and Drew Aldrich commit to join their lives together in love."

# 65. Spotting

Alone in her apartment, Abby brushes rubber cement on the back of the flowers she cut from a reclaimed greeting card. She arranges them and presses them into place surrounding the calligraphy she penned of one of her favorite verses, "Find contentment in yourself and you need not search for it elsewhere." She holds her work up and blurs her eyes. "Yes. I think she'll like it." She tapes the decorative sentiment to a mat she removed from a tossed picture and slides the entire piece into the accompanying frame. "Voila!" With a hint of pride, she reaches for wrapping, but stops short to answer the phone. "Hello?" Abby's mind races. *Who?*

Ellen's words cascade in tiny bursts between wet inhales. "Oh, Abby. I'm so glad. You answered."

"Els? Are you okay? Wait, what day is this? Sunday?"

"It's Saturday. I had to call."

"What's wrong? What's happened?"

"Oh, Abby. I don't know where. To start."

"At the beginning, Els. What happened?"

"It's over. Ted and I broke it off. What am I going to do?"

Abby focuses all her love and attention on her friend's grieving words. "What? Broke it off? The engagement or the whole relationship?"

"The whole—relationship. It was awful. I don't even know—how it happened. One minute we were talking—about a house we liked. And the next—he said—he didn't think he could—or should go through with it. I said, 'go through with what?' I thought he meant—putting an offer on the house. He said, 'the wedding.' I couldn't even speak. I mean, I know things haven't been perfect. But I thought we were working—toward the same goals. Had the same dreams. He said he doesn't want children! How could we have gotten this far? And he never told me that? As many times as we've talked about it! He never said. I just don't understand."

"Els, wait a minute. How did you leave it? I mean, you've been living together for what, three years? It's completely ended?"

"He just said—he was sorry. And rolled over. 'Sorry'?! Like he—stepped on my toe!"

"That's terrible, Els. You didn't deserve that. No one deserves that."

"What am I going to do? My heart and soul—are devoted to him. I left my home and my family. Moved all the way here. Pittsburgh. He's the only person. I know here. I don't even like my job. Oh, my family. What am I going to tell them? They warned me. Oh Abby." Ellen gives in and collapses into frenzied crying.

Abby digs deep into the far reaches of others' experiences and her imagination. "I know you feel like you can't get through this, but actually, now you're going to find out how strong you are."

"I don't want to be strong. I want someone—to take care of me."

"For now, that's not an option. You have to start over, imagine a new beginning. Take one day at a time."

"One day at a time? I can barely breathe. I laid awake—all night on the sofa. I could hear him. Snoring. Fast asleep. And I had to remind myself to inhale. One inhale at a time—is the best I can do."

"Then start there, Els. Inhale and exhale. You are an amazing person. This happening is awful, I know. You gave yourself and all your love and trust to him and were betrayed. He will regret this soon if he doesn't already. But you are worth more than he could ever afford. He doesn't deserve you. Now you have to learn how to appreciate yourself."

"You've said all these things before, haven't you, on your show?"

"No, not really. But I do know that people who call in the middle of a crisis call back some time later, maybe a week, or a year or longer and they tell me that things did get better. And you are at least as brave, as strong and as determined as they are. So I know you'll be okay. I know, you will look back on this day as maybe your worst day but also your best day. The day you started fresh, the day you chose your attitude and how you viewed the world around you. You'll be fine, Els. I know you will."

"Thank you, Abby. No wonder so many people trust you."

"I love you, Ellen. Believe me, you will smile and laugh and dance again."

Ellen catches her breath. "I love you, Abby, so much. Thank you. For being there. For talking me down. I guess I need to start packing. Oh, God. Packing! Okay, I can do this. I better go. I'll call from my mom's next weekend, okay? If she lets me move back. Oh, God."

"I'll look forward to hearing about the progress you've made. Keep facing forward. Remember, what you believe makes all the difference."

"Thanks, Abby!"

"Els, wait one second. Let's say a little prayer, okay?"

"Sure. As long as you're the one talking."

"Okay. Father God, Mother God, we come to you as believers in your power to heal and to renew brokenness and sadness. Please be with Ellen, one of your best creations, as she turns toward the life you have in store for her. Give her sensitivity to see your signs around her, in the faces and actions of your people. We ask this humbly and faithfully, as your daughters. Amen."

"Amen. Thank you, Abby. I love you."

"I love you, Els."

Abby hangs up the phone, "Please bless Els, dear God. Give her strength." Abby checks her watch. "Oh no, it's gotten late." She turns her attention back to wrapping Ellen's birthday gift, now more appropriate than ever. "Find contentment in your self and you need not search for it elsewhere." She walks, limping on swollen feet to her refrigerator. There she finds her Christmas card from Ellen, still held fast by her treasured green and white magnet. She reads it with sincerity. "'What you believe makes all the difference.' I think she'd like this, too." She wraps both gifts separately in reclaimed gift wrap and slides them into a reclaimed mailing envelope. She licks it to seal it. "Waste not. Want not. I'll drop these off on my way to the Y."

# 66. Anchor

Another week comes to an end. Staying clear-minded for two hours of problem-solving challenges every starved cell in Abby's skeletal body. She fixates on the passing of each minute. She paces back and forth between the stacks of her possessions giving her skin time to breathe. She decides to take a break from lifting other's burdens. "Welcome back to LifeLine, the call-in program directed by you. I'm your host, Abby Thompson.

"This weekend marks a significant day in the history of LifeLine. July 13, 1981 was the very first LifeLine program. It's so hard to believe we've been part of each other's lives for five years! I've been thinking a lot about this and I finally came up with a way I'd like to celebrate our special anniversary. During our time together, you and I have achieved more intimacy than many face-to-face relationships. Yet, we have no idea what each other looks like. To protect your privacy, I won't ask for your pictures, but I would like you to muster all your artistic gumption to create your vision of me. Choose any medium you want: crayons, pencils, paint, anything! Send those to WTOK to my attention. They'll be my treasures. Let's take a call. Welcome to LifeLine. The airwaves are yours."

"Hi Abby, I'm Tina."

"Hi, Tina. What's on your mind?"

"I wonder what I should do about these mean girls in my neighborhood. They don't pick on me, but there's a girl that they bully all the time. They call her names and take her things. It's terrible. I've decided I need to do something. I just don't know what."

"Tina, bullying is a terrible thing. Some consider being wounded by nasty words less hurtful than being physically injured. I disagree. The echoes of words can linger, long after they're first heard. And, the agony of being humiliated, especially in front of your peers, can take a lifetime to ease.

"I believe the best thing you can do is to befriend the girl you say is their target. Give her a different experience to focus on. Especially in the rough years of adolescence—when we all struggle to figure out who we are, what talents we have, and how we'll ever get to share them—critical comments can catapult us off course, send us reeling. By focusing on them, like focusing on the sharp edges of a single mosaic piece, we miss the big picture of our potential and the positive path we can choose.

"Your friendship will help her step back from that sharp, hurtful memory and see that it was part, but only a small part, of a much larger, beautiful life. Does that make sense?"

"Yes, I understand. But what about the bullies?"

"Unfortunately, bullies don't often care what anyone else thinks. They judge, injure and then gloat about the pain they've caused. Ignoring their actions and giving their gloating less power can help. But, creating a new story, that they are not a part of, negates their power. That leaves them stuck."

"I see. Dilute their meanness with goodness."

"Exactly! Once someone understands their worth, bullies lose their power. They are the ones left feeling weak and insecure. And, who knows, yours may turn out to be the friendship you have both been hoping for."

"Thanks, Abby. I'll give it a try."

"Thanks for your call, Tina. Well, that's all the time we have for today, friends. Please join me again tomorrow at ten for more LifeLine. Stay cool, Boston." Abby hangs up the phone and reclines on her sofa. Days with Y visits require extra sleep and extra feedings. Sleep first.

# 67. Red Point

Abby repays Stuart's favor as is their year-long custom. She wipes her hand on her pants, eases out of his car and grabs her swim satchel. She nods in his direction as he honks his farewell. He gives her a lift. She gives him a lift. Such consequences, of choosing not to renew her license when her photo came up for replacement, propagate unrelenting and inescapable regrets.

Yes, she swims, but never alone and never freely. Yes, she shops, but with an observer and for far fewer items. And although her scavenging remains a solo act, she now makes her rounds on foot, only in the dark and pushing a shopping cart. Most disruptive of all, despite her convictions to the contrary, she now attends Sunday services in Lizzie's stead, thereby relegating her conversations with Ellen to a coveted Saturday time slot.

When honesty forces her hand, Abby grudgingly recognizes the silver linings hidden among these clouds. While she finds his sexual arousal and orgasm bewildering and repulsive, Stuart's plentiful compliments and mindless conversation come close to balancing out her displeasure. Being forced to throw expired coupons away corrodes her nerves, but with the limits to her endurance getting more severe by the day, having Stuart's help to carry her groceries to her front door accounts for something. While she fights a constant battle against her compulsion to twice-daily visit every dumpster, walking her abbreviated rounds necessarily pares her route to something less life-threatening. And although her impulse to flee rages when anyone gets near her, going to weekly church service does supply her with at least temporary homes for her "gifts" among the mild-mannered members of the congregation.

But the true extent of the consequence of prioritizing time at the Y runs deeper still. For despite the emotional advantages of using her Y-visits as therapy, squandering her meager available energy to keep warm and afloat forces Abby to replace the organizing and tidying pieces of her jigsaw-puzzle life with periodic naps. The trade-off brings the edges of her space into her paths and onto her surfaces. She falters coming and going. She sleeps sitting and leaning. The spiral cycles downward.

Abby rinses her suit out in the sink and hangs it on the shower rod to dry. She smiles, eyes closed, remembering the feeling of lying back on the buoyant water, slowly moving her hands and feet just enough to keep herself afloat. "So relaxing." Her softened breaths become sighs of gratitude, imagining her skin tingling, pelted by the lavish, steaming shower. "Thank you, God." She swoons and reaching, catches her balance on the crowded vanity. *Time to feed.*

Stacked to shoulder height, relying on the orientation and resilience of the containers below, rows of towers of boxes, jars and cans wobble as Abby holds her breath to reach for this meal's fare - three cans of tuna, a jar of applesauce, a box of saltines and a bag of sandwich cookies. Barely gummed before swallowed, the solids soon reappear in the toilet bowl and once flushed, take their nutrients with them. The calorie balance tilts far from her favor. "Just a little nap."

# 68. Screamer

Abby stretches open her stinging eyes to see the streetlight beam colliding with the stack of rotund garbage bags looming at her front door. By curtain-filtered light, she feels her way carefully from her spot on the sofa toward the kitchen. She checks her clock. "Eleven-thirty?!" *That's not good.* Desperate to feed before heading out to scavenge, Abby awkwardly pivots back toward the living room to gather... The edge of a protruding shovel blade interrupts. She cries out. She lifts her weight from her grazed foot and falters as her center of gravity deserts her. Instinctively, she reaches out to the canyon wall to steady herself. The jars below her palm shift back, setting off a domino reaction as the jars and cans perched above teeter, then careen and collide with her bony shoulder and forearm on their fateful path toward the hardwood floor. Some graze her feet. Others land, crack and splinter into shards that protrude like dorsal fins from pools of juice and sauces. Abby's mind races as she tumbles down, her jagged memory of the cracking sound instantly predicting her agony. She watches a dark pool of her blood mingle with the mess. Her left hand and hip burn as the acidic liquids saturate her clothing and leach into her gaping wounds. The shock keeps her silent until the pain of sliced skin and flesh overwhelms her. In the darkness, she feels for and extracts the penetrating edges of the most egregious offenders. She moves to crawling, leaving a trail of blood in her shallow wake.

Once away from the disaster, she flips a light switch to see the full extent of the damage. Horrified by the sight, her anger gets the better of her.

"Oh God! I asked you to catch me!"

With blood flowing down her thigh, she pulls herself to standing at the sink, drops her shorts to the floor and grabs the iodine from the medicine cabinet. She empties it over the yawning gash in her hip, tinting the exposed bone and the floor tile below. The searing pain sends her reeling. She cries out and squeezes the gap shut. She uses her gums and right hand to unwrap three bandages and, when the iodine dries, tacks the edges closed, applying pressure until the bleeding slows. She rinses her left palm, dizzied with pain as the running water flushes the wound. She encircles it in multiple layers of salvaged gauze and closes her grip tightly to compress the wrap. Once the free flow of blood ebbs, she delicately glides her right hand over the remaining punctures and lacerations to find and remove the hidden shards tucked therein. Exhausted beyond rational thought, she lowers herself, sobbing, to the bathroom floor and leans against the tub like a marionette without strings. Sleep approaches and envelops her in.

# 69. Long Runout

Saturday. "Elizabeth, I'm here! Elizabeth?" Some way, though muddled by starvation, Abby senses, from deep within her nightmare, Stuart's muted calls and rhythmic banging to rouse her. Empty for too long, her body droops to horizontal, oblivious once more. "Are you in there? Elizabeth?!" Unsuccessful, he parts, discouraged.

Sunshine blazes through the pebbled bathroom window and diffuses onto the floor in a soft blanket covering Abby in natural warmth. She stirs and lifts her face an inch from the ceramic tile. Its imprint leaves red crosshatches behind. Through the slit between her eyelids, she notices gauze on her hand crusted with something black. Memories of her traumatic ordeal slowly drift into focus. She reaches to touch her hip. Two flies alight. The exposed, blood-caked, gaping laceration startles her. "I thought I bandaged that." She feels from buttock to thigh and finds two blood-soaked patches barely hanging on her skin. She pushes herself to sitting. "God help me." Twisting around to get a better view, she sees the orange iodine stain surrounding the wound but not within. *It must have bled away. I need to eat.*

Abby adjusts to all-fours and struggles to crawl, the acute pain caused by each retraction of her left thigh pales its pervasive ache. "Yogurt. Cookies. Peanut butter." Starvation forces her forward and slows her down. She arrives at the refrigerator and exerts herself to kneel. Leveraging her weight, she opens the door. Pushing herself higher, she manages to reach the yogurt container and nudge it off the top shelf. Miraculously, it lands unbroken, before her. She removes the lid and scoops the cool, creamy goodness into her mouth with her hand until every smear is consumed. "Cookies."

Abby aims her agonizing body toward the living room, careful to avoid the shards, stagnant maelstrom and coagulated blood, now feeding an assortment of flying and crawling arthropods. She ignores her phone when it rings halfway to her destination. *Sorry Els. I really need to eat.* She arrives at the stack of packages and gazes to the top, three feet above. "Not this again." Kneeling with her back fully extended, she wills her stretched arm and hand to pinch a seamed edge enough to pull it toward her. The stack sways but stays upright as her prize escapes her grip and hits the floor. She yanks it open and, accompanied by the rhythmic ringing, consumes one sleeve of chocolate-drizzled calories. Unable to resist her Pavlovian impulse to answer the phone any longer, she surrenders. "Hi." Abby uses her tongue to dig the chocolate goo from her gums.

"Hi, Abby? What's wrong? Are you okay? I've been ringing you for at least five minutes."

"Hi, Els. Sorry. Can I call you right back? I'm in the middle of something."

"Of course. You have my number, right?"

"I do." Abby considers the effort of reaching it. "Maybe you should call me back. Give me fifteen minutes. Actually, make it twenty-five."

"Sounds good. Are you okay?"

Abby hangs up the phone. She rips open the pinched seal and voraciously gorges on the cookies in the remaining sleeve. "Now, where's the peanut butter?"

With minute remnants of her meal racing to incorporate themselves into what's left of her body, Abby pulls herself onto the sofa and melts into relaxation. The ringing stops when she presses the speaker button. "Hi."

"Hi, Abby. What's going on?"

Abby adjusts her voice to match her guise. "I was just finishing my meal and then I had to purge. Sorry, I'm a little slower than usual. I took a fall and I'm still kinda sore. Thanks for calling back. How was your week?"

"A fall? Are you okay?"

"I will be. How was your week?"

"Not too bad, pretty good actually. I got that job we talked about, that uses my degree, and pays enough for me to move out on my own. Hard to believe it's been almost a year since Ted and I ended it. You were right. I am better off."

"That's great news! Congratulations! Remind me, where is it?"

"It's just off I-79, a bit south of Pittsburgh. My commute will be about the same."

Distracted by her physical aches and the creeping awareness of her perilous plight, Abby's mind wanders from the conversation. Clarity edges its way in between her meanderings. *The box.* She snaps back to Ellen, deftly smoothing over her absence.

"Unfortunately, parking will be more."

"That's too bad. Listen, Els. You know I collect lots of things from all over. I have something here that I want you to have."

"Abby, you know you don't have to give me anything."

"I know, but—I want to. Since you're moving, I'll hold onto it until you're settled. Then I'll send it along."

"That'll work. What is it?"

"A surprise, okay?"

"If you say so."

"Els, I'm sorry. I'm not feeling too well. Would it be all right if we cut this short today? I'll try to call during the week to finish our conversation."

"Are you okay? You seem distant."

"It's just that tumble has me sore. I'll call early in the week. Bye, Ellen. I love you."

"Bye, Abby. I love you, too."

Her prayers for deliverance match the rhythm in her wounds. *God help me. God help me. God help me.* The steady throb lulls her back to sleep.

Silently, shadows lengthen, marking the retreat of another day. Still submerged in a stupor, Abby unwittingly draws her arms and legs toward her stomach. Instead of comfort, the change to fetal position sends searing pain radiating from her hip in all directions. Her cry of anguish ejects her from tortured slumber back to torturing obsession. "Getting dark?" *I slept all day?* "I need to go out." *To do my rounds.*

Driven by a force impossible to resist, Abby rises and takes step after deliberate step, enduring the torment each movement causes. By the light over the bathroom sink, she unwinds the gauze hiding her wounds from view. She re-bandages her palm and hip, wary of the widening redness surrounding the lacerations on both. Strategizing to minimize stress on the gape in her thigh, she slides her left foot into her pant leg first taking care to lift the fabric over the fresh bandage on its way to her waist.

Finally dressed, she limps to the door and grasps the cart handle. A bolt of pain sizzles from her left palm through her forearm. "That's not good. How can I do this?" She takes hold firmly with her right hand and uses the fingertips on her left to pull and guide the cart to the door. It veers off course and chips the molding on its way through. "Damn." She leans down and uses her left forearm to steady the orientation. "That's not going to work." *I don't even have flesh to pad the bone! And, even if I manage to get it out the door, I'll never be able to guide it full over sidewalks and streets.* For the first time in nearly five years, the obsession that dictates her every waking movement lays vanquished. "I'll feed, then try again."

# 70. Dyno

Sunday. Fifteen hours, spent silencing the demon that drives her, leaves Abby weak and agitated. She limps to the seductive cart and grasps the handle for the fifth time since waking. "It's no use." She shakes her head in disgust. "I've got to get to the bins." She lays her right hand gently on the inflamed skin visible around her bandages. The temperature difference explains the taut, swollen, redness. "Not good." Abby hears a car pull up and quickly limps to eclipse the impending knock at her door. She squeezes out before Stuart reaches the threshold, bracing herself for his questions and against the jamb for support. "Good morning, Stuart."

"Hi Elizabeth." He scans her head to foot, oblivious to the bandaged hand tucked behind her back. "You're not ready? Where were you yesterday? I stopped by. Didn't you hear me knocking? I had a nice swim, but I missed you."

"I was here, but I couldn't come to the door."

"Another visitor?"

"No. I fell during the night. My hip was still throbbing."

"Ouch! Sorry to hear that. You're not coming to Sunday service, I guess? I'll ask everyone to pray for you. How bad is it?"

"It's not too bad. I just need to rest it."

"Okay. I'll see you later. Do I get a hug?"

Abby leans in as Stuart wraps his arms around her waist. His hands drift lower by reflex.

"Ow! Ow! Don't touch me there! That's right where it hurts most!"

"Oh, sorry. I didn't know." Stuart backs away. "Maybe I'll see you tomorrow?"

"I think I may take a few days off from swimming. Let my injury heal. Try me on Wednesday."

"Okay. I'll miss you."

"Thanks, Stuart. For everything."

"You're welcome, Elizabeth. I'll see you Wednesday."

Abby watches as Stuart shuffles to the curb and eases into his car. She waves as he drives off. "See you Wednesday."

# 71. Crux

Monday. For the third day and night in five years, the routine Abby lives by disintegrates. The empty cart sits idle to the right of her door. No scavenging. The rhythm of her feedings slows against her will. Less energy. A box labeled "Ellen Kincaid" rests at her feet. New priorities. Abby opens her bloodshot eyes. Daylight. She closes her left fist to test its deteriorating condition. "Hmmmm. I need to eat."

She slides her right leg off the sofa's edge and lets it dangle. Pushing her torso up with her right arm, she twists to ease her left leg. "Ahhhhh! Keep going." Her feet touch the floor in unison. She rocks gently back and forth to provide momentum to stand. The weight of her body barely lifts off her bottom. Her left hip seizes. She falters backwards. "Ahhhh!" She rocks again. "Reach!" Her weight lifts. She falters backwards, sobbing. "Heavenly Father, blessed Mother, where are you?" She pauses, tears rolling down her face, and listens for an answer. "Oh, you're coming to take me home." The corners of her weary mouth rise for an instant as sheer exhaustion envelops her again.

Blood relentlessly pulsing in her damaged hip awakens Abby with a start. "Oh no! What time is it?" She checks her watch.

"Nine twenty-five?" *If I'm going to do the show, I need to eat something.* Ignoring the now accepted pain, she scoots herself within reach of the food boxes stacked beside her. The mashed dry cereal cakes her gums and wedges in her throat. She forces it down by sheer willpower. Gastric juices churn and gnaw as the impulse that once restored peace-of-mind returns as a curse. She grabs a nearby bag in the nick of time, expelling the caustic fluids therein to mingle with the regurgitated grains. She answers the phone, running her burning tongue over her acid-etched lips and gums.

From deep within she recites the lines she memorized long ago. "Good morning, Boston. I'm Abby Thompson. Welcome to LifeLine, a radio program directed by you. We all have thoughts we're reluctant to share, even with those closest to us. Sometimes, especially with those closest to us. Without an outlet, these thoughts lie fallow. This is your outlet. This is where we nurture your thoughts and give you an opportunity to grow. I invite you to share what makes you human. The situations in your life that generate exuberance or agony, pride or fear. The number is 555-WTOK. Hi, the airwaves are yours."

"Hi, Abby. This is Phyllis. Can we talk about love? I'm getting to the point where I think I may never find it. I'm terrified."

"Of course, Phyllis. I bet other listeners will have ideas to add to make this a tremendous topic for today. So why are you terrified?"

"Well, because I've been open to love, but nothing's lasted long enough to name it."

"Do you have friends? From childhood or school? Do you have family members who can call on you for help, knowing you'd do everything possible to lift their burden and to whom you can reach out? Do you view the people around you as co-travelers on life's journey?"

"Well, yes. I guess I could answer 'yes' to all of those, some more than others, but yes."

"I'm single, Phyllis. And I get lonely sometimes, when the nights seem really long and dark. But when I'm feeling my worst, I remember how much love I have in my life that doesn't live in my home, but lives in my world. I have a trusted friend I've known since we were nine. We talk every week. I have a mother and brother who, though we've had troubles in the past, would come if I called. And I have all of you, who trust me enough to share your lives with me on LifeLine. So, no, I don't have Eros, erotic passionate love in my life, but I do have much love. And I think if you think about it this way, you'll find you have love all around you, too."

"But everyone always says that love never ends. I've been in relationships that I thought were the one, the one that would last, but they failed. I've gotten jaded about trying any more."

"Those same thoughts, the 'love never ends' line, got me thinking, too. I've come to imagine love as a never ending river. It flows through our lives and every once in a while it's enticing enough to lure us in. So, in we go.

"Sometimes we just float along and feel tranquil and safe. Those might be our friend relationships, with the ones that accept us unconditionally. Sometimes the flow speeds up and encounters boulders, it's exciting and dangerous and we're happy for the shot of adrenaline but also to make it out unscathed. Those might be the alluring liaisons we doubt could be lasting love, but we're willing to risk, if only for the thrill of the ride. Sometimes the altitude drops out from under us and the water falls onto jagged rocks below. Love ripped from our grasp, when we feel like we're drowning or wish we were. And sometimes it pools for a while in a lake of cool serenity where we can linger in security for years and years.

"And at any point, we can choose to get out of the river, to stand on the banks and watch it flow by. Or we can get in and see where we end up. But the river, the love, goes on and on. It never ends."

"You have thought about this, haven't you?"

"Yes."

"But what about trying and failing. I'm so cynical, some guy starts sweet-talking me and I look at him and think 'I've heard it all before.'"

"Truth be told, I've also thought a lot about the concept of failed loves. I think failure can't be used to describe any relationship where we learn something about ourselves or the people or world around us. I believe our main purpose on this Earth is to raise the empathy quotient of our souls. Sometimes it goes up in leaps, other times, inches. But, every relationship, lasting or momentary, has the potential to teach us something.

"Whether it's a marriage of fifty years or a mutual nod on the sidewalk with a stranger. The only failed relationships are the ones whose lessons are ignored. The ones where growth and empathy fail to move ahead. But relationships that end are not failures. They give us permission to move on to the next opportunity for growth."

"So, wow, that's a really different way of looking at it."

"I'm not saying it's the only way. But it's how I've come to understand what I've heard from all of you. When you call back after some horrible experience to say the sun finally made you smile, I think, okay, life is good. It's moving in a positive direction.

"As far as your longing for intimacy and passion, be patient. Be yourself, your true self, in all your relationships, because the one you are looking for is looking for you, too. You want to make sure you're recognized as your most authentic self so you can carry that self with confidence every day. I believe in you, Phyllis. Believe in yourself."

"Thanks, Abby. I believe in you, too."

"Thanks for your call. Who do we have next?"

After giving for what seems like years but lasts only two hours, Abby relinquishes her final pocket of available energy. "Well, I thank you all for reminding me how complicated but worthwhile the power of love can be. We've come a long way from the day I asked, as a newcomer, what places I needed to visit in Boston. It's an honor every day to share these two hours with you. I do love you, each of you, and I feel your love in return. Please stay safe out there. Hug each other and never, ever take love for granted. Until later, Boston."

Abby presses the disconnect button. Silence. Stillness. Slumber.

Abby shifts her body to ease the pressure on her side. Sleep lifts as her hand compresses a patch of something cool and wet on the sofa cushion. She twists to see a dark spot beneath her and on the fabric over her hip. "What's that?" She pulls the waistband of her pants out far enough to answer her own question. Her facial muscles relax. Her gaze drops. She dials her phone.

"Hi, Els. I have, some, news."

"Hi. What's happened?"

"I fell into broken glass the other night and did some serious damage."

"Last night?"

"No, actually, Friday. It's my hip and hand."

Confused, Ellen stammers, "But I talked with you on Saturday morning. You didn't mention anything serious, just that you fell and were sore."

"True. I didn't want to worry you. The other smaller cuts are healing, but the gash in my hip. Well. It happened before I was able to eat and I was so exhausted I just fell asleep on the bathroom floor. When I woke up the next morning, the bandages had fallen off, and I think flies were in the open cut. I could see the bone."

"What? Oh Abby! Did you go to the hospital to get it cleaned out? I mean, if it's that deep? You went, right? It must have needed stitches."

Abby keeps her voice measured, "It's too late for stitches now and besides, I'm not going to a hospital. They'll never let me out."

Desperate, Ellen's voice rises. "But Abby, what are you going to do?"

"Stuart can help. He's coming back on Wednesday."

"Wednesday?! That's two days from now! That sounds dangerous, especially if you think flies were in it."

"Yah, and I'm out of iodine. Well, I have no other choice. Els, I can hear your wheels turning, but whatever you do, do not call my mother. She'll just freak out. It's not worth upsetting her since she can't do anything."

"All of these sound like the worst ideas. I need to call your mom. She could be there in four hours."

"No! If she sees me, my apartment, she'll force me to do everything I promised I'd never do."

"But, Abby. Going to the hospital…"

"Promise me, Els. Promise you won't call her. I can't go to the hospital. I can't move back home."

"Okay, I promise, but I'm going to call again tomorrow to make sure you're still okay."

"That's good. That works for me. Thank you."

"Okay, I'll call tomorrow about this time."

"I'll be here. Thanks, Els."

"I love you, Abby."

"I love you, too."

# 72. Zipper

Tuesday. The rise and fall of Abby's chest barely registers. Her limbs lie still and limp. She opens her eyes enough to see the familiar streetlight shining through the visible section of her window. She dials the phone. "Hi, Linda, it's Abby. Sorry for the late notice, and sorry to have to leave this as a message, but I won't be able to do LifeLine today. I'm not sure about tomorrow either. I'm sorry for the inconvenience. Goodbye." Eyes close. Sleep returns.

Abby reaches toward the ringing phone. She presses the speaker button and fades to relaxation. "Hello?"

"Hi, Abby. Well, how are your cuts today? How's the one on your hip? Any better?

"It's not better. It's actually worse. It's been shedding a yellow discharge since yesterday."

"Abby! That means it's infected! You can't ignore that!"

"I know. Stuart will be here tomorrow. I'll ask him to get me some iodine. I'll be fine."

"It's too late for iodine. A doctor needs to look at it!"

"Els, you don't understand. One look at me and I'll be sent to the nearest psych ward. I look like a skeleton with skin, Els.

Remember, seventy-three pounds, no hair, no teeth, so little muscle you wouldn't believe."

"But,"

"Els. I have all those pills. If things get worse, I plan to take them. In case that happens, remember that I have something here that I want you to have. I'll tell my mother. I've decided to call her. Not to tell her about the fall, just to say a sort of goodbye. It's a box with your name on it, Els. I think you'll like it. Make sure, if anything happens to me, that you get it from my mother. I'll tell her it's for you."

"Abby, tell her about the fall. She'd want to know. She'd want to be there for you. She loves you."

"But my world will unravel, completely."

"It seems like it has already, Ab..."

Abby winces as she shifts her position. "Ellen, I need to go. Remember that I love you. So much. I will always love you. Goodbye."

"Oh Abby. Please don't hang up. I can't imagine never hearing your..."

Abby presses the button to disconnect the call. Tears stream down her face. "I love you, Ellen."

Abby dials the phone. "Hi, Mom."

Chloe perks up by reflex at the sound of Abby's voice. "Abby? Hi." Then quiets her voice by habit. "How are you? I haven't heard from you in a while."

Responding in kind, Abby's voice softens to a whisper. "Yes, I'm sorry about that. It's been pretty hectic here."

"Really? What have you been up to?"

"The usual. I've been going to the Y a lot. With my friend, Stuart. And to church with him."

Chloe brightens but keeps her voice down. "Oh, that's wonderful. Dad will be so happy."

Determined to leave no misunderstanding, Abby uses a tone saved for her journal. "Mom, please don't tell Russell. I don't want him to know. He'll think I'm going to church to 'get right with the Lord'. It's nothing like that. Besides, proving him wrong is the main reason I never tried to get better."

"Oh, darling. So, you're not any better?"

"No, Mom. I've actually. Well." Abby weighs the horrible choices before her. "Actually, I'm tired."

"Tired? Oh, me too! I don't sleep through the night more than a few times a week."

"No, Mom. I'm tired of everything."

Abby feels Chloe's tension build as her breathing deepens and her voice quakes. "Abigail. What are you saying?"

"I'm saying I'm tired of fighting this disease. And fighting battles against gravity and weather. I fell, Mom. And cut myself, badly. I think it's infected."

Chloe dives headlong into mothering mode. "Infected? Did you see a doctor?"

"I don't want to see a doctor. I…"

"Abby, I'll be there in…" Chloe discounts the obstacles in her way. "In, in three hours. I'll just throw some clothes in a bag and grab my toothbrush. Make up your sofa for company. I'll take care of you."

"But, Mom. No."

"I'll be there. I love you." Chloe disconnects the call.

In desperation, Abby calls back immediately but gets no answer. "Damn." Her hand releases the receiver. She scrounges amid her crumpled packaging and litter searching for her journal. Her pen.

> July 15, 1986, Dear Diary, The worst just
> happened. I called mom to tell her I love her but I
> told her about my fall. She's coming here. To sleep
> on my sofa! My sofa!!

Abby forces her hand to continue.

> *Dear Mom, If you're reading this, I'm already gone. I'm ready. I'm sorry for the mess I made of my life. I'm sorry you have to clean it up. There are boxes of journals under my bed. There are paintings under my mattress. There's a box for Ellen. Don't hide what happened to me. Telling my secrets could save lives. I knew, but I didn't know how. I love you. And Mark.*

The pen drops from her hand. Shadows.

From the darkness behind her eyelids, Abby hears an unfamiliar banging sound. For the first time in her life, someone's love for her pounds in desperation. For the last time in her life, she cannot respond.

# 73. Finish Line

Wednesday. A pair of cardinals takes turns caring for the noisy brood of hatchlings squawking in their nest. A thrifty tourist handles a jar of homemade marmalade comparing the price in her mind to the economy-sized store brand at home. A street sweeper mindlessly positions his dustpan ahead of a cigarette butt and flicks it in with a twist of the wrist. An orderly strips the stained sheets from an empty gurney, tucking in this morning as a meaningful memory. A woman sits listless at the microphone in a radio studio, chin raised, eyes closed. It is ten o'clock in Boston.

"Welcome to LifeLine. This is WTOK station manager, Linda Warner. It is. Today. I was informed early this morning that our wonderful Abby Thompson, the originator and host of LifeLine, has died. Friends will be received on Saturday morning at Morewood Funeral Home in Boston. Funeral services will be held at St. John's Church. Abby had two great passions in her life, you, her listeners, and classical music. Today's program will be a musical tribute to Abigail Thompson."

Drivers pull their cars over from the flow of traffic and sit staring ahead. Joggers find a park bench, then exchange hugs, with the ones already seated, when they arrived. Brooms rest. Pencils drop. Hearts break. Tears follow. It's ten-o-five in Boston.

# 74. Clean

Thursday. Stuart brings his car to a full stop at the intersection. He raises his sunglasses for a better view. "What's going on over there?" He pulls out slowly, careful to avoid the stragglers in the crowd of people gathered in small groups, with their eyes trained on the activity unfolding in front of them. He parks at a safe distance from the industrial-sized dumpster looming over his normal space. He pushes his way through toward Abby's front door, confused by the conversations he overhears about how surprising it is that Abigail Thompson was living this close and living this way. *Abigail? Abigail Thompson?*

Once in the clearing between threshold and street, Stuart notices a statuesque woman who bears a resemblance to his friend. He smooths back his hair and approaches with apprehension.

"Excuse me. I'm Elizabeth's friend Stuart. What's happened? Where's Elizabeth?"

The expression on Chloe's troubled face blends anguish and confusion. "Elizabeth? No one named Elizabeth lived here. This is the home of Abby, Abigail Thompson."

"But. She told me her name was Elizabeth."

Chloe's impatience quarrels with her curiosity. "Elizabeth was her grandmother's name. Maybe that's why she chose it."

Stuart persists, sure his confusion will clear with a few more answers. "But. Where is she? We were supposed to go swimming yesterday but she didn't come to the door when I knocked. What are you doing with all her things?"

Chloe's defenses crumble, her delicate facade of stability tumbles to dust. She grabs his hands and speaks through her tears. "Oh, you're Stuart! The person who took her swimming and shopping. And to church service! Stuart, I'm Abby's mother, Chloe. It's so good to meet you. She told me about your friendship. Thank you for the care you showed my daughter."

The combination of Chloe's breakdown and gratitude push Stuart past restraint. "But where is she?"

"Stuart, Abby died yesterday. She called me Tuesday morning and told me about a fall she had taken. I got here as soon as I could, but, it was too late. The medics on the ambulance did what they could, but the infection had spread and her body was already so fragile."

"Died? Eliz...Abby is gone? Wait, Abigail Thompson, from LifeLine? Elizabeth is Abigail Thompson? Oh, there are so many people in mourning today."

"Yes, that was her show. I've been in contact with the station. They have been very kind and supportive. She seems to have made quite a family for herself here."

"Oh, yes. She did."

"Stuart, if you'll excuse me, I have a lot to do to empty out her place. If you see anything that interests you, please take it. She would have wanted it that way."

"Thank you for that, but memories of our time together are good enough for me. I'm so sorry for your loss. Lizz…Abby was a remarkable person."

Chloe hears the phone ringing inside. "Thank you. I know. I've got to answer the phone. Please plan to come to the funeral home on Saturday. Morewood."

Chloe edges past the workman pushing an overloaded wheeled bin through the doorway. "Hello? Abby Thompson's residence. Who's calling?"

"It's Ellen, Ellen Kincaid. Who's this?"

"Oh, hello Ellen. This is Mrs. Thompson, Chloe."

"Mrs. Thompson? Where's Abby? Is she okay?"

With her reserves nearly empty, Chloe musters a wisp of strength. "I was going to call you earlier, but the workmen arrived and I got distracted." She takes a deep breath and bites her lip. Her heart races. "Ellen, are you sitting down? I have very."

Ellen instantly grows frantic. "What is it? Where's Abby?"

"Ellen, Abby died yesterday. The doctors said the infection was too widespread and her body didn't have any fight left in it. I know how important your friendship was to her. She loved you so much."

Ellen struggles to speak. "Abby's dead? But…?"

"She's at peace now, Ellen. She told me when she called that she was tired of fighting. I think she welcomed death. She was prepared to go. I know we're all going to miss her, but she's finally free, so we have to remember that while we grieve."

"How did she die? At home?"

"No, in the hospital, but without a lot of tubes and wires. She told me she was ready and didn't want to be forced to stay alive. It was the most difficult reality I've ever had to face. But, I love her, so I let her have her way. She died peacefully. She told me to make sure I gave you a box. It's here with your name on it. It looks like a set of china dishes. She said to tell you that she loves you and that she'll be waiting."

The line goes silent.

# 75. Beta

Friday. Chloe takes refuge in her car from the nauseating upheaved squalor of Abby's home. She opens her purse and hesitantly removes the worn journal she found on the sofa next to her daughter's emaciated, nearly lifeless body. With dread and anguish filling her consciousness, she opens the cover. Each page, as she turns, is virtually covered in ink. Minuscule groups of perfectly printed letters squeezed in between the lines. She turns to the last entry. Despondence. She returns to Abby's bedroom and, on her knees, peers under the bed.

# 76. Curtain Call

Saturday. Ellen sits watching cars arrive and park. The morning sun edges up, casting its warmth on the growing line of people waiting for the doors to open. Despite imagining this moment for years, she feels unprepared for the tumult of emotions raging inside. *I know I need to go in. To see the grief in Chloe's eyes, hold her hands, tell her how deeply heartbroken I am. To remind Mark how much his sister loved him, even from so far away. I need to go in.* Ellen wipes the tears from her face and takes a deep breath. "Oh, Abby." She slides a manila envelope into her purse. "I can do this." She pulls the handle and pushes her car door open. "For you."

The melody of Beethoven's Moonlight Sonata floats through the open doorway and gently caresses her weary soul. Without noticing, she passes arrangements of bright summer blooms set on either side of the threshold, framing the scene within. She mindlessly tilts the shiny gold poll to one side to slip around the red velvet rope and the hundreds of people waiting patiently for viewing hours to start.

With her attention dedicated to staying composed and finding Chloe, she misses Renee and Donna hurriedly tacking images to the suite's walls having already filled available display boards placed about the rooms. Nor does she notice Abby's watercolors of barren trees against the dark clouds of Boston Common, colorful boats moored in Gloucester Harbor, a deserted lighthouse on Cape Cod or the lonely solitude of a Provincetown beach leaning against the walls. Oblivious, too, is she to the heavy floral scent of mingling pollens dispersed into the crowded space by arrangements stacked floor-to-ceiling and wall-to-wall.

As she pauses to brace herself at the entryway for her next step, her heart drops and shatters to see the name of her beloved childhood friend, ABIGAIL THOMPSON, spelled out in small, white plastic letters on the marker at the door. "Abby." She inhales and holds her breath, finally letting the air leave her lungs one molecule at a time. Her eyes fill then overflow with tears. She swallows and presses her tongue to the roof of her mouth. Hard. Her face contorts into sorrow. She pivots slightly to enter.

Chloe's eyes instantly catch Ellen's brimming gaze in spontaneous understanding. As Ellen approaches, they blend their agony in weeping silence. Years of helplessness pour into their embrace. Hearing his mother's now familiar agony, Mark approaches and envelops the pair. Family. The quaking weave draws Russell's attention. From his seat, he motions to Mark and shakes his head. Mark registers the signal, but remains defiantly in place. Chloe and Ellen step apart, but stay connected, squeezing hands right-in-left, left-in-right. A circle of sorrow. A ring of support. Suddenly reminded of her goal to bring solace, Ellen loosens her hold and shows Chloe the packet. "Shall I put this on the stand beside her casket?"

"Yes, Ellen. Thank you so much for bringing it."

Ellen slides two pages of beautifully calligraphed writing between the protective sleeves on the display stand and returns to Chloe's side.

"It's so hard to believe she's gone."

"Maybe in body, Mrs. Thompson, but considering the number of people outside, I think her spirit has infused us all."

The funeral director consults his pocket watch. Ten o'clock. He unhooks the velvet rope dividing visitors from family, and respectfully stands aside. Adults and children of all varieties progress slowly in a line that extends around the building.

Soft murmurs build as Abby's Boston family reacts to the hundreds of diverse portraits of "our Abby Thompson" hung on every available surface. Some are clearly the work of toddlers who, new to faces, drew arms and legs where ears and bodies should be. Others place Abby against insightful settings—from behind a microphone to before an easel, from swimming at the Y to lounging at Tanglewood. Created in crayon and watercolor, acrylic and oil, pastel and charcoal. The size of a postcard, a score, a window or door. Abby with flowing, frizzy or close-cropped hair; blue, green, brown or hazel eyes; alabaster, cocoa or coffee skin. But always, always with a smile that radiates caring and love. Prompted by the intensifying hum, Ellen finally surveys her surroundings. "Abby. They are all Abby."

As the crowd grows, Ellen moves discreetly to slip away from Chloe's side to a more neutral spot. Stunned by the sheer number of visitors, Chloe automatically reaches for her hand and gently urges her back. The discomfort Ellen feels positioned in the family circle soon gives way to gratitude. For, from her observation spot, Ellen witnesses little pockets of couples and individuals spontaneously introducing themselves to each other and before long, with Abby as their common friend, she catches snippets of stories of risk-taking and triumph that permeate the gathering. And, as the line progresses, Chloe's gracious, "This is Abby's lifelong friend, Ellen," becomes the segue into welcomed stories of the impact Abby's open heart and caring soul had on each and every person who altered their Saturday routine to queue around a block in Boston.

Debbie stands in line fumbling with her notepaper, now soft with rolling and unrolling in sweaty hands. Jeremy slips his arm under hers and gently accepts the paper as the couple ahead of them steps aside. Debbie takes Chloe's outstretched hands in hers, looks directly into her eyes and bares her heart. "I'm so sorry for your loss. I want you to know that, I am the reason Abby arrived so late for Thanksgiving all those years ago. She talked with me for hours. I would not have made it through the day otherwise. Because of Abby, life for many of us will continue to get better even though she's gone. Thanks to her, inhales follow exhales follow inhales. Eyes blink and refocus on the world brought back into view. Because of her, twitches give way and vulnerable hearts may still panic but they also ease. She listened. Really listened. Thank you for sharing her with us."

Chloe tightens her grip and pulls Debbie in for a tender embrace and a knowing, tearful nod. "She never said what kept her. I knew it must have been important. I'm so grateful to meet you."

Feeling the relief of her message delivered, Debbie takes Jeremy's hand as they proceed to the casket. "Look at that smile. That must be her college portrait. You can see the love in her eyes, can't you?" They stand silently, each reading the words displayed before them, then move on.

One half-step by half-step, the line edges slowly forward. Cathy and Drew sway their weight in rhythm to the swells of Chopin. "Remember how much Abby loved classical music? It's so nice that they're playing it." Their turn arrives. Cathy steps into the family circle. She stands close enough to feel their grief. Her words flow from the heart. "You've probably heard from nearly everyone here how Abby helped them improve their relationships. Well, she taught me the value of letting go. How new boundaries could bring toxic relationships to an end. It's not the most pleasant lesson, but it gave me options in my life that would never have been possible."

Drew intercedes when Cathy's tears catch in her voice. "Abby gave Cathy and me permission to celebrate the love we felt for each other and to commit our lives to each other, to trust in that connection despite the scorn of others. We are so sorry she's gone."

"Thank you for sharing that. Abby learned that lesson very close to home. Thank you for coming."

Having said their piece, Drew and Cathy step closer to those in line ahead of them now stalled at the casket.

Two women, with similar features, talk quietly to one another. The elder steps aside to survey the situation. "Wow, Gina, I knew the line would be long, but, this is really a tribute. I need to go call off work."

"Okay, mom. I'll be here."

The woman goes in search of a phone leaving her daughter to inch along and admire and applaud the talents of Boston's myriad of artists. Gina approaches a pastel to better view the subtle blending. Her step back into line collides with an old man who apologizes with grace. "Excuse me, I'm so sorry. I'm Stuart, a friend of Abby's. This is Leo. We know Abby from the Y. She and I swam together."

"Hi, I'm Gina. I never met Abby in person, but I feel like she's a friend."

The woman weaves her way back through the crowd just in time to be introduced.

"My mom, Janice, this is Stuart and Leo, Abby's friends from the Y. Stuart says Abby liked to swim. It's weird. I never picture her anywhere but behind a microphone on LifeLine."

Stuart takes a breath, excited to elaborate, but Janice interrupts, "Abby's mom looks really tired. Why don't you go talk with her sister and brother. I'm going to find her mom a chair so she can sit down."

Gina steps up and connects with Ellen. "Hi, I'm so sorry for your loss. Your sister walked me and my mom back from a horrible cliff. I just need you to know how much she is already missed."

Ellen starts to make the correction, but accepts the compliment instead. "Thank you. I miss her already, too."

From his vantage point just above waistbands, Joey sadly points to a colorful grinning face hung at his eye level. "Look Mom, here's the one I made."

"Yes. That is yours. I wonder where mine is."

Just ahead, Harry moves solemnly alongside Ben and Sandy waiting patiently for his opportunity to express their loss, mentally running sentiments he fears may fall short. As the space between him and Chloe clears, he steps closer. "I'm so sorry, we —are so sorry that Abby has passed away. She saved our family, breathed life into fading hope. We owe her everything."

Betty, hugging their children at her sides, completes his thought, "We took her words to heart. They became our guiding path. 'Find your joy.' She gave so many the strength to keep going. She was our angel."

Chloe stands, though emotionally exhausted by the hours-long outpouring of grief, and struggles to maintain her poise, "Everyone I speak with has a story." Tears force their way. "She touched so many lives."

Betty releases her embrace of the children and wraps her arms around Chloe, one mother to another. "This is so, so awful. Abby would always say, 'Now you're going to find out how strong you are.' 'You can do this.' Reach out to Abby. I know she is watching over you, over all of us. I will pray with you."

Considerate of those still waiting, Betty reluctantly parts from Chloe and moves toward the casket. There, she stands silently reading the piece displayed on the stand. Joey rises to his tiptoes to see for himself. "This speech was de-live-red. Mom, what does it say?"

"Delivered. It says, this speech was delivered by Abigail Thompson on the occasion of her college graduation on June 9, 1981. 'We come to this day with our hopes outstretched, our hands prepared for giving back. Our lives have been fashioned by loving parents, devoted professors, supportive friends. Until now we have been receivers, accepting from others their gifts of time and talents. Beginning today we will enflesh the wisdom that it is indeed better to give than to receive. We enter the world's tapestry of life as teachers, physicians, scientists, artists, dreamers. We enter to encourage youth, to support the aged and to make the transition between the two as life-giving as possible. We enter the world's tapestry of life with tentative steps, gaining confidence with each success achieved each failure overcome. Our paths are determined not so much by our past as by our willingness, our determination, to embrace the changes that embrace us — both those pursued and those uninvited. Beginning today, we become irreplaceable, undeniable strands in the world's great tapestry of life.'"

# ACKNOWLEDGEMENTS

Every couple hundred lifetimes, a celestial constellation of individuals comes together for each of us to forward goodwill and love in the universe. I'm convinced *this* is that lifetime for me. While I have turned to all the stars in my life at one point or another, a certain several luminaries generously shared their ideas and skills with me to get this book out into the world. First, Diane Laemmle and Kathleen Burk who patiently read a tedious first draft of LifeLine and still managed words of encouragement. Then, Noretta Willig and Pamela Livingston, educators, bibliophiles and friends, whose input and enthusiasm gave me the motivation to refashion a second and third draft into the work you now hold. And to my dear sister Beth Giles, for reconnecting me to these two beloved high school teachers. Next, my loved, supportive sister Laurie A. B. Scheuring and dear Tasso Spanos who never, not for one moment, doubted my ability to put words in a compelling order to tell a story of value. Next, the talented and inspiring Erin Burkett, whose insights born of experience helped legitimize dialogues that otherwise would have sadly missed their mark. Erin also graced me with her artistic sensitivity in creating the cover art for the book. To Toni Weber, cherished and forever friend, who seized life by the elbow and left plenty of breadcrumbs to follow along the path she forged to self-publishing. To two voracious readers and longtime, treasured friends Deb Hennel and Kris Groves, who added the unfinished LifeLine to their summer reading list. To my dear, insightful friend MaryKay Meanor, who reminded me that life is indeed a tapestry. To my precious sons, Joel and Bailey Donovan, who while reading LifeLine with open hearts, offered sensitive editorial suggestions that always enhanced my storytelling. To my precious daughters, Molly and Hannah Donovan, who stood in my corner and cheered me on over lo these many years. And finally, to my anonymuse, who inspired me to tell the story of lives shaped by connection, acceptance, perseverance and love.

I thank you and love you all from the depths of my heart. I could not have done it without you. — Bobbi

# ABOUT THE AUTHOR

Bobbi Donovan was born and raised in Pittsburgh, Pennsylvania. She enjoys camping, jazz and spending time with her sisters, friends and four adult children, Joel Micah, Molly, Bailey and Hannah. She credits her A.P. English teacher Pamela Livingston with instilling in her the joy of writing.
To be, or not to be? Not "to be."

Made in the USA
Monee, IL
16 January 2022

89078991R00187